ZELDA OLIVER- MILES

the weight of **SILENCE**

ALSO BY ZELDA OLIVER-MILES

Amelia Gayle Gorgas: First Woman of Position

*My Headless Marriage: If I Knew Then
What I Know Now*

*Love Beyond Measure A 30-Day
Journey through God's Promises for Marriage*

Write the Book

ZELDA OLIVER- MILES

the weight of SILENCE

a novel

Five Oaks Publishing

Birmingham

The Weight of Silence
Copyright © 2024 by Zelda Oliver-Miles

Cover design by Zelda Oliver-Miles

Published in December 2024 by Five Oaks Publishing
ISBN: 979-8-89619-510-8

This book is published as a print-on-demand and ebook edition by Five Oaks Publishing.

Published in the United States of America

Printed in the United States of America

First Edition

DEDICATION

ACKNOWLEDGMENTS

First and foremost, I thank my Lord and King for the gifts He's bestowed and trusted me with.

This book would not have been possible without the love and support of so many incredible people:

To Wendell, my partner in life—your steadfast support and unwavering belief in me keep me challenged and inspired every day.

To my extraordinary children, Xenia and Yori—thank you for thinking I can change the world. You inspire me, and because of you, I strive to be better.

To my little sister, Rene—the fear is gone. It's done.

To my brothers, Dre and AJ—no matter how many times you say it, y'all are still my little brothers.

To my mom and dad—thank you for your endless love and support. I will always be grateful.

To Vanessa Davis Griggs—you will never know just how much your friendship has meant to me. From day one in Dr. Lewis's office until now, you've been a source of inspiration and encouragement.

To JoAnn Hagood—thank you for believing in me and my writing. My entry into journalism was because of you. (P.S. While I didn't write for the New York Times, I did contribute to an article it published—close enough, right? LOL.)

To my sisters from other mothers—you know who you are. Thank you for listening to my crazy ideas and helping me turn them into reality.

To my friends and the writing community—you've been my cheerleaders, my critics, and my family in every way that matters. A special thanks to my beta readers and critique partners; your insight and encouragement have refined this story into what it is today.

Dear Reader,

The *Weight of Silence* is the first installment in *The Breaking Free Series*, a journey of love, resilience, and the healing power of truth. While Zariyah and Sterling's story stands on its own, it also lays the foundation for a larger narrative about family, redemption, and self-discovery.

This book touches on difficult topics, including childhood abuse and its long-lasting impact. I approached these subjects with care and a desire to foster empathy and understanding. If you or someone you know is dealing with similar challenges, I encourage you to seek support. Resources and people are out there to help, and your voice matters.

As you read, I hope Zariyah and Sterling's journey reminds you that healing isn't linear, and it isn't perfect—but it is always possible. Each installment of *The Breaking Free Series* will explore the lives and loves of characters you've come to know, each overcoming their own silences and breaking free into their truth.

Thank you for picking up *The Weight of Silence*. Your support gives life to these pages, and I hope Zariyah and Sterling's story stays with you long after the last chapter.

—Zelda

Prologue

The NO TRESPASSING signs didn't stop her. At nine years old, Zariyah didn't need anyone to tell her she shouldn't be here. Her heart pounded as she darted deeper into the woods, her Keds barely making a sound against the hard-packed dirt. She had silently prayed they wouldn't come back to this place. But they always did.

What was happening wasn't right. Being back here wasn't right.

When she could, she ran.

The woods were supposed to be her safe place, the only place where the world couldn't reach her. But today, they felt like a trap, every snapping twig echoing the things she couldn't say.

Her name rang out in the distance, sharp and frantic. "Zariyah!" The sound bounced off the trees, growing faint as she pushed further into the shadows. She didn't look back. Her legs moved faster, her breath catching in her throat as she dodged low-hanging branches and briars. The honeysuckle-covered fence was just ahead. She had to reach it.

The vines wrapped tightly around the barbed wire, their

sweetness masking the sharp edges beneath. Her mother's voice echoed in her mind: Something can look soft and sweet but cut you just the same.

She slowed, the air thick and stifling, like it was holding its breath along with her. Sweat beaded on her forehead, mixing with the dirt streaked across her skin. Then, she fell.

"Dang it," she muttered, hitting the ground hard. A gnarled tree root jutted from the earth like a hand reaching to stop her, its bark rough against her scraped knee. She glanced at the fresh blood welling there, crisscrossing the scars already etched into her skin. How many times can you bleed before you run out of something to give?

She pulled herself up, swiping at the blood with trembling hands. The thorns from the briars had caught her legs, leaving tiny red scratches. Her fingers brushed them away carefully, but the sting lingered. Her eyes locked on the fence. It felt just within reach.

The sweet scent of honeysuckle wrapped around her like a protective blanket. She plucked a vine and brought it to her nose, inhaling deeply, desperate to drown out the other smell clinging to her—Camel cigarettes and stale sweat.

For a moment, the breeze cooled her skin, and the sweetness of the honeysuckle almost made her believe she was safe. She tilted her head back, eyes closed, a small smile breaking across her face.

Almost.

The smile faded as quickly as it had come, replaced by the weight of what she couldn't escape. If she had just listened, maybe her brother wouldn't have broken his leg. She thought of the scar running jagged across his shin, a reminder of the day she couldn't protect him. Mama had made sure she bore her share of the blame, her words cutting deeper than the tree branches ever could.

She sat on the same root that had tripped her, her fingers tracing its rough bark. A red bird landed on a branch ahead, tilting its head to look at her. Zariyah tossed petals from the honeysuckle onto the dirt, watching as they fluttered to the ground.

Her thoughts shifted to his words, the ones she couldn't stop hearing no matter how hard she tried: *Have you ever heard of a nine-year-old getting married?* It had sounded like a storybook gone wrong, something that couldn't possibly be real.

But even at nine, she knew better. She knew enough to understand what those words meant—and that terrified her more than the woods ever could.

The petals fell one by one from her hand as the weight of it all settled in her chest. Her jaw tightened, a resolve hardening inside her like concrete. *I'll never get married. Not ever. No matter what he says.*

Chapter 1

Twenty Years Later...

The woods were back. Not the way they were that day, but darker, thicker—silent in a way that felt suffocating. She could feel the sharp pull of thorns, the sting of branches cutting her skin as she stumbled through the underbrush. The weight of something unseen loomed just behind her, its presence pressing against her chest, making it hard to breathe.

She jolted awake, her heart hammering against her ribcage. The dream dissolved like smoke, but the unease it left clung to her chest like a heavy stone. Shadows loomed in the darkened room, broken only by the pale glow of moonlight filtering through the curtains.

Zariyah stayed still, her breath shallow, the faint scent of Sterling's cologne lingering in the air—a presence that felt both comforting and suffocating.

The woods always found her in sleep. Sometimes they were quiet, almost serene, but more often, they felt like this—dark, endless, and waiting. No matter how fast she ran, she never escaped them. And no matter how much time passed, the memory of the real woods—the ones from that day—always found its way back to her.

She blinked, dragging a hand over her damp forehead. The dream had already slipped beyond her grasp, but the feeling it left behind stayed, sinking deeper into her chest. For a moment, she sat there, still as the night around her.

Her gaze shifted to the glowing numbers of the bedside clock: 2:13 a.m. With a sigh, she swung her legs over the side of the bed, the cool hardwood grounding her. Her feet carried her down the hall and into the kitchen, her refuge in sleepless hours. The house was silent, save for the hum of the refrigerator.

She reached for a mug, her movements mechanical, until something on the fridge caught her eye.

A note.

The words were hastily scrawled on the back of a to-do list: "Honey, I'm sorry."

Zariyah stared at it, her chest tightening. This was what she got for trying? Hours of effort reduced to scraps. She crumpled the paper and tossed it into the trash with a sharp flick of her wrist. "You and your apology can go to hell," she muttered, her voice low.

Her gaze drifted to the French doors leading to the terrace. The string lights Sterling had insisted on buying last summer still glowed faintly. The table she had so carefully prepared just hours ago stood untouched—a perfect scene for an audience that never arrived.

Her jaw tightened at the memory.

Earlier that evening, Zariyah had spent hours in the kitchen, her brother Dominic and his team helping her prepare an elaborate dinner. Crab cakes with mustard sauce, grilled scallops, salmon Wellington, and a flawless chocolate soufflé. By seven o'clock, the terrace was set with lanterns and flowers, the table arranged with vintage silverware she had carefully selected from an estate sale.

By seven-thirty, the only person standing by that beautifully arranged table was her.

She tried calling Sterling, of course. No answer. No explanation. Just silence. By eight, she had sent the waitstaff home, and by nine, she had poured the rest of the Chardonnay down the drain, unable to stomach anything—not even the bitterness in her mouth.

Now, in the quiet of the kitchen, Zariyah's fingers tightened on the counter. Why do I keep doing this to myself? Her gaze shifted toward the terrace again, its emptiness mocking her. She turned away, her bare feet carrying her to the living room.

She sank onto the couch, wrapping herself in the throw draped across the armrest. Sleep came in uneasy fits and starts, leaving her mind restless even as her body succumbed to exhaustion.

The sound of birds roused her from her slumber. Zariyah blinked against the sunlight streaming through the curtains, her body stiff from the awkward angle she had slept in. The house was eerily quiet. She glanced at her phone—no messages, no missed calls.

Sterling's side of the bed had been cold when she left it. Now, it was clear he wasn't coming back anytime soon.

By the time she made her way into the kitchen, the pale morning light had softened the sharp edges of her frustration. She reached for the tea kettle, her movements deliberate. When she opened the fridge, her lips twisted at the sight of the neatly packed containers of leftovers—Sterling's silent olive branch.

Too little, too late.

Without hesitation, she dumped the containers into the trash, the clang of glass and metal breaking the morning's quiet. The sound startled her, echoing in the silence that surrounded her like a suffocating fog.

The whistle of the tea kettle jolted her back into the moment. She poured herself a cup, the steam curling into the air. Her gaze lingered on the trash can, where the note and leftovers sat buried. Why am I still doing this?

Zariyah crossed to the French doors, her eyes landing on the terrace. The table stood as it had the night before—untouched. The glasses sparkled in the early light, the napkins still neatly folded at each place setting. The sight twisted something deep inside her, a painful reminder of what had gone unsaid.

She pulled the curtains shut with a forceful tug, shutting out the view and the bitterness it stirred.

The silence of the house felt heavy, pressing down on her shoulders like the weight of the woods. The thorns weren't real, but sometimes they still felt like they were—pricking at her skin, reminding her of what she had buried deep but never truly escaped. In moments like this, the past felt closer than it should, as if it were just waiting for her to slip back into its grip.

Zariyah exhaled, her hand lingering on the curtain's edge. You've tried, she told herself, though the words felt hollow. Tried with dinner. Tried with their marriage. Tried with their home. And yet, she felt like the only one still fighting to keep it all together.

In her office, the only place she felt like herself, Zariyah settled into her desk chair. The wide windows overlooked the garden, its roses and hydrangeas blooming in bursts of color. Tending the garden had once been her therapy, a way to channel the chaos inside her into something thriving. But even that joy had dimmed.

She stared at her calendar, deadlines and projects

blurring into a sea of obligations. Her mind circled back to the note, the untouched table, and the empty space beside her in bed.

Her reflection stared back at her in the glass. How much longer can I keep pretending this is enough?

Chapter
2

The parking lot at Charades was beginning to clear as the lunch rush wound down, making it easier for Zariyah to slip inside without drawing attention. The Alabama sun beat down relentlessly, the heat clinging to her skin as she stepped out of the car. The brief reprieve of snagging a spot near the entrance felt like a small win, though her stomach churned with the weight of the morning.

Stepping into the cool interior of the restaurant, the familiar scent of Dominic's cooking wrapped around her like a comforting hug. Charades wasn't just a restaurant— it was a testament to her brother's talent, a culinary oasis in the middle of their bustling town. The blend of modern sophistication and Southern charm felt warm and welcoming, with polished wood accents, exposed brick walls, and pendant lighting that bathed the room in a soft golden glow. Ferns and trailing vines softened the industrial edges, breathing life into the space.

The dining area still hummed with energy as the last of the lunch crowd lingered. Silverware clinked against plates, and soft conversation ebbed and flowed, creating a soothing backdrop. Each table was meticulously set with crisp cloth napkins and delicate herb centerpieces. Zariyah's eyes swept across the room to the open kitchen, where Dominic's team moved with practiced precision, cleaning up from the busy service.

"Hey, Mrs. Ellis!"

The bright voice pulled her attention to the hostess stand, where Felicity, the restaurant's newest hire, greeted her with a warm smile and a quick hug.

Zariyah forced a smile in return. "Hey, Felicity. Is Dominic in his office?"

Felicity nodded, brushing a loose strand of hair out of her face. "Yep, he's been holed up in there all morning. Want me to let him know you're here?"

Zariyah shook her head. "No need, I'll head back. He's expecting me."

She slipped through the restaurant, her gaze briefly catching the controlled chaos of the kitchen. The clatter of pans and the low hum of conversation were the familiar rhythm of Dominic's world—a world he had built with relentless passion. Pride swelled in her chest, even as the knot of her own frustrations tightened. She needed him to listen today, to help her untangle the mess that had taken root in her life.

As she approached Dominic's office, the door was slightly ajar. She raised her hand to knock just as the door swung open. A woman she didn't recognize stepped out, her heels clicking softly against the hardwood floor. The scent of expensive perfume lingered in her wake as she offered Zariyah a polite smile before disappearing down the hall.

Dominic appeared in the doorway, leaning casually against the frame, his arms crossed over his chest. The knowing smirk on his face immediately softened her tense mood.

"Playin' it cool, huh?" he teased.

Zariyah arched an eyebrow, unable to resist the banter. "Playa, playa."

Dominic laughed, shaking his head. "You're ridiculous. Come on in."

His office, with its mix of practicality and personality, felt like a safe haven. The massive desk, which she had found for him during one of her estate-sale hunts, dominated the space, while framed photos of family and friends lined the shelves. Dominic perched on the edge of his desk, his sharp gaze fixed on her.

"Alright, Z. What's up? You've got that look." He gestured toward her, his tone light, though his concern was evident. "And don't bother sugarcoating it. Just tell me what Sterling did this time."

Zariyah's lips twitched at his directness, but the weight in her chest didn't budge. She sank into one of the leather chairs, the strap of her purse twisting between her fingers.

"He didn't show up last night," she said quietly, her voice wavering.

Dominic's brow furrowed, his expression darkening just slightly. He didn't interrupt, letting her speak at her own pace.

"I spent the whole afternoon getting ready for this dinner party—one of his big client things. I called in favors, asked your team to help with the menu. Everything was perfect. And then…" She trailed off, swallowing hard against the lump in her throat. "Nothing. No call, no text. He didn't even show."

Dominic's fingers drummed against the desk, his jaw tightening. "And then what?"

"He came home after two in the morning," she said, her voice barely above a whisper. "Didn't say a word. Just crawled into bed like nothing happened."

Dominic let out a slow breath, rubbing a hand over his head. "Z, that's—not okay. You shouldn't have to deal with this."

"I know," Zariyah replied, her voice trembling. "But I don't know how to fix it, Nick. I keep trying, but it's like nothing I do is enough."

Dominic stood, moving around the desk to sit beside her on the edge of the chair. He handed her a tissue, his hand squeezing her shoulder gently.

"You're more than enough, Z. You always have been."

Zariyah wiped her eyes, the tears she'd been holding back all morning finally breaking free. "I don't even know if I'm mad at him or at myself anymore."

"You're mad at him," Dominic said firmly. "And you have every right to be. But that doesn't mean you're giving up. It just means he needs to get his act together. You can't keep carrying this on your own."

She nodded, though the knot in her chest didn't loosen.

"You want me to talk to him?" Dominic offered, his tone a mix of protectiveness and frustration.

"No," Zariyah said quickly. "That'll just make things worse."

He sighed, leaning back slightly. "Alright. But you know I'm here if you need me."

"I know," she said softly. "Thanks."

Dominic handed her a to-go box, a small smile breaking through his concern. "Your favorite trio salad. I figured you could use it."

Zariyah laughed softly, her first genuine smile of the day. "Thanks, big brother."

As she headed for the door, Felicity waved her over to the private dining room. Though hesitant, Zariyah allowed herself to be pulled into a conversation about floral arrangements for an upcoming event. The lighthearted distraction was a welcome reprieve, giving her a moment to breathe.

By the time she returned to her car, the tension in her chest had eased, if only slightly. She slid into the driver's seat, pulling a business card from her wallet. The embossed lettering caught the light as her thumb traced over the name.

For a long moment, she stared at it, her thoughts churning. Her fingers trembled slightly as she tapped the number into her phone.

"Hi, can I see you this afternoon? ... I can be there in a few minutes."

As she hung up, she exhaled slowly, leaning her head against the seat. She was really doing this. There was no turning back now.

Chapter 3

Zariyah pulled up to the beige-and-cream Craftsman-style house, her fingers gripping the steering wheel as if it could anchor her. The quiet street was too still, almost mocking her with its calm.

Her gaze lingered on the house, taking in the neatly trimmed hedges and flowerbeds bursting with early spring blooms. It was charming, inviting even. But to her, it felt like a threshold she wasn't sure she should cross.

Was she really ready to do this?

The question twisted in her mind, each loop tightening the knot in her stomach. She pressed her phone to silent and shoved it into her purse, burying it beneath the mess of receipts and lipsticks as though the device itself could betray her.

Her heart raced as she glanced at the house numbers again. They matched. She wasn't in the wrong place. But something about being here felt… dangerous.

What am I doing?

Her fingers hovered over the ignition, debating whether to turn the key and back out of the driveway before anyone knew she had come. But no. She was here for a reason.

She had a right to be here.

Didn't she?

She exhaled sharply and reached for the door handle, her movements stiff and mechanical. The late-afternoon sun warmed her skin as she stepped onto the pavement, but it did nothing to soothe the chill creeping up her spine. Her eyes darted to the neighboring houses, wondering if anyone was watching.

With every step toward the porch, her pulse quickened. She climbed the stairs slowly, her heels clicking too loudly against the wood, each sound hammering at her resolve.

She stood at the door for a long moment, her finger hovering over the doorbell. What would happen if she just… left? No one would know. No one would judge her.

But deep down, she knew the truth: she wasn't ready to walk away. Not from this. Not yet.

The bell chimed before she could second-guess herself again. She stepped back, her chest tightening as she waited.

The door clicked open, revealing the soft glow of the interior. Vanilla and lavender drifted out, wrapping around her like a whisper of comfort.

And then, Dr. Monroe appeared in the doorway, her warm smile immediately softening the jagged edges of Zariyah's nerves.

"You made it," she said gently, stepping aside to let Zariyah inside. Zariyah swallowed hard and nodded, crossing the threshold. She could feel her chest easing with every step into the calm space.

Dr. Monroe was tall, elegant, and strikingly composed. Her tailored dress accentuated her graceful curves, and her short, silver-tipped waves framed her face with an effortless sophistication. Her deep-set eyes held an unspoken understanding, one that made Zariyah's throat tighten.

"You don't have to say anything just yet," Dr. Monroe said, stepping into the room with measured ease. Her voice was gentle but firm, like the kind you didn't question.

Zariyah managed a small nod, her feet carrying her to the sofa. She sank into its softness, the tension in her body loosening just slightly. The iced tea was cool in her hands, grounding her as she took a small sip.

Dr. Monroe settled into the chair across from her, crossing her legs with effortless grace. She rested her hands lightly on her lap, her gaze steady but kind. "Take your time, Zariyah. Start wherever you need to."

Zariyah's fingers tightened around the glass. She stared down at it, watching the condensation form tiny droplets that slid toward her fingers. The words felt stuck, tangled in her throat.

"I'm tired," she said finally, her voice barely above a whisper.

Dr. Monroe nodded, her expression encouraging. "Tired of what?"

Zariyah hesitated, the weight of the truth pressing down on her.

"Of being invisible. Of feeling like nothing I do matters."

Dr. Monroe leaned forward slightly, her eyes intent. "You feel invisible?"

The knot in Zariyah's chest tightened. "With Sterling. In this marriage. I don't even know if I'm angry at him or at myself anymore."

The admission hung in the air between them, heavy and raw.

"What happened?" Dr. Monroe asked softly.

Zariyah's gaze dropped to the glass again. The memory was sharp, cutting through her defenses. The untouched table, the cold candles, the empty seats.

"He didn't show up," she said, her voice trembling. "I planned this dinner party for him—for his clients. I called in favors. I made everything perfect. And he didn't even bother to show. No call, no explanation. Nothing."

Dr. Monroe's expression softened, concern etched in her features. "And how did that make you feel?"

"Like I don't matter," Zariyah whispered. "Like everything I do is just… a waste."

Her hands shook as she set the glass down. Tears pricked at the corners of her eyes, but she blinked them away.

Dr. Monroe didn't rush to fill the silence. She waited, her presence steady and calm, giving Zariyah the space to unravel her thoughts.

"Why do you think you feel that way, Zariyah?"

The question lingered, cutting deeper than Zariyah expected. She opened her mouth, but the words refused to come. She shook her head, retreating. "I don't know."

Dr. Monroe tilted her head slightly, her silence an invitation for more.

But Zariyah couldn't go there—not yet. Instead, her mind drifted back to Sterling. To the early days when his charm had swept her off her feet, when his grand gestures had seemed like the height of romance. Back then, she thought she had everything she ever wanted.

But now? Now those gestures felt hollow, like distractions from the real issues he refused to face.

"Zariyah?"

Dr. Monroe's calm voice brought her back to the present. The room felt smaller, the walls closing in as the weight of her emotions pressed harder.

Dr. Monroe's gaze was steady, unyielding but kind. "Is this about more than just Sterling?"

The question landed like a stone in her chest.

Zariyah looked away, her throat tightening. She wanted to answer, but the truth was too big, too heavy. She wasn't ready to face it—not yet.

Her fingers brushed against the edge of the sofa, grounding her as she forced herself to meet Dr. Monroe's gaze. "I don't know," she lied, though they both knew the truth was lurking somewhere just beneath the surface.

Zariyah sat in her car long after leaving Dr. Monroe's office, her hands resting limply on the steering wheel. She wasn't ready to drive yet—not ready to face the silence of home or the questions Dr. Monroe had stirred to the surface.

The session had left her raw, vulnerable in a way she hadn't expected. Dr. Monroe's words still echoed in her mind. Is this about more than Sterling?

Chapter
4

The space beside her was empty when Zariyah awoke the next morning, but the lingering traces of Sterling's presence were unmistakable: the faint scent of his cologne, a damp towel draped over the bathroom counter, and an empty coffee mug abandoned on the kitchen island.

Once, these little remnants of him had felt like threads tying their lives together. Waking up to the hum of his routine had been comforting, a quiet reminder of their shared world. Now, it felt like a series of ghostly signs pointing to how far apart they'd drifted.

She picked up the mug and placed it in the sink, letting the cold ceramic press against her palm. Her fingers lingered, the sharp contrast to the warmth of her memories cutting through her. How had they come to this?

The house, large and silent, felt too big for the growing void between them. Once, its understated elegance had mirrored their vision of a perfect life together. The sprawling one-story European-style home, with its four bedrooms, marble countertops, and pristine chef's kitchen, had been the backdrop for countless dinner parties, family holidays, and late-night talks over glasses of wine.

But now? It felt more like a museum of their past life, carefully curated and dusted but devoid of life.

Zariyah wandered into the family room, the open floor plan giving way to floor-to-ceiling windows that framed the backyard. Spring's early blooms dotted the edges of the garden, and the waterfall at the far end of the pool shimmered in the morning light. It was a view she had once cherished, but today, it felt distant and detached.

Her gaze lingered on the wrought-iron arbor at the edge of the garden, its climbing roses just beginning to bud. Beyond it, the octagonal gazebo stood surrounded by azaleas and hydrangeas—a space that had once been her sanctuary.

But the magic of her garden, like so much else in her life, felt muted.

With a sigh, Zariyah turned toward her office. This room was hers, untouched by Sterling's presence. It was a small reprieve, a space where she could breathe freely and focus on the parts of her life she still controlled.

She had barely settled at her desk when her phone buzzed, its sharp tone shattering the fragile silence. The name on the screen made her stomach twist.

Her mother.

Zariyah sighed and pressed the speaker button. "Good morning, Momma. What can I do for you?"

"Don't get smart with me," her mother snapped. "Why didn't you answer the first time I called?"

Zariyah pinched the bridge of her nose, already feeling the familiar ache building behind her eyes. Noni's calls were rarely kind. They were reminders of what Zariyah hadn't done, of the ways she had failed to meet her mother's expectations.

And she knew exactly where this conversation was going.

As Noni launched into complaints about overdue bills, Zariyah's mind drifted, the sharp criticisms pricking her skin like tiny needles. Her mother's voice filled the room, overpowering the quiet calm Zariyah had sought in her office.

"You need to get checked out," Noni said suddenly, her tone sharp. "Something must be wrong with you if Sterling hasn't given you any babies yet. A man like him? You should've had a house full of children by now."

Zariyah's stomach clenched, her nails digging into her palm. The words hit harder than they should have, cutting deep into wounds she tried desperately to ignore.

"Mom," she interrupted, her voice strained. "I'll put the money in your account later."

Without waiting for a response, Zariyah hung up and exhaled sharply, pressing her hands flat against the desk. The ache in her chest refused to ease, the weight of her mother's words settling heavily on her shoulders.

The sound of the security chime startled her. Someone had entered the house.

Zariyah glanced at the clock. Ms. Emma, their housekeeper, wasn't due in today. That meant one thing: Sterling was home.

He appeared in the doorway of her office, leaning casually against the frame. He looked effortlessly handsome, his T-shirt clinging to his broad shoulders, his jeans perfectly fitted. The scruff on his jaw added an edge to his clean-cut appearance, a detail that might have once made her smile.

Now, it only deepened the ache in her chest.

"You having a good day?" he asked, his tone casual, as if their life hadn't unraveled thread by thread.

"I was," Zariyah replied, the bitterness in her voice sharper than she intended.

Sterling frowned slightly, his gaze flicking to the round table in the corner of her office. It was her space, the place where she worked, planned, and kept things in order. His presence here felt like an intrusion.

"Still upset about the other night?" he asked, his voice tinged with exasperation. "You know there was nothing I could do."

The pencil in Zariyah's hand tapped against the desk, her only response. She didn't trust herself to speak.

Sterling sighed, running a hand through his hair. "I'll be right back."

She watched him leave, her body tense with anticipation. A gesture was coming. A peace offering. It always did, as if something tangible could paper over the widening cracks in their marriage.

When Sterling returned, he carried a tray of sandwiches and a pitcher of sweet tea. He placed everything carefully on the round table, the arrangement meticulous, almost performative.

"Come. Let's eat," he said, pulling out a chair and waiting for her to join him.

Zariyah hesitated, her feet heavy as she crossed the room. This table, her sanctuary, was now part of Sterling's script. She sat, though her appetite had vanished.

Sterling filled the silence with small talk—stories from work, apologies for missing the dinner. His words felt rehearsed, like lines memorized for a performance.

Then, he pulled out a small velvet box and placed it beside her plate.

"I'm really sorry about the other night," he said, his voice softer now. "I should've called. You went to all that trouble, and I let you down."

Zariyah stared at the box, her heart heavy.

"Where were you?" she asked quietly, the question slipping out before she could stop it.

Sterling faltered, his eyes shifting away. He opened his mouth to respond but closed it again, the silence between them louder than any excuse.

Zariyah pushed her chair back, her sandwich untouched. Sterling reached for her arm, but she pulled away, the physical distance a mirror of the emotional gulf between them.

She turned without a word, her movements deliberate but unhurried, as if trying to hold onto the last shreds of her composure. The soft scrape of her chair against the floor echoed in the quiet room, filling the silence Sterling didn't dare break.

Her footsteps were steady, but with each step toward the door, her chest tightened, the weight of the conversation pressing harder with every inch she put between them.

Just as her hand brushed the door handle, his voice cut through the air like a whip.

"You think I'm the only one to blame here? Maybe you should ask yourself why things are the way they are."

Zariyah froze, her hand hovering above the doorknob, Sterling's words hanging in the air like a slap. The ache in her chest sharpened, twisting into something darker—anger, frustration, maybe even guilt. But guilt for what? For trying? For caring? For not walking away sooner?

She turned slowly, her eyes locking on his. "You really think that, Sterling? That this is my fault?"

He didn't answer immediately, his jaw tightening as he folded his arms. For a moment, he looked like he might respond, but instead, he shook his head and walked past her toward the family room.

"That's not what I said," he muttered, though his tone

was anything but apologetic.

"Sure sounds like it," she called after him, but her voice cracked on the last word.

Sterling didn't look back, and she didn't wait for him to. The moment she stepped out of the room, she felt like she could breathe again. But the relief was fleeting, replaced by the weight of everything unsaid, everything unresolved.

The night passed in silence, each corner of the house feeling like a separate battlefield. Sterling spent most of it in the family room, the sound of muted sports commentary filtering through the closed door. Zariyah stayed in her office, burying herself in work she couldn't focus on.

By the time she finally crawled into bed, Sterling was already there, his back turned to her. The chasm between them felt wider than ever, the air thick with words neither of them would say.

Zariyah tightened her fingers on the steering wheel as she pulled into the driveway of Dr. Monroe's house, the beige-and-cream Craftsman just as inviting as it had been the day before. But today, the sight of it didn't soothe her. Today, it felt like a mirror, forcing her to look at the parts of herself she wanted to avoid.

She sat in the car for a moment, staring at the house's familiar lines, the neat flowerbeds, the wind chimes that swayed gently in the breeze. Her mind replayed Sterling's words from the night before, each syllable like a thorn digging into her skin.

You should ask yourself why things are the way they are.

She had asked herself that, over and over again. And no matter how many ways she turned it around, she always came back to the same conclusion: she couldn't fix this alone.

Taking a deep breath, Zariyah grabbed her purse and

stepped out of the car. Her chest felt tight as she climbed the porch steps and rang the bell. She wasn't sure what she'd say today—how much she was ready to admit—but at least here, she didn't have to carry it all alone.

The door opened, and Dr. Monroe's warm, steady presence filled the space.

"Come in," she said, her smile soft but inviting. "You're right on time."

Zariyah nodded, stepping inside.

Chapter
5

The warmth of Dr. Monroe's office felt almost stifling today, the vanilla scent heavy in the air as Zariyah sat on the navy sofa. She clutched the glass of iced tea in her hands, the condensation slick against her palms.

She had replayed the morning's argument with Sterling countless times on the drive over, every unanswered question and unspoken truth gnawing at her. His silence. The unopened velvet box. That final, cutting remark.

You think I'm the only one to blame here? Maybe you should ask yourself why things are the way they are.

The words clung to her like a bruise, tender and unshakable.

Dr. Monroe's voice pulled her back to the present. "Where would you like to start today?"

Zariyah hesitated, her fingers tightening around the glass. "We fought again," she said quietly.

Dr. Monroe nodded, her expression attentive but neutral. "What happened?"

"It's like… he doesn't get it. He doesn't see me. He thinks gestures fix everything, but they don't. Not when he's not really listening."

As the words spilled out, Zariyah felt both relief and a strange sense of guilt. Saying it out loud made it feel too real, like she couldn't take it back. Like she was betraying him, even though he'd betrayed her first in so many small, quiet ways.

She stared into the glass, her grip tightening as she continued. "He brought lunch to my office, made it all perfect—like a stage set for reconciliation. But it didn't matter. It didn't fix the way he dismissed me. And when I asked where he was the night before, he didn't answer. That silence… it was louder than anything he could've said."

Dr. Monroe leaned forward slightly, her gaze steady. "What did that silence remind you of, Zariyah?"

The question made her chest tighten. Zariyah hesitated, staring at the glass of tea in her hands. "It's just… when he ignores me, it's like I'm invisible again." She paused, her voice dropping. "Like I was back then. Like nothing I did mattered."

Dr. Monroe's voice was calm, measured. "Back then?"

Zariyah looked away, the faint flicker of a memory tugging at the edges of her mind. "It's hard to explain. I've been having these… dreams. Not dreams, really— nightmares."

Dr. Monroe tilted her head slightly, her expression one of quiet encouragement. "What are the nightmares about?"

"I don't know," Zariyah lied, her throat tightening. "I wake up, and I just feel… this heaviness, like something terrible happened, but I can't quite place it."

Dr. Monroe waited, her silence gentle but expectant. Zariyah's fingers tightened around the glass. "It's not just the nightmares, though. It's the way I feel when Sterling doesn't see me. It's like… I'm back there again. Waiting. Hoping. And no one ever comes."

Zariyah's voice cracked on the last word, and she quickly wiped her eyes. "I thought I'd moved on from that part of my life. But it feels like it's still there, just waiting to creep back in."

Dr. Monroe nodded, her tone even. "Sometimes, when trauma isn't fully processed, it manifests in different ways—through dreams, through feelings we can't quite explain.

It's your mind's way of saying it's still there."

Zariyah swallowed hard, her hands trembling slightly. "I'm not ready to go there, Dr. Monroe. Not yet."

Dr. Monroe leaned back, her gaze steady. "That's okay, Zariyah. Recognizing it is the first step. We'll go at your pace."

As she left Dr. Monroe's office, Zariyah's chest felt lighter, though her thoughts remained tangled. She climbed into her car, staring out at the flowerbeds lining the driveway.

When her phone buzzed, she reached for it hesitantly. Sterling's name flashed on the screen.

We need to talk. Tonight.

Her grip tightened on the phone, her stomach twisting. Hope and dread warred inside her, each pulling in opposite directions. What did he want to say? And was she ready to hear it?

With a slow breath, Zariyah put the phone down and turned the key in the ignition. The road ahead felt as uncertain as her next steps.

Leaving Dr. Monroe's office, Zariyah felt the weight of the session still pressing against her chest. The sun was warm, casting long shadows on the driveway as she walked to her car, but it didn't ease the tension knotted in her stomach.

She replayed the conversation in her head as she drove home, the connections Dr. Monroe had drawn between her past and her present looping like a song stuck on repeat.

By the time she pulled into her driveway, the sense of clarity she'd found in therapy had dulled, replaced by the familiar ache of unresolved feelings.

* * *

An hour later, Zariyah returned to her office, thankful that Sterling wasn't home. The silence of the house wrapped around her like a heavy blanket, equal parts relief and weight.

She moved to the window, her gaze settling on the waterfall in the backyard. The steady cascade of water over the rocks had always been soothing, but today, even its rhythmic flow couldn't quiet her thoughts.

How had we gotten here?

Zariyah and Sterling had been happy once—or at least she thought they had. But lately, their lives felt like two parallel lines under the same roof, growing further apart with each passing day. She had tried, time and time again, to bring them back together, but every effort was met with the same distance, the same walls.

She turned back to her desk, her eyes catching on the small velvet box Sterling had left earlier. She hadn't opened it yet, but she knew what it was—another piece of guilt jewelry, another attempt to patch over the cracks in their marriage without ever addressing the foundation.

Her fingers hovered over the box before flipping it open, revealing a sapphire and diamond pendant with matching earrings. They were stunning, as always. But this time, beauty wasn't enough.

Zariyah set the box down, her chest tightening as frustration bubbled up inside her. *He thinks this will fix it?* The gesture felt hollow, like the apology he hadn't fully given.

Next to the box was a note, hastily scribbled in Sterling's familiar handwriting: *I'm running out for a bit. See you later. — S.*

The words were simple, almost dismissive. Like she didn't deserve more.

Her phone buzzed on the desk, Aimee's name flashing across the screen.

"Girl, why do you sound like you've lost your best friend? Is everything all right over there?" Aimee's voice was bright, but a thread of concern wove through her tone.

Zariyah forced a smile into her voice. "Everything's peachy," she replied, using their code for *don't ask.*

"I could say the same about you," Zariyah said, trying to keep her voice light.

"Shouldn't you be closing another big deal?"

"I did! Closed a three-million-dollar deal this morning, thank you very much." Aimee's laughter filled the line, and for a moment, Zariyah felt a pang of envy. Aimee had a way of making everything seem effortless.

"Congratulations! I know you've been working on that one for a while."

"Two years," Aimee said, sighing dramatically. "And now I'm ready to spoil myself. Come with me. I'm headed to Saks for some retail therapy."

"I don't know, Aimee. I've got a lot on my plate—"

"Z, come on. You need this. I'll even buy you a drink after. We haven't had girl time in forever."

Zariyah hesitated. Aimee's energy was contagious, but her own mood was weighed down by thoughts of Sterling and the widening gap between them. Still, maybe she needed the distraction. Aimee always had a way of pulling her out of her head, even if just for a little while.

* * *

"Fine," Zariyah relented. "But only for a little while."

She sighed, tossing the note aside. She reached for her phone and typed a message: Gone shopping with Aimee. Having dinner with her afterward. *Thanks for the pendant and earrings. They're beautiful.*

She didn't wait for a response before slipping the jewelry back into the box and heading out to meet Aimee.

* * *

Inside Saks, Zariyah tried to match Aimee's energy as they browsed through fragrance counters and evening gowns. Aimee flirted with the staff, her laughter echoing through the dressing room, while Zariyah's mind wandered back to the sapphire pendant sitting on her desk.

When Aimee settled on a silver one-shoulder dress, Zariyah couldn't help but smile at her friend's confidence.

"You're going to steal the show," she said, trying to let herself bask in Aimee's joy.

"For once, I deserve to," Aimee replied with a wink, her eyes lighting up as the stylist brought over matching rhinestone stilettos.

* * *

Over dinner, Aimee leaned back in her chair, her sly smile hinting at something she'd been waiting to reveal.

"So," she began, swirling the last of her drink in its glass. "I have a date for the Jasper Ball."

Zariyah raised a skeptical brow. "Oh? Who's the lucky guy?"

"Richard Walker."

Zariyah nearly choked. "Richard Walker? That Richard Walker?"

"The one and only," Aimee said, her smile widening.

Memories of Aimee crying over Richard flashed through Zariyah's mind—the heartbreak, the promises he hadn't kept, the way he'd disappeared and left Aimee in pieces.

"You swore you'd never speak to him again," Zariyah said, her disbelief evident.

Aimee shrugged. "People change. He's divorced now. Shared custody of his kids, and yes, I've seen the papers."

Zariyah wanted to believe her, but doubt lingered. Her own marriage felt like it was sinking, and the idea of giving Richard a second chance felt like another bad omen. But she didn't voice her concerns. Aimee was a grown woman. She could make her own decisions. Even if Zariyah feared this one would end the same way the others had.

It wasn't the first time Aimee had fallen hard for the wrong man. And it wasn't the first time Zariyah had been the one to pick up the pieces.

Zariyah's mind drifted to the night three years ago, when

Aimee had shown up at her doorstep, mascara streaked down her cheeks and clutching an overnight bag. Her hands trembled as she knocked, and when Zariyah opened the door, the look in her eyes had been enough to make Zariyah's heart drop.

"I don't want to talk about it," Aimee had said quickly, brushing past her into the living room. "Don't even start with your I told you so."

"I wasn't going to say that," Zariyah replied, shutting the door softly. "But now that you've mentioned it…"

Aimee let out a choked laugh that turned into a sob, sinking onto the couch. Her hands covered her face, her whole body shaking.

"He's married, Z." Her voice cracked as she forced the words out. "He's married, and I didn't know. I didn't—"

Zariyah sat down beside her, heart sinking as she wrapped an arm around her friend. "Oh, Aimee…"

"I caught him," Aimee continued, her words spilling out between sobs. "At that little Italian place on Third. He said he was meeting a client, but it was her. They were—" She broke off, burying her face in her hands again.

For a moment, Zariyah couldn't find the words. She had always known Aimee had a knack for falling for the wrong men, but this? A married man? It was worse than she could have imagined.

"I'm such an idiot," Aimee whispered. "How could I not see it? All the times he canceled plans, all the excuses… I should've known."

"You're not an idiot," Zariyah said firmly. "He's the idiot. And a liar. And a piece of—"

Aimee cut her off with a bitter laugh, wiping her cheeks. "Save it. I've already called him every name in the book."

They sat there in silence for a moment, the weight of the

betrayal hanging heavy between them. Then, Aimee sighed, leaning back against the couch.

* * *

"Why does this keep happening to me, Z? Why do I keep falling for men like this?"

Zariyah didn't have an answer. All she could do was reach for the wine they kept for emergencies like this, pouring two generous glasses and handing one to Aimee.

They had stayed up until the early hours of the morning, dissecting every moment of Aimee's relationship with the man—every lie, every red flag she had ignored. Zariyah listened, offered advice where she could, and let her friend cry until she finally fell asleep on the couch.

Even now, sitting across from Aimee in the restaurant, Zariyah could see traces of that night in her friend's eyes. The same vulnerability, the same flicker of hope that maybe this time would be different.

Zariyah took a sip of her drink, swallowing the words she wanted to say. Aimee might be a grown woman, but she still had a knack for finding new ways to break her own heart. And Zariyah had always been the one to pick up the pieces.

* * *

Later that evening, Zariyah returned to a quiet house. Sterling was sprawled on the family room sofa, fast asleep. The faint smell of barbecue lingered in the air, though there was no evidence of his dinner left behind.

She stood in the doorway for a moment, watching him. He looked so peaceful, his chest rising and falling with the rhythm of sleep. But the sight didn't bring her comfort. If anything, it deepened the ache in her chest—the feeling of being alone, even when he was right there.

In their bedroom, Zariyah washed the day's makeup from her face, the steam from the shower curling around her like a fog. Her reflection in the mirror caught her off guard—tired eyes, a heavy heart.

By the time she slipped into bed, exhaustion weighed her down, but sleep didn't come easily. Moments later, Sterling slid in beside her. He turned his back to her, falling asleep within seconds, the physical distance between them mirroring the emotional gulf she couldn't seem to cross.

Zariyah stared at the ceiling, the silence pressing down on her like a suffocating force. She couldn't shake the feeling that something was about to give—and when it did, everything would change.

Chapter
7

Zariyah hadn't slept well. She had tossed and turned, her thoughts spinning like a carousel, replaying the laughter she shared with Aimee and the silence she returned to at home. The contrast gnawed at her, leaving her restless and drained.

When she finally opened her eyes, the light filtering through the curtains did little to soothe her. She turned over, her gaze falling to Sterling's side of the bed. Empty. Again.

The quiet emptiness beside her mirrored the growing gulf between them. She let out a breath, forcing herself to sit up, even as the ache in her chest lingered.

Zariyah wrapped herself in her robe and padded downstairs, her footsteps echoing through the stillness. The house was spotless, as though it had erased every trace of Sterling's presence. Even his cologne, faint and fleeting, felt like it was slipping away.

She paused at the kitchen island, where the small velvet box still sat, unopened since she'd shown it to Aimee. Her fingers traced the soft fabric absentmindedly, but the sight of it only made her chest tighten. Sterling's gift, like his words, was beautiful on the surface but hollow underneath.

Her phone buzzed on the counter, breaking the silence. A message from Sterling: Have a good day. Let's talk when I get home tonight.

Zariyah stared at the screen. The words were too familiar, too rehearsed. How many times had they had these conversations? The apologies, the promises, the temporary peace before it all unraveled again.

She texted back a simple Okay, but her heart wasn't in it.

* * *

Later that morning, Zariyah sat at her desk, trying to lose herself in work. She had deadlines looming—branding concepts for a client's conference—and she welcomed the distraction. But no matter how many times she stared at her screen or sketched out new ideas, her thoughts drifted back to Sterling.

The conversation they were supposed to have loomed over her like a dark cloud. Would this time be any different? Could it be?

She pushed her chair back and stood to stretch, her gaze drifting toward the window. Outside, the waterfall shimmered as it cascaded into the pool below, its steady rhythm mocking her restless thoughts.

The familiar buzz of her phone jolted her out of her reverie. Her mother's name flashed across the screen.

Zariyah hesitated. She knew what this call would bring. It always did. After a few seconds, she swiped to answer.

"Hi, Mom," she said, keeping her tone neutral.

"Well, it's about time you answered. I've been trying to reach you for days," Noni's voice rang out, sharp and clipped.

Zariyah braced herself. The conversation unfolded predictably: complaints about the landscaping, demands to fix the water heater, and a reminder that the car insurance payment was due.

"I'll send what I can," Zariyah replied quietly, forcing herself to stay calm.

"Make sure you do," her mother added before abruptly hanging up.

Zariyah set the phone down, her hand trembling slightly. The pressure from her mother, the emotional distance from Sterling—it was all too much. She felt like she was being crushed under the weight of everyone else's needs, her own buried so deeply she couldn't even find them anymore.

Zariyah sat at the dining table, her stomach churning as she replayed Sterling's message from earlier: We need to talk.

Her mind had run wild all day. Was he going to say he wanted a divorce? Admit he was cheating? Or worse, somehow twist everything around to make it her fault?

The sound of the front door opening made her heart lurch. She straightened in her chair, her hands gripping the edge of the table as Sterling's footsteps moved through the house.

He appeared in the doorway, his expression hard to read, and the air between them seemed to thicken. He didn't sit right away, instead pacing to the counter where the velvet box still sat. His eyes flicked to it, then back to her.

"We need to talk," he said, his tone sharp and clipped.

Zariyah's pulse quickened. "So talk," she said evenly, though her voice betrayed a slight tremor.

Sterling's jaw tightened as he finally took a seat across from her. He clasped his hands together, his knuckles white. "I can't keep doing this, Zariyah. The tension, the distance—it's suffocating."

Her heart dropped, the words hitting harder than she anticipated. "You can't keep doing this?" she repeated, incredulous. "What exactly is this, Sterling? Me trying to hold our marriage together while you disappear into your work and your silence?"

Sterling's eyes flashed, and he leaned forward, his voice rising. "Don't turn this around on me. You think I'm not trying? You think it's easy coming home to someone who's constantly pushing me away?"

Zariyah blinked, the accusation cutting through her anger. "Pushing you away?" she repeated, her voice rising. "How am I pushing you away, Sterling? By asking for your attention? By begging you to talk to me?"

Sterling slammed his hands on the table, his voice booming. "By making everything my fault! Every look, every word—it's like you've already decided I'm not good enough for you anymore!"

"That's not fair," Zariyah shot back, standing abruptly. "I've been here, trying to hold us together, while you shut me out over and over again. How can you say I'm pushing you away when you're the one who's never here?"

Sterling rose to his feet, his voice growing colder. "And how am I supposed to be here, Zariyah, when all you ever do is remind me of how much I'm failing you?"

Zariyah froze, his words landing like a slap. "Failing me?" she said, her voice trembling. "The only thing you've failed at, Sterling, is showing up. Showing up for me, for us. I've been screaming for you to notice me, to hear me, but you just disappear. Every. Single. Time."

Sterling's face darkened, and he took a step closer. "And maybe I disappear because every time I try, I'm met with that same wall, Zariyah. The one where nothing I do is enough. No matter what I say, no matter what I give, it's never enough for you."

Her chest tightened, her breath coming in sharp bursts.

"That's bullshit, Sterling, and you know it."

"Do I?" he challenged, his voice dropping. "Because lately, I feel like I'm just the guy paying the bills while you're off building your perfect little world—without me."

Zariyah felt the sting of his words but refused to let them sink in. "You don't get to rewrite history. Where were you the night of the dinner party? Or all those late nights when you didn't bother calling? Where were you, Sterling?"

Sterling's jaw clenched, his hands forming fists at his sides. "Don't," he said, his voice low and warning.

"Why not?" Zariyah pushed, stepping closer to him. "Because you don't have an answer? Or because you know I'm right?"

The silence that followed was deafening. Sterling's nostrils flared, his chest rising and falling as if he were trying to hold something back.

"You think I'm the only one who's failing here?" he said finally, his voice venomous. "You've been checked out for months, Zariyah. Don't stand there acting like this is all on me."

She stared at him, her chest heaving. "What the hell is that supposed to mean?"

"It means," Sterling snapped, "that maybe if you stopped pointing fingers for two seconds, you'd realize you're not as perfect as you think you are."

The words hit her like a blow, and for a moment, she couldn't find her voice. Sterling turned on his heel, walking toward the family room.

"I'm done talking," he said over his shoulder, his voice cold.

Zariyah stood there, her heart pounding as the echo of his words settled into the quiet house. She didn't know whether to scream, cry, or let the silence consume her.

Her gaze fell to the velvet box on the counter, its lid slightly ajar. The sapphires caught the light, mocking her with their brilliance. She picked it up, her hands trembling, and hurled it into the sink with a sharp clatter.

The room felt too small, too heavy, and Zariyah could barely breathe. She grabbed her phone, her fingers hovering over the screen, wanting to call someone—anyone—to release the pressure building inside her.

But she didn't. Instead, she sank into the nearest chair, burying her face in her hands as the weight of everything she'd been holding onto finally crashed down.

Chapter

8

Zariyah woke the next morning, her body stiff and her head heavy with exhaustion. She blinked against the sunlight streaming through the bedroom window, her eyes settling on the empty side of the bed.

Sterling was gone. Again.

The memories of the night before pressed heavy on her chest—the way they'd collided physically, as though trying to silence everything unsaid. For Sterling, it had been enough. For her? The ache in her chest was proof that it hadn't been.

She lay still, staring at the ceiling, the weight of yesterday pressing down on her like an anchor. The argument played on a loop in her mind—his accusations, her anger, the way his words had hit her deepest wounds.

Zariyah ran a hand over her face, letting out a slow breath. She didn't have the energy to be angry anymore. All that was left was a dull ache, the kind that comes from wanting to fight but knowing it wouldn't change anything.

She had snuggled against Sterling's solid chest sometime during the night, his arms wrapped tightly around her like a fortress. His warmth had enveloped her, but the memories of the previous night came rushing back, sharp and unyielding.

Why do I let this happen? she thought, trying to shift away. But the moment she moved, Sterling's arms tightened, pulling her closer.

"Don't," he muttered sleepily, his voice low and rough. "Stay."

"Sterling, I need to get up," she murmured, though her words lacked conviction.

"You're just trying to escape me." His lips brushed her temple, trailing slowly down to her collarbone. "You don't have to run, Z."

His voice, rich and persuasive, struck something deep in her—a reminder of the man she once believed he was, the man she sometimes thought she still loved.

She wanted to resist, to push him away, but Sterling knew how to unravel her defenses. He kissed the hollow of her neck, his touch firm yet tender, and she cursed the way her body responded despite everything.

"You don't get to charm your way out of this," she said, glaring at him. But her voice faltered as his hand slid down her side, possessive and insistent.

Sterling smirked, his dark eyes gleaming. "Are you sure about that?"

Before she could respond, his mouth captured hers, his kiss deep and urgent. It was a familiar dance—one where desire masked their unresolved anger. She hated how easily her body betrayed her, responding to him even as her mind screamed no.

Their movements were frantic, fueled by frustration as much as passion. When it was over, Zariyah lay still, staring at the ceiling as Sterling's breathing slowed beside her. The room was quiet again, but the storm inside her hadn't settled.

For him, the connection had worked like a reset button, a way to move past the fight without actually addressing it.

But for her, it was just another reminder of how far apart they'd drifted.

Sterling had fallen asleep beside her, his arm draped across her waist, but Zariyah had lain awake for hours, staring into the darkness. By the time she drifted off, exhaustion had replaced her anger, though the ache in her chest remained.

She pushed herself up and swung her legs over the side of the bed, letting her feet touch the cool hardwood floor. The sound of footsteps broke the quiet. Sterling appeared in the doorway, carrying a tray with a steaming mug and a plate of muffins. His pajama bottoms hung low on his hips, showing off the broad planes of his chest and arms. The six-pack he still maintained was a shadow of the twelve-pack he used to have, but he was no less magnetic. His cinnamon-toned skin gleamed in the soft morning light, rich and warm, and Zariyah hated how much her body responded to him, even now.

"Good morning," he said, setting the tray on the nightstand.

His voice was calm, teasing, as though nothing had happened the night before. It grated on her nerves, but she stayed silent, watching as he poured cream and sugar into her tea with practiced ease.

"You look like you could use this," he said, pouring cream and sugar into her tea as though they hadn't been at each other's throats less than 12 hours ago. "Figured it might smooth things over."

Zariyah raised an eyebrow, folding her arms across her chest. "Smooth things over?"

Sterling handed her the mug, his expression disarming. "Life's too short to stay mad."

She accepted the tea but didn't take a sip. Instead, she studied him—his easy smile, the slight twinkle in his eye, the way he could brush past an argument as if it hadn't left scars.

"Sterling," she began, her tone sharp, "last night—"

"Let's not, Z," he interrupted, his voice soft but firm. "Not first thing in the morning."

Zariyah's jaw tightened. "So we're just going to ignore it?"

"No," he said, sitting beside her on the bed. His hand rested on her knee, warm and steady. "We're going to let it breathe. Give it space."

Her chest tightened at his words, the familiar blend of frustration and longing twisting inside her. Sterling leaned in, his voice dropping lower.

"I know I'm not perfect," he said, his lips brushing her temple. "But I love you, Z."

Her breath caught, her resolve faltering. He kissed her cheek, then her jaw, his hands sliding to her waist.

"Sterling," she said, her voice trembling. "We can't keep doing this—"

But his lips silenced her, his kiss slow and deliberate, like he was determined to remind her of everything they once had.

* * *

Later, as Zariyah sat alone in the shower, the water cascading over her, she tried to untangle the knot of emotions twisting inside her. The sex had been like it always was with Sterling—intense, consuming, a temporary reprieve from the storm.

But that was all it was: temporary.

For him, the connection had worked like a reset button, wiping the slate clean. He had fallen back into his easy charm, kissing her forehead before leaving the room to start breakfast, as though the fight had never happened.

For her, it had been something else entirely—a reminder of how easily she gave in, how much she wanted to believe in a version of them that no longer existed.

Zariyah scrubbed her hands over her face, willing herself to let the water wash away the regret that clung to her. But as she stepped out of the shower and caught her reflection in the mirror, the ache in her chest told her that nothing had really changed.

She took her time getting ready, her movements deliberate. Sitting at the vanity, she swept concealer under her tired eyes and blended it carefully, taking care to erase every trace of the previous night's emotions. A few swipes of bronzer sculpted her cheekbones, and she added a soft pink blush for a touch of life.

Her eyeliner was sharp, her mascara lengthened and defined, and her lip color—a bold crimson—was the final layer of armor. As she leaned back to inspect her reflection, she looked polished, composed. Not a hair out of place.

She dressed in a black pencil skirt and a fitted top that hugged her figure perfectly. Her three-inch open-toe sandals clicked across the hardwood floors as she moved back to the bedroom. At the dresser, she dropped her lipstick and other items into her purse, her motions efficient and sharp.

As she stepped into the bedroom, Sterling, who was sitting on the edge of the bed, stopped scrolling on his phone. His hand hovered over the screen for a moment before he set it down, watching her in silence. His gaze lingered, taking her in, but she didn't spare him a glance.

"I've got meetings out of the office all day, and I won't be home for dinner. I'm going to Dominic's."

Her voice was cool, measured, like a blade slicing through the stillness.

Sterling stood, blocking her path with a single step, his

eyes narrowing slightly as confusion clouded his expression.

"You're going to make me late for my meeting. Move, Sterling."

She didn't raise her voice, but the sharpness in her tone left no room for argument.

He stared at her for a long moment, his jaw tightening before he stepped aside. "I'll be here when you get home."

* * *

Charades was beginning to wind down from the lunch rush when Zariyah arrived. The warm glow of pendant lights and the faint hum of jazz music wrapped around her like a familiar hug. The scent of grilled seafood and fresh herbs lingered in the air, a signature of her brother's culinary mastery.

The staff greeted her warmly, and she made her way to her brother's office in the back. The door was open, and she knocked lightly, peeking her head in.

Dominic looked up from a pile of paperwork, his face breaking into a smile. "Hey, Sis, what brings you by?"

"Just stopping by to see my brother," Zariyah said, plopping down into the chair opposite his desk.

Dominic leaned back in his chair, his eyes narrowing slightly as he studied her.

"Everything okay?"

Zariyah shifted in her seat, fiddling with the edge of her napkin. "Yeah, just... stuff with Sterling. Nothing I can't handle."

Dominic raised an eyebrow but didn't press. Instead, he leaned forward, resting his elbows on the desk. "Well, you're here now. Let's focus on the good stuff—like me."

She couldn't help but laugh, the tension in her chest loosening just slightly. That was Dominic for you, always finding a way to distract her.

As they made their way to the kitchen, Dominic filled her in on the latest happenings at the restaurant, his usual humor putting her at ease.

Once they sat down with plates of food, Dominic leaned in, lowering his voice. "So, I wasn't going to bring this up, but... Ciara called me yesterday."

Zariyah's stomach turned at the mention of Dominic's ex-wife. Ciara had been trouble from the start—ungrateful, manipulative, always making Dominic jump through hoops.

"What did she want?" Zariyah asked, trying to keep her tone neutral.

"I don't know. I haven't called her back yet," Dominic said, frowning. "But I'm not sure if I even want to."

"Good," Zariyah said firmly. "Don't. You know she's just going to try and get something out of you."

Dominic sighed, rubbing his hand over his shaved head. "Yeah, you're probably right." He paused, but the flicker of uncertainty in his eyes lingered, as if Ciara's shadow still hung over him.

They spent the next hour catching up, swapping stories about their mother's latest antics and the usual family gossip. By the time Zariyah was ready to head home, she felt lighter. Visiting Dominic always had that effect on her.

As Zariyah drove home, Sterling's final words echoed in her mind. "I'll be here when you get home."

But something about the way he'd said it made her stomach turn.

Chapter 9

The house was dark when Zariyah returned home that evening. Sterling's car was in the driveway, just as he'd said it would be, but seeing it only added to the heaviness she carried.

Inside, the faint glow of the living room lamp spilled into the hall, leading to their master suite. Sterling was sprawled across the bed, his head tilted back and his laptop still open beside him. A half-eaten takeout container sat on the nightstand, the smoky aroma of barbecue lingering faintly in the air.

For a moment, Zariyah lingered in the doorway. His face was peaceful, soft in sleep—so unlike the man who had pulled her close that morning, as though a single act could erase the widening gap between them.

She stepped closer, carefully closing the laptop and setting it aside. Her fingers hovered over the container, and she hesitated before picking it up. The barbecue sauce smeared across the edges of the box was a strange reminder of how he could so easily leave a mess for her to clean up— literally and figuratively. She dropped it into the trash can by the door, her movements deliberate and quiet.

Sterling stirred slightly but didn't wake. Zariyah hesitated, the ache in her chest sharp and unrelenting. The bed felt like it had grown larger overnight, the distance between them as vast as ever.

With a sigh, she turned off the lamp and retreated into the bathroom. She let the hot water wash over her, scrubbing at her skin as though she could cleanse more than just the day's grime.

The sweet smell of cinnamon and coffee pulled Zariyah out of her thoughts the next morning. She followed the aroma into the kitchen, where Ms. Emma was already pouring coffee and setting a plate of cinnamon rolls on the counter.

"Morning, Ms. Emma," Zariyah said, stepping into the older woman's open arms for a hug. Ms. Emma's familiar scent of peppermint and menthol wrapped around her like a comforting blanket. Ms. Emma's hug lingered, offering wordless comfort Zariyah needed.

"Sit with me a minute. I've got fresh coffee and a roll with your name on it," said Ms. Emma as she handed her the plate with the biggest cinnamon roll Zariyah had ever seen.

Zariyah sat, grateful for the distraction. Ms. Emma placed a steaming cup of coffee in front of her, its rich aroma mingling with the sweetness of the cinnamon roll.

As they sat in the soft morning light, Zariyah found herself relaxing into the familiar rhythm of Ms. Emma's gentle chatter. It was always the small things with Ms. Emma—stories about her family, updates on the latest neighborhood gossip, or complaints about the high price of groceries.

This morning, Ms. Emma seemed particularly intent on discussing her grandson, Joshua, who had just landed his first internship. "I told him he needs to keep his head down and work hard, no matter what they throw at him. You know how these young folks get—they want to be CEOs in six months!"

Zariyah laughed softly, the sound feeling foreign after the heaviness of the past few days. "He's lucky to have you in his corner, Ms. Emma."

"And you, baby girl, what's got you looking so heavy this morning?" Ms. Emma asked, her tone softening as she fixed Zariyah with a knowing look.

Zariyah hesitated, picking at the edge of the cinnamon roll. She wanted to tell Ms. Emma everything—about Sterling, about the ache in her chest that wouldn't go away—but the words caught in her throat.

Instead, she smiled weakly and said, "Just work. You know how it is."

Ms. Emma didn't press, but the look in her eyes said she wasn't fooled. "Well, don't let that man or that job steal your joy," she said firmly. "You're too good for that."

Zariyah looked away, blinking quickly. She hated how easily Ms. Emma saw through her, how the older woman always managed to dig beneath the surface.

"Sometimes," Ms. Emma continued, her voice softening, "we hold on to things that aren't good for us because we're scared to let go. But, baby girl, you can't let fear keep you in a place that's hurting you. Life's too short for that."

The words hit Zariyah harder than she wanted to admit. She nodded, unable to trust herself to speak. Ms. Emma didn't press further, letting the moment pass without demanding answers Zariyah wasn't ready to give.

Instead, she stood, smoothing her apron. "Now, you get back to your day, and I'll handle this house. Don't you worry about a thing."

Zariyah watched Ms. Emma move around the kitchen,

her steps purposeful and her energy unwavering. For a moment, she envied the older woman's clarity, her ability to cut through the noise and focus on what mattered.

She leaned back in her chair, letting the cinnamon-sweet air fill her senses as a welcome memory surfaced.

* * *

It had been three years ago, not long after Zariyah and Sterling moved into the house. Boxes were still scattered everywhere, and Zariyah had been struggling to organize her office while Sterling made endless phone calls for work.

She'd been carrying a stack of books when the knock came at the front door. Zariyah sighed, brushing dust off her hands as she made her way to answer it.

Standing on the porch was a petite, silver-haired woman dressed in a crisp blazer and skirt, her blouse buttoned neatly to the top despite the sweltering August heat. She held a wicker basket in one hand, and her sharp eyes immediately began surveying the foyer as soon as Zariyah opened the door.

"Excuse me," the woman said, her voice soft but firm. "You moving into this big ol' house by yourself, young lady?"

Zariyah blinked, momentarily thrown by the stranger's directness. "No," she finally managed. "My husband and I just moved in."

The woman nodded, stepping inside uninvited. "I see. Well, you'll be needing a housekeeper."

Zariyah stood frozen as the woman moved through the house with an air of authority, her eyes darting to the high ceilings, the crystal chandeliers, the gleaming hardwood floors.

"My name's Emma Jewel," the woman continued, handing Zariyah a business card with elegant script. "Call me after you talk it over with your husband. I can start

Monday."

With that, Ms. Emma turned and left as abruptly as she'd arrived, leaving Zariyah standing in the foyer with the card in her hand.

Zariyah stood in the foyer for a moment, staring at the card in her hand. That evening, she showed it to Sterling over dinner, half-expecting him to laugh at the audacity of Ms. Emma's pitch.

Instead, Sterling had smirked, flipping the card between his fingers. "Anyone bold enough to walk in here like she owns the place is probably worth hiring." He leaned back in his chair, his eyes twinkling with amusement. "Call her tomorrow."

But Zariyah had hesitated. The house already felt overwhelming, like a weight pressing down on her shoulders. Boxes still cluttered the halls, and even simple tasks seemed insurmountable. A housekeeper sounded like a luxury they didn't need—until the following day, when she found herself staring at the piles of dishes and unopened boxes.

Two days later, Sterling had called Ms. Emma himself. She arrived Monday morning with a basket of cinnamon rolls and a loaf of banana bread. "I always bring a little something sweet for new beginnings," she'd said with a smile.

Back then, Zariyah had thought Ms. Emma's arrival would solve everything—the disarray, the constant feeling of being behind. She hadn't realized how much more she'd come to rely on the older woman—not just for the house, but for herself.

Zariyah's lips quirked into a small smile at the memory. Ms. Emma had been right, of course. The house had been overwhelming at first, and Sterling had quickly come to rely on the older woman's efficiency and discretion. But for

Zariyah, Ms. Emma had become much more than just a housekeeper.

It wasn't just her skills—it was the way she could see through Zariyah's carefully constructed façade, offering comfort in a way that no one else could. Ms. Emma had a knack for knowing what Zariyah needed, even when Zariyah herself didn't.

But even Ms. Emma's warmth couldn't touch the growing distance in her marriage. The cracks were there, spreading silently beneath the surface, no matter how much Zariyah tried to ignore them.

The sound of the vacuum whirring to life down the hall snapped her out of her thoughts. She drained the last of her coffee and pushed herself to her feet, steeling herself for the day ahead.

* * *

Back in her office, Zariyah stared at her laptop screen, the cursor blinking on an open email draft. She was supposed to finalize the design proposal for a client by noon, but her thoughts kept drifting.

Ms. Emma's words echoed in her mind: *You can't let fear keep you in a place that's hurting you.*

Her phone buzzed, pulling her attention. It was a message from Sterling: Looking forward to dinner. Let's try to reconnect.

Zariyah stared at the screen, her heart tightening. She didn't know if reconnecting was even possible anymore, but the thought of trying felt both exhausting and necessary.

She sighed and reached for her planner, flipping through the pages until her eyes landed on her next appointment with Dr. Monroe. Two days. Just two more days.

For a moment, she let herself imagine sitting in Dr. Monroe's calming office, untangling the thoughts that clung to her like cobwebs. The idea felt both daunting and strangely comforting.

With a deep breath, she set the planner aside and turned her attention back to her email. *One step at a time.*

Chapter
10

Later that afternoon, restlessness got the better of Zariyah. She grabbed her keys and headed to Dominic's.

Over lunch, Dominic leaned back in his chair, a mischievous glint in his eye. "So, I hear you're going to the Jasper ball this year."

Zariyah paused mid-sip of her drink, her brow furrowing. "How do you know that?"

"Because your husband texted me last night," Dominic said with a smirk. "He's already making plans to impress the board, or whatever it is he's always trying to impress."

Zariyah rolled her eyes but didn't respond right away. Instead, she thought of the sticky note Sterling had left on her vanity that morning. The message had made her stomach tighten—not with excitement, but with uncertainty.

"Yeah, he wants us to go," Zariyah said, setting her drink down. "I'm still thinking about it."

"Thinking about it?" Dominic raised an eyebrow. "Since when do you need to think about going to the Jasper Ball? It's practically a family tradition—at least for the two of us."

Zariyah shrugged, avoiding his gaze. "It's not that simple."

Dominic studied her for a moment, his teasing demeanor softening. "Is everything okay with you two?"

She hesitated, not sure how much she wanted to share. "It's... complicated."

Dominic leaned back, folding his arms. "Well, here's something to make it more complicated—I got the catering job for the ball."

Zariyah's eyes widened. "You're catering the Jasper Ball? Why didn't you tell me sooner?"

"I just found out this morning," Dominic admitted, grinning. "I was thinking about asking Aimee to go with me as my date."

Zariyah nearly choked on her drink. "Aimee? With you? At the ball?"

Dominic laughed at her reaction, shaking his head. "Don't make it sound so ridiculous. I figure it's a win-win. She gets to dress up and enjoy the night with one of the suavest chefs around."

Zariyah raised an eyebrow. "Aimee doesn't need you for that. She's already going with Richard Walker."

Dominic's grin vanished, replaced by a look of pure disbelief. "Richard Walker? You've got to be kidding me."

Zariyah sighed, shaking her head. "Wish I was. She told me last week."

Dominic's jaw tightened, his usual lightheartedness replaced by something darker. "Of all the guys... Why him?"

"You think I don't ask myself the same question?" Zariyah said, her voice tinged with frustration. "But you know how she is. Once she makes up her mind, there's no stopping her."

Dominic sat back, rubbing a hand over his head. "That guy doesn't deserve to be anywhere near her. He already proved that the first time around."

"I know," Zariyah said quietly. "But she's convinced he's changed."

Dominic let out a bitter laugh. "Yeah, I've heard that one before."

They sat in silence for a moment, the weight of their concerns for Aimee hanging between them.

"Guess I'll just have to keep an eye on her while I'm catering," Dominic muttered, though his tone lacked its usual bravado.

"Good luck with that," Zariyah said softly.

* * *

It was early evening when Zariyah finally pushed away from her laptop, her neck stiff from hours at her desk. The faint aroma of something savory wafted through the house—a comforting reminder of one of the many perks of having Ms. Emma around. Before she'd left for the day, Ms. Emma told her that she'd left their dinner in the oven and set the table.

Zariyah stretched her arms above her head, her thoughts still tangled in work, when the soft creak of footsteps pulled her attention. She glanced toward the doorway as Sterling appeared, still in his suit, his tie loosened and a familiar ease in his posture.

"Dinner smells good," he said, his voice cutting through the quiet. He glanced at her, his expression unreadable. "Ms. Emma?"

Zariyah nodded, meeting his gaze briefly before turning her attention back to her desk.

Sterling leaned against the doorframe, crossing his arms. "I'll change and meet you in the kitchen."

The table was as impeccable—crisp linens, polished silverware, and a small vase of hydrangeas sat at the center, adding a touch of softness to the space. It was funny how

Ms. Emma knew exactly what she liked and how she liked it.

She slipped on oven mitts and pulled out the casserole dish, the rich aroma of baked chicken and creamy macaroni and cheese filling the air. On the stove, a Le Creuset Dutch oven simmered gently, filled with tender country green beans cooked with onions, smoked turkey, and just the right amount of seasoning.

Sterling joined her moments later, now dressed in sweatpants and a fitted T-shirt that hinted at his athletic build. He poured two glasses of wine and set them on the table, his movements calm and deliberate.

"Ms. Emma didn't just cook, she cooked," he remarked, lifting the lid on the Dutch oven and inhaling deeply.

"She always does," Zariyah replied, setting the dish on the table before sitting opposite him.

They served themselves in silence, the clinking of utensils filling the void. Sterling broke the quiet first.

"How was your day?"

"Productive," she said flatly, avoiding his gaze.

"How's Dominic?" Sterling asked, cutting into his chicken.

Zariyah paused mid-bite, caught off guard by the question. She glanced at him, trying to gauge his tone. "He's fine, why?"

Sterling met her eyes briefly before returning his attention to his plate. "I called him earlier."

Her fork hovered in mid-air as her brow furrowed. "You did?"

Sterling shrugged, his tone casual. "Just to check in. It sounds like you've been spending a lot of time at the restaurant."

Zariyah stiffened, setting her fork down deliberately. "Dominic's my brother, Sterling. I don't need permission to see him."

"I didn't say you did," he replied evenly, though there was an edge in his tone. He set his knife down and leaned back in his chair, crossing his arms. "I'm just wondering if there's something I need to know about."

The words hung in the air, sharp and unexpected. Zariyah blinked, her stomach twisting as her mind raced to catch up.

Sterling's gaze didn't waver. "It just feels like you're more involved lately."

Zariyah's expression tightened, her mind flashing back to the early days of Charades. When Dominic decided to chase his dream of owning a restaurant, she'd been there from the start, stepping in as a silent partner to help him bring it to life. Sterling had only gotten involved later, stepping up as a private investor when unexpected setbacks during the remodel threatened to derail everything.

"I've been spending time with my brother because I need someone to talk to. It's not about the restaurant, Sterling. Not everything has to be about business."

Sterling studied her for a moment, his jaw tightening. "You need someone to talk to? I'm your husband, Zariyah." He leaned forward, his tone sharp but controlled. "What do you talk to Dominic about that you can't say to me? Or am I the problem?"

Zariyah stiffened, her frustration bubbling over. His question hung in the air, heavy and piercing, forcing her to confront feelings she'd tried to push aside. The anger and sadness she'd been suppressing threatened to spill over. She set her fork down deliberately. "It's not about Dominic. It's about us. You're so wrapped up in everything else that I don't even know where I fit into your life anymore."

"We don't talk, Sterling. Not really. You're here, but

you're not... here. We barely see each other. You come home late, we sleep, and then we do it all over again."

Her voice cracked, but she pressed on, the words spilling out before she could stop them. "We're growing apart, and you don't even seem to notice. Or care."

Sterling leaned back in his chair, exhaling sharply as his hand dragged down his face. "Oh, really? I'm working my ass off to give us a good life, and it's still not enough?"

Zariyah's eyes narrowed, her arms crossing. "You think money makes up for everything? That I should just sit here, smile, and be a grateful little wife? You're always somewhere else—working and I'm here, feeling more alone than I ever did before we got married."

Sterling's jaw clenched, his gaze flickering to her but not holding. The silence between them grew heavy and suffocating. Finally, he stood, his movements deliberate as he picked up his plate. "I don't want to fight tonight."

He walked to the sink without another word, leaving Zariyah at the table, her chest tight and her appetite gone.

Chapter
11

The past two days had been strained. Zariyah and Sterling hadn't exchanged more than a few polite words, their interactions cordial but hollow. At night, they stayed on their respective sides of the bed, the silence between them stretching wider with each passing moment. For Zariyah, the nights were the worst. The nightmares were back—more vivid and suffocating than ever, pulling her into a darkness she couldn't escape.

This morning, she found herself once again in Dr. Monroe's office, seeking solace she wasn't sure how to claim. The soothing jazz playing faintly in the background and the warm, cream-colored walls did little to ease the tension knotting her shoulders.

"Good morning, Zariyah," Dr. Monroe greeted her with a gentle smile as she settled into her usual chair. "How have you been since we last met?"

Zariyah hesitated, running her fingers over the armrest. "Not great," she admitted, her voice subdued. "Things at home have been... strained."

Dr. Monroe nodded, her gaze steady and supportive. "Tell me what's been happening."

Zariyah glanced down at her hands, gathering her thoughts. "We're stuck in this cycle. Polite conversations, going through the motions. But it's like... like we're strangers sharing the same space. And I don't know how to break it."

Dr. Monroe leaned forward slightly, her presence grounding. "It sounds like there's a lot of distance between you and Sterling right now. Do you feel like it's something new, or has it been building for a while?"

Zariyah sighed, her fingers tightening around the armrest. "It's been building. I think I've just been too busy pretending everything was fine to notice how bad it's gotten."

Dr. Monroe's voice was calm, but there was a firmness in her tone. "Sometimes we distract ourselves to avoid confronting painful truths. But avoidance only works for so long."

The words struck a chord, and Zariyah felt a lump rise in her throat. She thought of the nightmares, of the way she jolted awake each night, her heart pounding and her chest tight.

"The nightmares are back," she admitted, her voice faltering. "They're worse now. I wake up... feeling like I can't breathe. Like I'm trapped."

Dr. Monroe's brow furrowed slightly, her attention laser-focused. "What are you experiencing in these nightmares?"

Zariyah hesitated, the images flashing behind her closed eyes. "It's the same one I've always had. I'm in a house, and I can hear someone coming, but I can't see them. I try to scream, but nothing comes out. I try to move, but my legs won't work. And then... they're there, standing over me, but I can't see their face."

Her voice cracked, and she exhaled shakily. "I wake up, and it's like I'm still there. Still that little girl. Helpless."

Dr. Monroe's voice was gentle but firm. "Nightmares like

that often resurface when there are unresolved emotions or memories. Do you think it's tied to something from your past?"

Zariyah's throat tightened as the words she'd avoided for years hovered on the edge of her tongue. "I think so," she whispered. "I think it's tied to... something that happened when I was nine."

Dr. Monroe nodded slowly, giving her the space to continue. "Something traumatic?"

Zariyah's chest constricted, and for a moment, she couldn't speak. Her hands trembled as she clenched them in her lap. "Yes," she finally admitted, her voice breaking. "There was a man... someone my mother trusted. He... hurt me. And I've never told anyone."

The weight of the confession settled between them, heavy and unyielding. Dr. Monroe didn't look away, her expression a mix of compassion and quiet strength.

"Zariyah," she said softly, "thank you for trusting me with that. What happened to you was not your fault. You were a child, and the responsibility was on the adults around you to protect you. They failed you, but you didn't fail yourself. You survived."

Tears welled in Zariyah's eyes, but she blinked them away. "I've carried it for so long. I thought if I just ignored it, it would stay buried. But now... it's like I can't outrun it anymore."

Dr. Monroe leaned forward slightly, her voice steady. "You've been in survival mode for a long time, Zariyah. And survival mode is powerful—it helps us get through the worst of times. But it doesn't leave room for connection, for vulnerability. That mode protected you when you needed it most, but now, it's keeping you from fully living."

The tears spilled over, and Zariyah didn't bother to wipe

them away. "I don't know how to stop feeling this way. I don't even know where to start."

"We start," Dr. Monroe said, her voice unwavering, "by acknowledging that what happened to you was real. And that it wasn't your fault."

The words settled over Zariyah like a blanket—warm but unbearably heavy. She nodded, her lips trembling as she fought to steady her breathing.

"It feels like admitting it makes me weak," she confessed, her voice barely audible. "Like I should've been stronger. Smarter."

Dr. Monroe's gaze was unwavering, her words deliberate. "What you endured required incredible strength. But strength doesn't mean carrying the weight forever. It means knowing when to put it down. You don't have to keep holding it, Zariyah. You've carried it long enough."

Zariyah let out a shuddering breath, the knot in her chest loosening ever so slightly. For the first time in days, she felt a flicker of hope—a faint glimmer of what healing might look like. The weight of the past wasn't gone, but for the first time, it felt like something she might be able to carry—not alone, but with the support she'd been too afraid to ask for.

As she left Dr. Monroe's office, Zariyah glanced at the sun breaking through the clouds and whispered to herself, "One step at a time."

Chapter
12

The weight of yesterday's session clung to Zariyah like a heavy fog as she walked into her office the next morning. Therapy had opened a door she'd spent years trying to keep locked, and now, there was no way to close it.

Her fingers hovered over her keyboard, but her mind was elsewhere—pulled back to the long, hot summer days. Uncle Ben. He wasn't her real uncle, just one of Noni's closest friends. Noni always said he was family because he'd been around since before Zariyah was born. He'd helped fix things around the house, and stayed late for dinners, especially after her daddy died. He and Noni never had a romantic relationship as far as she knew.

To everyone else, Ben was charming, dependable—the kind of man you could call on when you needed something. But to Zariyah, he was a shadow. A looming presence whose cigarette smoke clung to her nostrils and whose voice still crawled under her skin when she let her guard down.

She'd never said his name in therapy, not yet. But yesterday, when she'd admitted her nightmares were getting worse, she could feel the weight of his presence in the room, even after all these years. Just the thought of him now made her stomach twist, nausea creeping into her throat as she stared blankly at the blinking email notifications on her screen.

A request for a last-minute redesign from one of her biggest clients popped into her inbox. She knew she should jump on it—she always did—but the thought of diving into another branding overhaul felt impossibly daunting.

Her phone buzzed, breaking her spiral of thoughts. Aimee: *Dinner tonight? I need to vent.*

Zariyah's lips quirked into a faint smile. If anyone could take her mind off her unraveling emotions, it was Aimee. She typed back a quick yes and set her phone down.

For now, she could compartmentalize—shove the therapy session and the tangled mess of her marriage to the back of her mind. But deep down, she knew the floodgates weren't just open—they'd burst, and the memories weren't going anywhere.

* * *

Zariyah glanced at the clock on her desk, realizing she needed to get going if she didn't want to be late for dinner with Aimee. She hesitated for a moment, then reached for her phone.

Out of courtesy, she texted Sterling: Having dinner with Aimee. Don't wait up.

The reply came faster than expected: Okay. Be safe.

She stared at the screen for a moment, the brevity of his response hitting harder than she expected. No questions, no offer to join her, no follow-up. Just okay.

It was the kind of exchange that perfectly encapsulated where they were now—polite, distant, almost like strangers sharing a house instead of a marriage. She sighed and set her phone down, her thoughts already shifting to Aimee.

Whatever foolery Richard Walker was up to now,

Zariyah could feel her blood pressure rising just thinking about it. Aimee's text hadn't gone into detail, but she didn't need to. Richard had a way of dragging chaos into every room he entered, and if he'd managed to hurt Aimee again, Zariyah wasn't sure how much more patience she had left for the man.

She grabbed her purse and keys, determined to get the full story—and maybe a stiff drink to go with it.

Zariyah met Aimee at their usual spot, a cozy bistro with dim lighting and a surprisingly good wine list. Aimee was already on her second glass when Zariyah arrived, and she wasted no time diving into her frustrations.

"Richard's being a total ass," Aimee said, punctuating the statement with a dramatic sigh. "One minute, he's all over me, and the next, he's cold as ice. I don't know if I'm wasting my time or if he's just playing games."

Zariyah sipped her wine, nodding as she listened, but the parallels between Aimee's words and her own struggles with Sterling gnawed at her. The hot-and-cold dynamic, the push and pull—it felt all too familiar.

"What do you think I should do?" Aimee asked, tilting her head and narrowing her eyes.

Caught off guard, Zariyah blinked. She'd been lost in her own thoughts, and now, Aimee's question dragged her back to the present. "I think you need to ask yourself if this relationship is meeting your needs," Zariyah said, her voice steady but distant. "If it's not, maybe it's time to let it go."

Aimee frowned, swirling her glass. "It's not that simple, Z. Walking away feels... impossible. Like, what if this is as good as it gets?"

Zariyah's throat tightened. She knew that feeling all too well—the quiet resignation of settling because the alternative seemed too daunting. She reached across the table, her fingers brushing Aimee's. "It's not impossible. It's scary, sure, but staying in something that hurts you? That's harder in the long run."

Aimee studied her for a long moment, her lips pressing into a thin line. "You're right. I just... I hate that you're right."

Zariyah let out a soft laugh, but it didn't reach her eyes. "I know."

As the evening wound down, Zariyah walked to her car, her mind drifting back to her own crumbling marriage. The conversation with Aimee had been a welcome distraction, but it had also forced her to confront the cracks she'd been ignoring in her own life.

One thing was certain: pretending everything was fine was no longer an option.

* * *

It was after ten o'clock, and Sterling still wasn't home. Zariyah found herself grateful for the quiet. She made a cup of tea, the warmth of the mug grounding her as she climbed into bed. Her fingers tightened around the mug as Dr. Monroe's voice echoed in her mind: "You can't keep running from this, Zariyah."

She set the mug on the nightstand, the tea's warmth lingering in her body but doing little to calm the storm inside. The sound of the front door opening broke the stillness. Sterling's familiar footsteps moved through the house—the click of his shoes on the hardwood floor, the soft rustle of his jacket as he hung it up. It was a rhythm she used to find comforting. Tonight, it only magnified the distance between them.

When Sterling entered the bedroom, Zariyah shut her eyes, feigning sleep. He paused in the doorway, and for a moment, she thought he might say something. The air seemed to shift, heavy with the unspoken. A few minutes later the bed dipped as he slipped under the covers beside her. His arm draped over her waist, pulling her close, but his touch felt different tonight—tentative, unsure.

Zariyah's chest tightened. She wanted to lean into him, to let his presence soothe her.   But the weight of the past, of everything left unsaid, kept her frozen.

Tomorrow, she thought again. *Tomorrow, I'll tell him everything.*

But when sleep finally claimed her, it wasn't the peaceful reprieve she had hoped for.

* * *

The dream began innocently enough—the soft hum of crickets, the scent of honeysuckle drifting through the warm summer air. But as the scene shifted, unease crept in. She was back in the woods, running. Her breath came in sharp, panicked bursts, her raggedy sneakers slipping over the uneven ground.

She could feel him behind her. He wasn't chasing her—not this time—but the fear gripped her all the same, coiling in her chest like a vice.

Her foot caught on a root, and she stumbled, falling hard into the dirt. The once sweet scent of honeysuckle turned bitter, tainted with something darker—acrid stench of cigarettes, rancid pee, and sweat.

She tried to move, but her limbs were leaden, pinned down by an invisible weight. Panic surged as she heard his voice, low and familiar, calling her name. It was soft at first, almost tender, but it grew louder, sharper, until it drowned out everything else.

Her mouth opened to scream, but no sound came. The silence of the woods was absolute, oppressive. His shadow loomed over her, closer, closer, until—

Zariyah woke with a start, her chest heaving, the air thick with remnants of the nightmare. Sweat clung to her skin, and the bedroom's darkness felt suffocating, as though the dream hadn't fully let her go. She pressed a trembling hand to her chest, willing her breath to slow, but the images lingered—the woods, the voice, the crushing weight of fear.

Beside her, Sterling stirred but didn't wake. His arm still rested loosely over her waist, his breathing deep and even. Once, his presence had been her anchor. Now, it was a reminder of everything slipping through her fingers.

She stared at the ceiling, her heart pounding, the sound of her pulse loud in her ears. She couldn't keep running—from the memories, from the past, from herself.

Her breath hitched as she whispered to herself, Tomorrow. No more running.

Chapter 13

The next morning, Zariyah woke to the sound of Sterling moving quietly around the room. She opened her eyes just enough to see him slipping on a crisp shirt, the light from the window catching the sharp lines of his silhouette. He'd come in late the night before, long after she'd pretended to be asleep.

Now, his usual routine felt both familiar and distant—like watching a stranger in her home. Zariyah leaned against the headboard, her mind swirling with doubts she couldn't voice. Tamia's "Stranger in My House" played faintly in her thoughts: "And he wouldn't treat me like you do. He would adore me, he wouldn't ignore me."

The words hit too close to home, capturing the aching gap between who Sterling used to be and who he seemed to be now. It was almost eerie, how perfectly the song mirrored her unease.

"Morning," he said, glancing over his shoulder as he adjusted his cuffs. His tone was casual, almost too light for the undercurrent of tension between them.

"Morning," she mumbled, sitting up slowly.

Sterling walked over, kissed her forehead, and leaned

back slightly, his expression unreadable. "Did you see my note about the ball the other day?"

"I did."

A small smile tugged at his lips. "And?"

Zariyah shrugged, keeping her tone casual. "Already have hair and nail appointments. So, yeah."

Sterling blinked, momentarily caught off guard. "Wait, seriously? You've got everything set?"

She nodded, not looking up as she smoothed the edge of the blanket. Sterling exhaled dramatically, clutching his chest in mock relief. "Thank God. I thought I was going to have to beg like some lovesick fool."

Zariyah's lips curved into a faint smile at his theatrics, but it faded just as quickly.

The tension between them lingered, unspoken but palpable. Sterling's gaze lingered on her, his expression shifting as though he wanted to say more.

"You're not... excited about this, are you?" he finally asked, his tone quieter, almost tentative.

Zariyah forced a shrug.

Sterling studied her for a moment longer, then nodded, his smile returning, though it lacked its usual warmth. "I'll see you for dinner," he said, his voice casual as he turned toward the door.

"Sure," she said, her tone clipped.

As the door closed behind him, Zariyah stared at the ceiling, and tried to ignore the ache in her chest.

* * *

Zariyah retreated to her office, determined to lose herself in work. The hours slipped by unnoticed, the clicking of her keyboard and the muted hum of the house her only companions. The project in front of her—normally something she'd find invigorating—felt like more of a chore, but she kept at it, welcoming the distraction. It wasn't until her stomach grumbled loudly that she realized she hadn't eaten.

She glanced at the clock—nearly one o'clock—and sighed, standing to stretch. The motion sent a dull ache through her back and shoulders, a reminder of the restless night she'd had.

In the kitchen, she found Ms. Emma folding laundry in the family room, earphones in as she worked. Zariyah leaned against the counter, watching the older woman move with a practiced ease that always seemed to bring a sense of calm to the house.

As if sensing Zariyah's presence, Ms. Emma pulled out one of her earphones and turned with a smile. "Good afternoon, Ms. Zariyah," she said, neatly placing the folded towels in the basket. "Thought I'd finish up the laundry before tackling the dusting."

"Good afternoon, Ms. Emma," Zariyah replied, returning the smile. The warmth in Ms. Emma's voice was a soothing contrast to the unease that had settled in her chest.

Ms. Emma gestured toward the dining table. "I left your menu for the week, and your salad's in the fridge for lunch. Joshua's bringing the groceries by later."

Zariyah chuckled softly. "You spoil me, Ms. Emma."

"Not spoiled, just well taken care of," Ms. Emma said with a wink before slipping her earphones back in and gathering the laundry basket. "I'll get out of your hair now."

Zariyah watched her disappear down the hallway, the comforting hum of her presence lingering even after she was gone. Ms. Emma's reliability was like a balm, soothing the parts of Zariyah that felt frayed and unsettled.

She retrieved the salad from the fridge and sat at the kitchen table, the sunlight streaming through the windows highlighting the floral centerpiece Ms. Emma had placed there earlier in the week. But despite the beauty around her, Zariyah's appetite was nowhere to be found. She pushed the greens around with her fork, her thoughts drifting back to the morning with Sterling, to the tension that lingered beneath their polite exchanges.

Her phone vibrated against the countertop. A text from Sterling: Wrapping up early. I'll be home soon. Need anything?

Zariyah stared at the message, her fingers hovering over the screen. She wanted to believe Sterling was just being thoughtful, but something about it didn't sit right. His small acts of affection lately felt off—calculated, as if he were trying to hide something rather than smooth things over.

No, I'm good, she finally typed back, hesitating before hitting send.

Sterling walked in less than an hour later, carrying a massive bouquet of daisies, yellow roses, tulips, and white hydrangeas that hid his face. Zariyah's suspicions flared instantly. Sterling only bought her flowers on two occasions: her birthday and Military Spouse Appreciation Day. This was neither.

"These are for you," he said, setting the crystal vase on the counter and kissing her cheek.

"Thank you," Zariyah murmured, her eyes lingering on the bouquet.

Sterling disappeared into the bedroom for a few minutes. Zariyah returned to absently pushing her salad around with her fork as her thoughts churned. Was he trying to cover something up? Distract her from noticing what wasn't being said?

She heard Sterling return, now dressed in a T-shirt and faded jeans. He grabbed a salad from the refrigerator and, slid onto the bar stool beside her.

He reached for her hand, giving it a brief squeeze before bowing his head to bless his food. The silence between them grew heavy, punctuated only by the occasional scrape of utensils on plates.

Zariyah watched him out of the corner of her eye, her heart pounding with questions she couldn't yet bring herself to voice. His smile was soft, but it didn't reach his eyes.

The doubt gnawed at her. Was he hiding something?

* * *

Zariyah excused herself shortly after, muttering something about needing to check on a client project. She slipped back into her office, grateful for the physical distance from Sterling. The bouquet on the table lingered in her mind, a symbol of something she couldn't quite name but couldn't shake either.

She sat at her desk, her laptop open, but the work in front of her blurred as her thoughts spiraled. Was he trying to make up for something, or was this just Sterling's way of brushing over their issues? Either way, the gestures felt hollow, a bandage on a wound that needed stitches.

The faint sound of the front door opening pulled her from her thoughts. She glanced up as Sterling's voice drifted down the hall. "I'll be back in a bit—just running a quick errand," he called.

"Okay," she replied, her voice flat, not bothering to look up. The sound of his retreating footsteps and the soft click of the door felt like a small relief.

The house settled into silence, and Zariyah used the quiet to ground herself. She needed to focus—on work, on something that didn't make her chest ache. But even as she dove into a new project, the tension remained, coiling in the back of her mind like a predator waiting to pounce.

* * *

The doorbell rang as Zariyah finished typing an email. She glanced at the clock—it was later than she realized. Ms. Emma's grandson, Joshua, had probably arrived with the groceries. Stretching, she walked to the door and opened it to find a tall young man standing there, balancing a crate of neatly packed paper bags.

"Ms. Zariyah," he greeted with a broad smile. His resemblance to Ms. Emma was uncanny—same sharp features, same warm eyes.

"Joshua," she said, stepping aside to let him in. "Thanks for bringing these by."

"No problem," he said, setting the bags on the counter with practiced ease. "Grandma says you're her favorite client. I think she sends me over just to keep me out of trouble."

Zariyah chuckled, appreciating his easy demeanor. "How's the internship going?"

"Busy, but I love it," Joshua replied, straightening up. "They've got me doing everything from drafting proposals to running data analysis. Grandma said I'd better not mess it up."

"She has a way of keeping people in line," Zariyah teased, earning a laugh from him.

"She does," he agreed. "But I wouldn't have it any other way."

As he headed out, he paused at the door. "If you need anything else, just let me know. I'm only a call away."

"Will do. Thanks again, Joshua."

He nodded and walked back to his car, leaving Zariyah with a faint smile. Ms. Emma had raised him well, and it was a reminder of the quiet strength she brought into Zariyah's life every day.

* * *

By the time Sterling returned, the sun had dipped below the horizon, casting long shadows across the house. Zariyah was in the kitchen reheating dinner when he walked in, carrying a garment bag draped over his arm.

"What's that?" she asked, nodding toward the bag.

Sterling smirked. "Just a little something I picked up for myself. Figured I'd need to step up my game for the ball."

Zariyah arched an eyebrow. "You already own a tux."

"True," he said, setting the bag aside and walking over to the stove. "But I thought this year deserved something different." He grabbed the plates she had set out and started serving the food, his casual tone catching her off guard.

They sat down to eat, the clinking of silverware filling the quiet as Zariyah waited for the inevitable shift in conversation. Sterling cleared his throat as he reached for his glass of wine. "I've been thinking," he started. "Maybe we should make a weekend out of it—go shopping for your gown, take in some sights, just... us."

Zariyah paused mid-bite, the fork hovering in front of her. "You want to go shopping? With me?" The disbelief in her voice was hard to mask.

Sterling chuckled, setting down his glass. "I know, shocking, right? But I figured it'd be a good way to spend time together. Plus, it's been a while since we've had a getaway."

Her instincts bristled at the suggestion, suspicion creeping in again. "That's... unexpected."

"Is it really that hard to believe I just want to spend time with my wife?" Sterling's tone was light, but there was a hint of challenge in his eyes.

Zariyah sighed, pushing her plate aside. "It's not that. It's just... out of character, that's all."

Sterling leaned forward, his gaze steady. "Maybe I'm trying to be more in character. Can we give this a shot, Zariyah? Just one weekend."

She stared at him, her emotions a tangled mess. On one hand, his effort felt genuine. On the other, the timing couldn't feel more calculated.

"I'll think about it," she said finally, her tone carefully neutral.

Sterling shook his head, a small smile tugging at his lips. "Don't think about it too long."

Chapter
14

The morning light spilled across the veranda, golden and serene, but Zariyah's heart felt anything but. She clutched her tea cup, staring at the faint tendrils of steam that spiraled upward. Dr. Monroe's words still echoed in her mind, urging her forward, but it was the weekend plans with Sterling that twisted unease into her chest.

He had been so earnest, so charming—just like the man she'd fallen for all those years ago. But was the trip really about reconnecting, or just another way to smooth over the cracks? She wasn't sure if she wanted to know the answer.

Her mind was still restless, filled with fragmented memories of her childhood— all the buried memories of her past surged to the forefront, demanding attention. She thought back to the years they'd been together—how she'd buried herself in work, in being the "perfect" wife, trying to distract herself from the dark parts of her past. But the more she tried to hide it, the more it seemed to creep into every corner of her life.

The sound of soft footsteps behind her pulled her back to the present. Ms. Emma appeared, carrying her ever-present bucket of cleaning supplies, her expression warm but curious.

"You all right, sweetie?" Ms. Emma asked, as she stood in the doorway.

Zariyah forced a small smile, brushing a stray curl from her face. "Just thinking."

Ms. Emma set the bucket down and poured herself a cup of tea. The older woman didn't sit, but her presence lingered like a balm. She stirred her tea slowly, her eyes flickering to Zariyah with quiet understanding.

"Sometimes talking helps," Ms. Emma said after a pause. "And sometimes, just sitting still does, too."

Ms. Emma settled into the chair opposite Zariyah. For a moment, they drank in companionable silence, the weight of Zariyah's thoughts hanging heavy in the air.

Zariyah's smile faltered, gratitude warring with the weight of her unspoken words. "Thanks, Ms. Emma," she whispered.

Ms. Emma stood and gave her a gentle pat on the should before taking the used tea cups inside with her. Zariyah stared off at the garden, her thoughts as murky as the brew.

Zariyah's phone pinged again, the sharp chime breaking through the stillness of the veranda. Then another. And another. The relentless cascade of notifications made her pick it up, already dreading what awaited her on the screen.

Aimee's messages flooded her phone:

Aimee: *Z! I need you to talk me down before I lose my mind. Richard came over last night, DRUNK, rambling about how I "knew what this was" and shouldn't expect more from him. Like, excuse me?! But THEN he starts talking about how he wants a future with me— like, pick a lane, sir!*

And to top it all off, his phone was blowing up the whole time, and when I asked him who it was, he said, "Nobody." NOBODY?! Z, I swear, if I find out it's some hussy texting him… Why can't I just leave him? He knows exactly how to keep me stuck, and I hate that I let him have this power over me. HELP ME. I need your wisdom and some wine.

Zariyah's chest tightened as she stared at the screen, her breath catching in her throat. You knew what this was. The words landed like a slap, conjuring shadows of feelings she'd tried to suppress. Memories she didn't want to face crept in—ones of powerlessness, of cycles she couldn't seem to escape. And Richard's phone—blowing up—brought a new weight to her thoughts, unearthing Sterling's late nights, his quick excuses, and the way he so often slid his phone just out of her reach.

The sharp buzz of another notification jolted her back, breaking through the growing haze in her mind. Aimee needed her now, and though Zariyah's emotions swirled dangerously close to the surface, she forced herself to focus. Her thumbs hovered over the keyboard, and with a deep breath, she began typing.

Zariyah: *Hey, girl. You know I've got your back. He's crossing lines, and you deserve so much better. I can't do dinner tonight, but let's do lunch tomorrow, okay? My treat. We'll talk it out, vent, and figure out a plan. Don't let him keep you feeling stuck—you're stronger than you think.*

Zariyah set the phone down, her fingers lingering over the screen as if the weight of Aimee's words still clung to her hands. I can't do dinner tonight. It wasn't entirely a lie. She'd been too restless, too raw since her session with Dr. Monroe, and the thought of sitting across from Aimee, hearing about Richard's drunken antics, felt like more than she could handle.

But it wasn't just that.

She hated how much of herself she saw in Aimee sometimes—the hope, the disappointment, the cycle of wanting more but settling for less. And tonight, Zariyah didn't trust herself to mask her own unraveling. Aimee needed support, not Zariyah's unresolved mess bleeding into the conversation.

Still, there was more to it. If she was honest, the thought of leaving the house, of engaging with anyone, felt suffocating. Her sanctuary was small and fragile right now, and she wasn't ready to let anything—anyone—disrupt it.

The sound of keys jingling sent a ripple of tension through her. Sterling was home earlier than she expected, the sight of him with his every move—toss jacket on chair, set down bag, go through the mail, check his phone—was so predictable. For a moment, she thought about slipping back into the house to greet him. But the unspoken thoughts that had consumed her all day—the doubts, the unease—kept her rooted to the chair.

When Zariyah finally ventured into the kitchen, she found him pulling ingredients from the fridge, his back to her. His movements were smooth and practiced as he set chicken and fresh vegetables on the marble island.

"Hey, you," he said, flashing her a smile that once made her heart race. He nodded toward the ingredients. "Thought I'd beat you to dinner tonight."

She nodded, watching him with a mix of nostalgia and detachment. The kitchen—oversized and pristine—felt like a backdrop to a life she wasn't sure they still shared. Sterling moved around it with ease, the hum of the Wolf range and the rhythm of his chopping filling the silence.

"You want to help, or are you just going to supervise?" he teased.

"I'll set the table," Zariyah replied, her tone neutral.

As she moved to the dining nook, she took her time arranging the napkins, silverware, and crystal glasses. The soft light filtering through the windows illuminated the room, making it feel warmer than her heart did. The faint sound of the waterfall in the garden outside added to the serene atmosphere.

As Sterling moved about the kitchen, Zariyah found herself watching him—not his actions, but the spaces between them. The gaps felt wider these days, like invisible walls they both pretended weren't there. She wanted to say something, anything, to bridge the distance. But instead, she reached for the napkins and set the table, her hands trembling just enough to remind her of how much she was holding back.

Chapter
15

Dinner smelled as delicious as always—Sterling had a way of making even the simplest dishes feel like an occasion. Tonight he'd made roasted chicken, fresh bread, and sautéed vegetable. But Zariyah's appetite was nowhere to be found. She forced herself to cut into the chicken, but every bite felt heavy. Across the table, Sterling ate with ease, oblivious to the weight she carried.

The conversation was equally sparse until Sterling finally broke it.

"About the weekend…" he began, setting his fork down.

Zariyah blinked, pulled from her reverie. "Hmm?"

"You didn't change your mind, did you?" he asked, a hint of playfulness in his tone.

She shook her head. "No."

Sterling chuckled, relief evident on his face. "Good. I was worried you'd back out."

"I didn't say yes, either," she countered, her voice soft but firm.

Sterling leaned back, a grin tugging at his lips. "You've never turned down a weekend trip before, a shopping trip no less."

She didn't respond, instead offering a faint smile as she sipped her water. The memory of simpler times lingered, unspoken between them.

She thought back to the first time she met Sterling. It had been her junior year, and he'd walked into her life with the kind of effortless charm that demanded attention.

She'd been flustered, juggling her books and notes as she made her way to class, barely noticing the path ahead until she collided with someone solid. Her things scattered, her breath hitched, and then there he was—crouching to gather her papers, his movements quick but deliberate.

"I didn't see you," she'd said, trying to compose herself under his steady gaze. "Sorry about that."

"No harm done," he'd replied, his voice warm, but his smile... it had been electric. Like he knew the effect he had on people and wasn't afraid to use it.

At the time, she'd been drawn to the way he seemed larger than life—not just in stature, but in presence. His easy confidence had filled the space around him, and for a fleeting moment, she'd felt like the center of his universe.

But looking back now, she couldn't ignore the undercurrent she'd missed. That same charisma that once made her feel special now felt calculated. Sterling had a way of steering every conversation, controlling the narrative without ever seeming forceful.

The warmth she'd felt then now felt... hollow.

Zariyah blinked, the memory fading as reality came rushing back. The ache in her chest deepened as she thought about how far they had drifted from that initial spark, that youthful excitement. She missed that feeling—missed them.

After dinner, Sterling busied himself outside while Zariyah cleaned up. She caught glimpses of him through the window, pacing the backyard with his phone pressed to his ear. The sight of him only deepened the ache in her chest.

By the time Sterling returned, Zariyah had settled on the sofa with a blanket and a movie she wasn't really watching. He joined her, sitting closer than usual, his arm draped over the back of the couch. She felt the slight shift of the cushions under his weight, the faint scent of his cologne encasing her.

"You okay?" he asked, his tone gentle.

Zariyah nodded, avoiding his gaze. "Yeah, just tired."

Sterling didn't press, instead leaning back with a sigh, his presence warm but heavy with unspoken tension. Zariyah closed her eyes briefly, trying to silence the storm in her mind. The weight of her secrets, her silence, pressed down harder than ever.

His hand drifted to the buttons of her sweater, absently toying with the top one as he talked about his day—the landscaper's mistakes, the weekend plans, the latest hiccup with the contractors on some project. His fingers brushed lightly against her collarbone, his touch familiar, almost instinctual. Zariyah's breath hitched.

Sterling's voice softened as he leaned closer, his lips brushing her temple. "You're quiet tonight," he murmured, his hand sliding just slightly lower, to the second button.

The small, teasing gesture sent a ripple of tension through her. For a moment, she wondered if this was his way of grounding them in something simple, something physical. But the thought was fleeting. The layers between them were too thick, the distance too wide.

And then, the shrill ring of the phone shattered the moment.

Sterling groaned, pulling back to grab the handset from the coffee table. "It's your mom," he said, glancing at the screen. "You want to take it?"

Zariyah shook her head, folding her arms across her chest. "No."

Sterling sighed, answering the call with a practiced ease. "Hey, Ms. Noni," he said, his tone instantly light. "No ma'am, she can't do that next weekend. I'm whisking her away," he added, a chuckle escaping as he glanced at Zariyah. He patted her belly playfully, and she rolled her eyes, knowing exactly what her mother had asked—again.

When Sterling hung up, he stretched out again, this time resting his head in her lap. The ease with which he shifted back into what he'd been doing was infuriating—a reminder of how effortlessly he could compartmentalize what she couldn't.

For a while, they sat in silence. Zariyah's fingers absentmindedly stroked his hair, but her thoughts churned with unrelenting intensity. The articles she'd read about sudden gestures of affection—flowers, gifts, small surprises— came rushing back, warning signs wrapped in pretty bows. How often did they signal guilt?

Her chest tightened as she recalled Sterling's late nights, the times he'd slipped through the door with a curt excuse, heading straight for the shower like he needed to scrub something away. The seeds of doubt, planted long ago, had taken root, and now they spread, creeping into every quiet moment, every unexplained gesture.

She stared down at him, fast asleep now. Once upon a time, the sight of him so at peace in her presence would have melted her. Now, it grated on her nerves.

The movie's happy resolution unfolded on the screen, but it felt like a cruel joke. Forgiveness, redemption, love rekindled—it all seemed impossibly out of reach. Zariyah shifted, letting her legs slide off the ottoman. The movement woke Sterling, his head lifting slightly as he blinked up at her, confusion etched across his face.

"What's wrong?" he asked, his voice groggy but concerned.

Zariyah hesitated, her throat tightening. "Nothing," she said, her tone flat. "The movie's over. I'm going to bed."

Sterling sat up instantly, the fatigue slipping from his features. He extended a hand, his expression softening with concern. "Z, talk to me. What's going on?"

Zariyah stared at his outstretched hand for a beat too long before accepting it. He pulled her to her feet, his touch lingering as he searched her face. The weight of his gaze was unbearable, pressing against the walls she'd so carefully built.

"I'm fine," she whispered, brushing past him.

Sterling didn't follow her immediately, but she felt his eyes on her back as she walked away. His silence felt like both a relief and a burden, his patience a cruel contrast to the storm raging inside her.

In the sanctuary of the bedroom, Zariyah sat on the edge of the bed, gripping the edge of the mattress as if it could steady her. Her chest heaved with unspoken words, her mind a swirl of shame, fear, and longing. She wanted to tell him—about Uncle Ben, about the nights she spent wrestling with nightmares and memories that refused to stay buried. But the enormity of it all was paralyzing.

She heard Sterling's soft footsteps approach. He paused in the doorway, his shadow stretching across the room. "Whenever you're ready, Z," he said quietly, his voice tinged with something she couldn't quite place—hope, maybe, or resignation. Then, just as quietly as he'd come, he retreated.

Zariyah exhaled a shaky breath, her resolve crumbling. How could she tell him everything when she could barely admit it to herself?

Chapter 16

The Birmingham skyline stretched out before her, the glass window cool beneath Zariyah's fingertips. Morning sunlight bathed the city in a deceptive glow, contrasting sharply with the storm churning inside her. Dr. Monroe's words from their last session echoed in her mind: You're not running anymore, Zariyah. It's time to face it.

But this morning, it wasn't just Dr. Monroe's voice haunting her.

"I spoke to Sterling," Noni's sharp tone had crackled through the phone earlier. "He's ready. When are you going to make that appointment?"

The memory of that call twisted in her chest. Noni had a way of weaving guilt into every conversation, like a master craftsman working a loom. And when she'd casually asked for more money, dismissing Zariyah's hesitation with a biting, "Well, you're his wife. You should have plenty," Zariyah's grip on her patience had nearly snapped.

"I can't keep doing this," she whispered to the empty office, though the words felt more like a confession to herself than a declaration.

The soft click of the door closing behind her signaled Dr.

Monroe's arrival. "I see that look, Zariyah," she said, her voice calm but perceptive. "What's on your mind?"

Zariyah turned, clutching the armrests of the chair as if they could anchor her. "It's Noni," she began, the words coming in a rush. "She's been calling about money again. And kids. She even called Sterling about it. I just... I can't."

Dr. Monroe tilted her head slightly, her expression a mixture of understanding and curiosity. "And how does that make you feel, hearing her pressure you like this?"

"Like I'm not enough," Zariyah admitted, her voice trembling. "Like I'm failing at everything she thinks I should be. She has this way of making me feel... small."

Dr. Monroe nodded thoughtfully. "It sounds like her words are striking a deeper chord. Do you think that pressure, that feeling of helplessness, could be tied to your past?"

Zariyah's chest tightened. She knew where this was going, and she wasn't sure if she could go there today. "It's not just Noni," she whispered. "It's everything. I've been trying to keep it together, but... it's too much."

"Let's unpack that," Dr. Monroe said gently. "You've carried so much for so long—your past, your mother's expectations, your relationship with Sterling. But burying it hasn't made it go away, has it?"

Zariyah shook her head, tears welling up.

Dr. Monroe leaned forward, her gaze steady and kind. "You start by giving yourself permission to feel what you've buried. You mentioned Uncle Ben before, but we haven't fully explored that. Can you tell me more about how his actions have shaped the way you feel now?"

The mention of his name made Zariyah's stomach knot. She pressed her lips together, fighting back the wave of nausea that always accompanied the thought of him.

"It's the powerlessness," she finally said, her voice breaking. "The feeling that someone else has control over me."

Dr. Monroe nodded, her expression thoughtful. "That sense of powerlessness often stays with survivors, manifesting in different ways. Research shows that survivors of childhood sexual abuse are three to four times more likely to experience heightened feelings of helplessness or a lack of agency as adults. It's not just about the trauma itself—it's about how the brain and body learn to respond in similar situations, even years later."

"So it's not just... me?"

"No," Dr. Monroe said gently. "It's not just you. It's a natural response to the trauma you endured. But recognizing it is the first step to breaking the pattern. You don't have to live in that space of powerlessness anymore."

Zariyah looked down at her lap, her fingers gripping the fabric of her skirt. "It feels like... I can't trust my reactions sometimes. Like, I get overwhelmed, and I just... freeze."

"That's completely normal," Dr. Monroe reassured her. "What you're describing is a freeze response, part of the body's natural reaction to fear or stress—fight, flight, or freeze. For many survivors, the freeze response becomes ingrained because, as children, they had no control over the situation. It's important to remember that it's a learned response, not a failing on your part."

Zariyah nodded slowly, her chest tightening. "But how do I stop it? I feel like I've been stuck there for years."

Dr. Monroe leaned forward slightly, her voice calm but firm. "The first step is awareness—recognizing when it's happening and what's triggering it. From there, we work on grounding techniques to help you reconnect with the present moment. For example, deep breathing exercises can calm the nervous system when you start to feel overwhelmed."

She paused, letting her words sink in before continuing. "Another strategy is reframing. When you notice yourself feeling powerless or frozen, try to identify one thing—just one—that you do have control over in that moment. It could be as simple as deciding to leave the room, drink a glass of water, or even say no to something that doesn't feel right."

Zariyah tilted her head, considering the suggestion. "But what about... the bigger things? Like with Sterling? Or Noni? It feels like there's no way to fix those things."

Dr. Monroe's eyes softened. "Start small. Boundary-setting is a skill, and it takes time to develop. With Sterling, for instance, you might begin by sharing how you're feeling in small, manageable pieces instead of waiting until everything boils over. With Noni, it might mean being firm about what you're able to give—emotionally, financially, or otherwise—and sticking to it, even if it feels uncomfortable at first."

Zariyah sighed, her shoulders slumping slightly. "I don't know if I can do that with Noni. She's... relentless."

"She sounds like it," Dr. Monroe acknowledged. "And that's where preparation helps. Before you talk to her, take a moment to rehearse what you want to say. Write it down if you need to. And remind yourself that it's okay to repeat your boundaries as many times as necessary. You're not responsible for her reaction—only for holding your ground."

Zariyah's lips quirked into a faint smile. "Easier said than done."

"It always is," Dr. Monroe agreed, her tone lightening. "But each time you take a small step—whether it's setting a boundary, using a grounding technique, or even just acknowledging how you feel—you're reclaiming control. It's not about doing it perfectly; it's about giving yourself permission to try."

Zariyah exhaled, feeling the faintest glimmer of relief. "I

guess I can start there."

Dr. Monroe smiled warmly. "That's all I'm asking."

Dr. Monroe reached into her desk drawer and handed Zariyah a leather-bound journal. "Start here. Write down everything you've been holding back—just for yourself. You don't need to share it with Sterling yet, but seeing it on paper can help you find clarity."

Zariyah took the journal, her fingers brushing over its smooth surface. "Okay," she whispered. "I'll try."

"You're not alone in this anymore," Dr. Monroe said, her voice full of quiet encouragement.

Zariyah nodded, blinking back tears. As she left the office, clutching the journal to her chest, the cold November air hit her like a wake-up call. She wasn't sure if she felt lighter or heavier, but she knew one thing for certain: she couldn't keep running.

That evening, as she packed for their weekend getaway, her hands trembled slightly. Each piece of clothing she folded felt like a small act of hope, a promise to herself to try—to be brave, even if it terrified her. As she zipped her suitcase shut, Dr. Monroe's words lingered in her mind: Change isn't always bad. But was she ready to embrace it?

Chapter
17

The soft hum of the private jet filled the cabin, a constant, lulling rhythm that should have been soothing. Yet, Zariyah's fingers gripped the armrest, her knuckles pale against the dark leather. Sterling sat across from her, scrolling through his phone, the picture of ease.

She glanced out the window, watching the clouds stretch into endless horizons. The thought of this weekend—their weekend—filled her with a strange mix of anticipation and dread. Sterling's gestures were always grand, always polished, but she wondered: What was he trying to prove this time? To her? To himself?

The flight attendant appeared, offering champagne. Zariyah declined with a polite smile, her stomach too knotted to enjoy it. Sterling glanced up, his brow quirking slightly. "You okay?"

"I'm fine," she replied, the word slipping out before she could consider how untrue it was.

Sterling raised an eyebrow but didn't press. Instead, he returned to his phone, tapping out a quick reply to a message. Zariyah's eyes flicked to the champagne glass resting untouched on the tray beside her. The flight attendant had poured it with a flourish earlier, but the thought of drinking it turned her stomach. This weekend—the grand getaway Sterling had meticulously planned—felt more like a performance than a retreat.

She forced herself to focus on the present. The flight, the suite, the city—it was all perfectly orchestrated. Sterling had gone above and beyond, just as he always did. But somewhere beneath the surface, Zariyah could feel it: an unanswered question, a lingering doubt. Was this trip really about them reconnecting, or was it Sterling's way of avoiding the deeper cracks in their relationship?

When they arrived, a concierge greeted them at the airport, ensuring every detail of their stay was handled. From the sleek car service to the executive suite at the Four Seasons, everything had been arranged with meticulous care.

Sterling had thought of everything—everything but the one thing Zariyah most needed: a moment to break through the silence that had been building between them.

The suite was breathtaking, with floor-to-ceiling windows framing the Atlanta skyline, casting a warm golden glow over the room. Zariyah admired the plush king-sized bed, the grand chandelier, and the comfy leather seating and dining area.

As she lingered by the window, Sterling wrapped his arm around her waist, his chin resting on her shoulder as they both took in the view. "What do you think?" he asked, his voice filled with pride.

"It's beautiful," Zariyah replied softly, her eyes on the skyline but her mind elsewhere.

"You deserve it," he said, his tone affectionate as he kissed her temple and moved to unpack before disappearing into the bathroom.

The view was stunning, but the tension knotting her chest wouldn't loosen. This suite, this trip—everything Sterling had planned felt perfect on the surface. Yet, underneath, a quiet unease hummed.

Moments later, he emerged, his sleeves rolled up and his tie loosened. "I ran you a bath," he said, his voice casual but warm. "And room service is on the way. You've had a long week. Go relax while I handle dinner."

The simple gesture caught her off guard, tugging at something deep within her. "You didn't have to do that," she murmured.

Sterling stepped closer, brushing a strand of hair from her face. "I wanted to," he said, his smile soft. "Go on. I'll let you know when dinner gets here."

Zariyah hesitated, then nodded, retreating to the bathroom. Her fingers trailed along the edge of the marble sink as she turned off the faucet. Steam rose from the tub, curling into the air as the warm lavender-scented water beckoned her. But even as she slipped into the soothing warmth, her mind remained restless.

The luxury of the suite, the grand gestures from Sterling—it should've felt safe, even indulgent. But instead, the hot water did little to quiet the doubts in her mind. How could she open up to Sterling about everything she had buried? How could she share her truth without destroying the image he had of her?

Zariyah undressed slowly, folding her clothes with an absent-minded precision. As she stepped into the hot water, the warmth enveloped her, coaxing the tension from her muscles, but doing little to soothe the storm in her chest. She turned on the jets, watching the bubbles swirl and churn like the thoughts she couldn't quiet.

Her hands rested on the edge of the tub, her fingers

tracing the cool marble as Dr. Monroe's voice surfaced in her mind: You've built this wall to protect yourself.

The words felt like a challenge, an accusation, and a plea all at once. Zariyah leaned her head back, her gaze drifting to the ceiling. Had she been protecting herself all this time—or just hiding? And from what? Sterling? Herself? The truth she'd buried so deeply, it had become part of her?

The jets pulsed gently against her skin, but the sensation only seemed to amplify the ache inside her. She thought about the past few days, Sterling's gestures, the way he had planned every detail of this trip. The effort was unmistakable—he was trying, wasn't he? And yet, the gap between them still felt vast, like two dancers out of step, moving to the same music but never in sync.

Why can't I just let go? she thought, frustration bubbling up alongside the guilt. It wasn't as if Sterling hadn't tried. He was here, doing everything he could to remind her of who they used to be. But every time she felt herself leaning toward him, something pulled her back—a whisper of doubt, a shadow of fear.

The water's heat pressed against her, wrapping her in a cocoon of steam and silence. She closed her eyes, the faint scent of lavender curling around her like a lullaby. Her mind drifted back to the sessions with Dr. Monroe, to the moments when she'd felt that flicker of hope—when she believed, however briefly, that healing was possible.

But sitting here now, the idea of sharing her truth with Sterling felt insurmountable. She imagined the look in his eyes—shock, confusion, maybe even pity—and her chest tightened. What if he didn't understand? What if he couldn't? The thought alone made her throat constrict.

She rubbed her temples, trying to will the thoughts away, but they persisted, each one sharper than the last. Memories of Uncle Ben slithered through the cracks, unbidden and relentless. The weight of them threatened to pull her under, and for a moment, Zariyah thought about climbing out of the tub, escaping the suffocating swirl of her mind.

Instead, she leaned forward, letting the jets hum against her back, her hands gripping the edge of the tub like a lifeline. What would it take to tear the wall down? she wondered. Was it bravery? Trust? Or was it something she didn't yet have—something she wasn't sure she'd ever find?

The faint knock at the door pulled her back. Sterling's voice carried through the bathroom. "Dinner's here. Take your time, okay?"

Zariyah exhaled, her breath trembling as she nodded to herself. "Okay," she called back, her voice steadier than she felt.

She stared at the bubbles one last time, the swirling patterns mirroring the chaos inside her. Dr. Monroe's words lingered: It's keeping you from the intimacy you crave.
And for the first time, Zariyah wondered if tearing down the wall would mean losing the only protection she'd ever known.

Chapter
18

Zariyah exited the tub, her skin warm from the soak, and wrapped herself in the plush robe hanging nearby. The lavender scent still clung to her as she padded out to the dining area, where Sterling had plated their meals with care.

On the table were seared salmon fillets glazed with miso and honey, a delicate side of asparagus spears topped with shaved parmesan, and a basket of warm, crusty sourdough bread with a pat of salted European butter. The aroma was rich yet comforting—a perfect balance of indulgence and simplicity, just the way she liked it.

"You barely touched your food," Sterling said, his tone light but edged with concern as he poured her another glass of chilled sauvignon blanc.

"It's good," she replied, setting down her fork after picking at the asparagus.

Sterling reached across the table, his hand brushing hers. "Z, I planned this whole weekend for us. To reconnect. No distractions. Just us."

His sincerity should have eased her doubts, but instead, it only magnified them. The tension in her chest coiled tighter. She nodded, forcing a smile. "Thank you, Sterling. Really."

He smiled back, but the lingering weight between them refused to lift. The clink of utensils against plates filled the silence as they finished the meal in an uneasy quiet.

Later that evening, Sterling turned on the radio in the suite, letting the sultry strains of a jazz ballad seep into the air. The melody wrapped around them, warm and inviting, as he extended his hand toward her, his eyes smoldering with intent.

"Dance with me," he murmured, his voice rich and low, like the bassline of the song.

Zariyah hesitated, the weight of her thoughts anchoring her to the couch. But the look in his eyes—familiar, commanding, and full of unspoken promises—drew her in. She slipped her hand into his, and he pulled her to her feet with ease, guiding her close until her body molded to his.

One arm circled her waist, the other clasping her hand against his chest. His warmth seeped into her through the soft silk of his pajama shirt, the faint hint of his cologne mingling with the clean scent of his freshly showered skin. She inhaled deeply, letting herself be drawn into his orbit as they swayed in perfect synchronicity.

The song dipped into a deeper rhythm, and Sterling tightened his hold, his lips brushing against her temple. "You remember this song?" he asked, his voice rough and edged with desire.

Zariyah nodded, her cheek brushing against the firmness of his chest. It was the same song that had played the night he proposed, in a candlelit room that felt a lot like this. The memory sent a shiver down her spine, and when Sterling's hand slid lower, resting at the curve of her hip, the warmth that followed was undeniable.

"You're so beautiful," he whispered against her ear, his lips grazing the sensitive skin just below it. The sensation made her pulse flutter, her body leaning instinctively closer.

"Sterling..." she started, but her voice faltered as his mouth traced the line of her jaw, his kisses slow and deliberate, his free hand finding the small of her back and pressing her firmly against him.

"Shhh," he breathed, his lips barely brushing hers. "Let me show you how much I've missed you."

Before she could respond, his mouth captured hers, soft and teasing at first, then deepening as the tension between them dissolved into something hotter, hungrier. His fingers tangled in her hair, tilting her head back as he claimed her fully, the music a faint hum compared to the pounding of her heart.

The space between them disappeared entirely as Sterling's hands explored her curves, his touch leaving a trail of heat in its wake. Zariyah's breath hitched when his lips moved down the column of her throat, her hands clutching at his shoulders to keep herself steady.

He backed her toward the bed, his movements deliberate and unhurried, as though savoring every second of their connection. When the backs of her knees hit the edge, he paused, his hands framing her face, his gaze locking onto hers.

"I love you, Z," he said, his voice rough with emotion and something deeper, something primal.

Her lips parted, her chest heaving with the weight of everything she felt and everything she wasn't ready to say. "I love you too," she whispered, the words barely audible but charged with meaning.

Sterling's lips curved into a smile—soft, knowing—as he leaned down to kiss her again. This time, there was no hesitation, no lingering doubts. Only the heady rush of heat and the unspoken promise that, for tonight, they would find each other again.

Zariyah's breath caught as Sterling's hands slid beneath the edges of her robe, his touch warm and sure against her skin. She closed her eyes, leaning into the moment, letting herself get lost in the feel of him—the safety, the heat, the longing that neither of them could fully voice.

Sterling guided her gently onto the bed, the silk of the sheets cool against her back. His lips never left hers, moving with a quiet urgency that spoke volumes. It wasn't just desire driving him; it was something deeper, a need to bridge the gap that had grown between them.

As his kisses trailed lower, Zariyah threaded her fingers through his hair, her mind warring with her body. She wanted to stay in this bubble of warmth and intimacy, to let it wash away the doubts and fears that had been eating at her for weeks. But as the moments stretched, the weight of what she wasn't saying grew heavier, pressing against her chest like an invisible hand.

Sterling paused, sensing the hesitation in her touch. He looked up, his brow furrowing slightly. "Z?" he asked softly, his voice laced with concern.

Zariyah opened her eyes, meeting his gaze. The tenderness in his expression made her heart ache. She wanted to tell him everything—to break down the walls she'd spent years building. But the words wouldn't come.

"I'm okay," she said, her voice shaky but resolute. She reached for him, pulling him back to her. "I need . . .just need you."

Sterling hesitated for a moment longer, then nodded, pressing a soft kiss to her forehead. "I'm here," he whispered, and for now, that was enough.

Their movements slowed, becoming less about urgency and more about rediscovery. Sterling's touch was deliberate, his hands and lips tracing paths between her full breasts that reminded her of how deeply he knew her, how intimately they were connected. It was as though he was saying everything he couldn't put into words, reassuring her in the only way he knew how.

When they finally lay tangled in the sheets, their breathing soft and steady, Zariyah rested her head on Sterling's chest, listening to the rhythmic beat of his heart. His fingers stroked her back absentmindedly, his other arm draped around her shoulders.

"You okay?" he asked again, his voice a murmur in the dark.

Zariyah nodded, but the truth felt more complicated. She was okay in this moment, wrapped in his warmth, feeling the steady rise and fall of his chest. But the questions lingering in her mind—the doubts, the fears—still cast a shadow.

As Sterling's breathing evened out and he drifted into sleep, Zariyah stayed awake, her thoughts swirling. Tonight had been a reprieve, a moment of connection in the midst of their distance. But she knew it wasn't enough. Not yet. Tomorrow, I'll try to tell him, she told herself.

But even as she made the promise, part of her wondered if she'd ever find the courage to truly let him in.

In the stillness of the early morning, Sterling stirred, his hand instinctively seeking Zariyah beside him. She hadn't fallen back asleep, her body warm against his but her thoughts racing. His fingers traced the curve of her arm, slow and deliberate, drawing her attention back to him.

Zariyah's heart pounded as his lips traveled along her neck, lingering in a way that made her toes curl. His hands followed, exploring her curves with a confidence that came from knowing every inch of her. His touch felt different—

like he was savoring her, rediscovering her.

"You've always been so beautiful," he whispered against her skin, his voice rough and full of need.

His words sent a shiver down her spine, and she climbed on top of him, her hands gliding over his toned chest. Sterling chuckled, a low, deep sound that vibrated against her fingertips.

"Taking charge, huh?" he teased, his eyes dark with mischief and desire.

"Somebody has to," Zariyah shot back, her lips curving into a smirk. But the playful moment was fleeting, replaced by a hunger that neither of them could deny.

Sterling pulled her closer, capturing her lips in a kiss that was all-consuming. His hands roamed over her body. He rolled her over, pressing his body against hers. The warmth of his skin, the strength in his arms was intoxicating. She tangled her fingers in his hair, pulling him closer as he kissed her deeply, their movements growing more urgent.

As Sterling's lips traveled lower, a flicker of unease darted through Zariyah. The unspoken truths she carried threatened to surface, their weight pressing against the fragile intimacy they had built tonight. She stiffened for a brief moment, and Sterling paused, his hand brushing her cheek in silent question.

"I'm okay," she whispered quickly, pulling him closer, as though she could drown her doubts in the heat of the moment. He didn't press, but his eyes lingered for a heartbeat too long before he continued. Her heart clenched, but she let the moment sweep her away.

Sterling's breath hitched as her nails dug into his shoulders. His hands explored her thighs, her hips, his touch igniting a fire that burned away the doubts lingering in her mind.

Their bodies moved together in a rhythm that felt both familiar and electric, as if they were discovering each other all over again. Sterling's touch was confident, yet reverent, his kisses leaving trails of heat wherever they landed. Zariyah responded with equal intensity, her hands and lips exploring him as if trying to memorize every detail.

When they finally collapsed against the sheets, their bodies spent and tangled together, Sterling pressed a kiss to her forehead, his arm wrapping possessively around her waist.

"Now that's what I call reconnecting," Sterling murmured, his voice low and full of satisfaction.

Zariyah let out a soft laugh, her cheek resting against his chest. But as she lay there, the word reconnecting felt foreign, as though it belonged to someone else's relationship. Could this truly be them again? She wanted to believe it, to hold on to the warmth of this moment, but the gap between their bodies and hearts still loomed.

But as the silence settled over them, the weight of her unspoken truths crept back in, reminding her that this was only a temporary escape.

Chapter 19

The morning sun filtered through the sheer curtains, painting soft golden streaks across the room. Zariyah stretched, her body sinking deeper into the plush sheets as the faint aroma of freshly brewed coffee drifted toward her. She blinked, her gaze falling on Sterling, who was seated near the window, a cup of coffee in one hand and the complimentary newspaper in the other.

Sterling Ellis looked every bit the picture of composed elegance. His crisp button-down shirt, unbuttoned at the top, revealed just a hint of his chest, while his navy slacks emphasized his athletic frame. The morning light played against the cinnamon tones of his skin, making him look almost unreal. His neatly trimmed beard framed his strong jaw, and the subtle tousle in his curly, cropped hair hinted at the passion that had unraveled between them hours before.

For a moment, Zariyah lingered on the sight of him, allowing herself to feel the warmth of his presence. But as he glanced up, meeting her gaze with a smile that reached his eyes—a rare thing lately—her heart tightened. Was this him being present, or was it just Sterling back to his usual role of orchestrating perfection?

"Morning, beautiful," he said, his voice low and playful. "Hungry?"

The question made her cheeks warm, a reaction she wasn't used to anymore. She nodded, brushing her hair back as she sat up, watching as Sterling folded the newspaper and stood. The ease with which he moved, the way he could command a space without trying, had always drawn her in. But today, it left her feeling... cautious.

"Breakfast downstairs, then shopping?" he suggested, placing a steaming cup of tea on the bedside table for her. He leaned down, brushing a soft kiss across her temple. "I want to spoil you today."

Zariyah cradled the cup in her hands, letting the warmth seep into her palms. Sterling could be attentive, but sometimes his grand gestures felt more like distractions.

By midmorning, they were strolling through the bustling streets of Atlanta. Sterling, normally impatient with long shopping trips, was uncharacteristically engaged. He held her bags without complaint, offered opinions on every dress, and even teased her with a pair of oversized sunglasses that made them both laugh.

At one boutique, a gown in a deep navy-blue shade caught Sterling's eye. The fabric shimmered subtly under the lights, reminding him of the sapphires he'd just bought for Zariyah. He instinctively knew it would look good against her cafe au lait skin. When Zariyah went into the dressing room to try on some cocktail dresses, he purchased it and had sales associate ship it to his office, to arrive before the ball.

Zariyah had chosen a sleek emerald-green dress for their evening out. It fit her like a dream, the fabric hugging her curves in all the right places while still feeling effortlessly elegant. She couldn't remember the last time she'd felt this good in something.

Exhausted from the day's excursions, Zariyah stretched out on the bed, her body sinking into the luxurious comforter. The soft murmur of Sterling's voice as he made a quick call in the corner of the room became a soothing backdrop, and she let her eyes drift shut.

It wasn't long before she felt the warm press of Sterling's lips against her neck. "You've got forty-five minutes to get ready, Sleeping Beauty," Sterling teased, his voice thick with affection. He rolled out of bed and headed for the bathroom, already wrapped in one of the hotel's plush robes.

Zariyah stretched, rubbing the sleep from her eyes as she took in the soft glow of the room. She wouldn't deny that she was enjoying this—the pampering, Sterling's attentiveness. It was a stark contrast to the past few years. Pushing those thoughts aside, she focused on getting ready for the evening.

* * *

She stood in front of the vanity, her fingers grazing the emerald-green cocktail dress she'd chosen earlier that day. The sleek satin fabric shimmered softly in the light, its rich hue reminiscent of a freshly polished gemstone. The halter neckline framed her shoulders elegantly, the delicate gathering at the collar giving way to the long, flowing tie that draped down her back. It hugged her frame perfectly, the subtle sheen accentuating her curves while the mid-length hemline hinted at understated sophistication. The dress felt like armor—elegant and powerful—but it couldn't shield her from the questions swirling in her mind.

Zariyah turned her attention to her hair. Her molasses-toned curls, rich with subtle golden undertones, cascaded around her face, their natural texture framing her features like a halo. She reached for a touch of cream, running it through the strands to define the coils even more. After some thought, she decided to pull the sides up loosely, pinning them with delicate emerald-jeweled clips that mirrored the tone of her dress. The style was effortless yet polished, allowing her natural beauty to shine.

Standing back, she examined the final look. The combination of the deep green dress, the gleaming clips, and her cascading curls was stunning, but it was the way it all highlighted her warm, glowing skin that made her pause. For a fleeting moment, she allowed herself to appreciate what she saw: a woman who, despite her doubts, carried herself with grace and resilience.

She reached for a pair of gold strappy heels, slipping them on and adjusting the delicate straps. A soft spray of perfume followed—something warm and musky, with hints of jasmine and vanilla. As the scent settled around her, she couldn't help but feel a flicker of confidence ignite, however small.

When she caught her reflection once more, she straightened her shoulders. Tonight, she would play the part. Elegant. Composed. Radiant. Even if the questions and doubts lingered beneath the surface, tonight she would be the Zariyah Sterling had always admired.

She sighed, brushing a touch of rose-gold highlighter across her cheekbones, the faint shimmer catching the light perfectly. A swipe of mascara enhanced her already striking eyes, while a soft, nude gloss completed her look.

Zariyah reached for her earrings, delicate drops that Sterling had gifted her early in their marriage, their simplicity still managing to feel timeless. She was securing the clasp on one when Sterling appeared in the doorway.

"You look incredible," he said, his voice low and full of admiration.

Zariyah turned to face him, and for a moment, her breath caught. Sterling looked like he had just stepped off a runway—his navy-and-white striped shirt, paired with a tailored navy suit, accentuated the sharp angles of his jawline. The flicker of pride in his eyes, the easy confidence in his stance—it all felt magnetic, pulling her in.

Sterling stepped closer, his movements slow and deliberate, a small velvet box in hand. "Turn around," he instructed softly, his tone intimate.

Zariyah obeyed, her breath hitching slightly as she lifted her hair. Sterling's hands were steady as he fastened a delicate diamond necklace around her neck, the cool touch of the jewels sending a shiver down her spine. The weight of the necklace settled between her breasts, a perfect accent to the neckline of her dress.

Their eyes met in the mirror, his gaze lingering on her with something deeper than admiration—something closer to reverence.

"You take my breath away," Sterling murmured, his voice barely above a whisper, yet heavy with meaning. His fingers brushed her shoulders, tracing the edge of the dress with a touch so soft it made her skin tingle.

Zariyah's heart fluttered at his words, a warm blush creeping up her neck. For a moment, she let herself believe him, let herself bask in the adoration in his eyes. But just as quickly, the familiar doubts tugged at the edges of her mind. Was this moment real, or was it just another beautiful illusion?

She managed a soft smile, willing herself to stay in the moment. "Thank you," she said, her voice barely steady, but sincere.

Sterling leaned down, pressing a kiss to her shoulder. "You don't need to thank me," he murmured, his lips lingering for a heartbeat longer. "You're everything."

For a moment, Zariyah let herself believe him, let herself sink into the warmth of his gaze and the weight of his hands. But as quickly as the thought came, her mind pushed it aside, the doubts creeping back like shadows at the edges of her reflection. She forced a smile and turned to him, placing a hand lightly on his chest. "You clean up pretty nicely yourself."

Sterling reached for her hand and kissed her knuckles, his lips lingering for just a moment. "Meet me in the lobby when you're ready," he said, flashing her one last smile before leaving the room.

Zariyah remained still, staring at her reflection in the mirror long after Sterling left the room. Her hazel eyes, always so expressive, seemed to shift with her mood—an unsteady mix of excitement and doubt flickering in their depths. The diamond necklace sparkled brilliantly against her skin, but it felt heavy in more ways than one. She forced a soft sigh from her lips. "Tonight, let's just pretend you're as exquisite as this diamond," she whispered to herself, attempting to silence the doubts clawing at the edges of her thoughts.

Stepping into the elevator, Zariyah took a deep breath, smoothing the folds of her dress. The silk fabric skimmed her legs like liquid elegance, but even its luxurious touch couldn't ease the tightness in her chest. As the doors opened, two sharply dressed men waiting in the lobby glanced up. One of them let out an appreciative whistle.

"Damn," he muttered, not bothering to hide his admiration.

Zariyah's cheeks heated, but she kept her gaze forward, locked on Sterling, who stood just a few feet away, his posture easy but his eyes firmly on her.

When she reached him, Sterling gave the two men a subtle nod—a quiet acknowledgment that said, She's with me.

Zariyah smiled up at him as he handed her a single white rose, its delicate petals cool against her fingers. She caught the faintest whiff of its soft fragrance, a reminder of innocence and beauty—so unlike the knots twisting inside her. Yet, when she met Sterling's gaze, the sincerity in his expression unraveled something within her, if only for a moment. She smiled, letting herself relax into his steady presence.

* * *

The limo ride to the theater was quiet, punctuated by Sterling's occasional glance at her, as though he couldn't believe she was sitting next to him. After the performance, they arrived at the rooftop restaurant. The city skyline stretched like a sea of diamonds against the deepening twilight, the stars above mirroring the lights below. Zariyah marveled at the glittering view, her breath catching at the beauty, but the soft hum of piano music in the background couldn't quite drown out her inner voice.

The candle flickered between them, casting dancing shadows across their table and onto Sterling's face. He looked impossibly handsome, his features softened by the golden glow, his eyes warm and attentive.

Sterling reached across the table, his fingers brushing hers before taking her hand fully in his. His thumb grazed her knuckles in slow, deliberate circles, sending a small shiver through her. "I've missed this. Us," he said, his voice low but steady. His gaze locked onto hers, a quiet intensity behind his words. "I want you to know I'm here for you, Z. Whatever you need from me, I'm here."

Zariyah's chest tightened. She wanted to believe him—

wanted to let his words erase the unease that had lingered in the back of her mind for weeks. The weight of his touch, so familiar yet foreign, felt both comforting and suffocating. She offered a soft smile and murmured, "I've missed us too." The words felt both honest and inadequate, carrying more weight than she intended but somehow not enough.

After dinner, Sterling led her to the dance floor, his hand resting gently on the small of her back as he guided her through the other couples. The soft strains of the music wrapped around them as his arms encircled her waist, pulling her close. His warmth seeped through the silk of her dress, grounding her in the moment.

"You remember this song?" he murmured, his breath brushing against her temple.

She nodded, the melody tugging at memories she thought she'd forgotten. It had played at their wedding reception, back when everything had felt so simple, so sure. Now, the notes felt like fragments of something they'd both lost but were too afraid to name.

Sterling tilted his head, his lips brushing the edge of her ear. "You're everything to me, Z," he whispered, the words weighted with emotion.

Zariyah closed her eyes, leaning into the moment, willing herself to believe it. For a brief second, she allowed herself to melt into the rhythm, the warmth of his touch, the comfort of his familiar scent. But even as their bodies moved as one, a hollow ache pulsed in her chest. The doubts crept in again, uninvited and relentless.

As they swayed under the stars, Zariyah's thoughts spiraled. Maybe it wasn't Sterling. Maybe it was all me.

The realization stung, a sharp pang that lingered even as Sterling pulled her closer, as though trying to shield her from the very doubts she couldn't escape.

* * *

The suite welcomed them with dimmed lights and the faint, soothing melody of a soft jazz instrumental playing from the speakers. Zariyah sank into the leather sofa, slipping off her shoes as Sterling disappeared into the adjoining kitchenette. Moments later, he returned with a tray of chocolates, a small bowl of strawberries, and two glasses of champagne.

Sterling placed the tray on the table and sat beside her, his knee brushing against hers. "A little snack before bed," he said, his voice warm, his tone laced with suggestion as he handed her a glass.

Zariyah picked up a piece of dark chocolate and held it between her fingers, the rich aroma filling the space between them. "If you keep this up," she teased, her voice light, "you'll ruin my appetite for brunch tomorrow."

Sterling chuckled low, leaning closer. "I'm not worried," he murmured. "You'll always find room for something sweet."

His words wrapped around her like a caress. She sipped her champagne, its crispness fizzing against her tongue as Sterling reached for a strawberry. He brought it to her lips, his eyes locked on hers, daring her to take a bite. Slowly, she leaned forward, her teeth sinking into the ripe fruit as its sweetness mingled with the champagne.

Sterling's thumb brushed her bottom lip, catching a drop of juice before leaning in to taste it himself. His lips were warm, the kiss starting soft but deepening as he cupped the back of her neck, drawing her closer. The tray and glasses were forgotten, the space between them dissolving as his touch ignited every nerve in her body.

Zariyah gasped as his hand slid along her thigh, the silk of her dress shifting beneath his palm. "Sterling…" she started, but her voice faltered as he pressed a kiss to the sensitive spot just below her ear, his breath hot against her skin.

"Shh," he whispered, his tone commanding but tender. "Let me take care of you."

He stood, scooping her into his arms effortlessly, carrying her toward the bed. The champagne flutes sat untouched on the table, their bubbles slowly fading, much like Zariyah's resolve to keep her guard up.

Sterling laid her gently on the bed, the silk sheets cool against her skin as he hovered above her, his fingers trailing along the curve of her jaw. "You're so beautiful," he murmured, his voice rough with desire. His lips followed the path of his fingers, pressing soft kisses to her neck, her collarbone, the delicate line of her shoulder.

Zariyah arched beneath him, her hands tangling in his hair as he slowly peeled away the emerald dress she'd chosen so carefully. His touch was deliberate, reverent, as though rediscovering her for the first time.

"Every time I look at you," he said softly, his lips brushing against hers, "it's like I'm seeing you all over again."

Their movements became a symphony of passion and tenderness, every kiss and touch a wordless conversation. Zariyah let herself surrender to the moment, to the heat between them, to the way Sterling made her feel like the only woman in the world.

Hours later, they lay tangled in the sheets, Sterling's arm draped over her waist as he pressed a lazy kiss to her temple. "I'm not sure I'll ever get enough of you," he murmured, his voice heavy with sleep and satisfaction.

Zariyah smiled faintly, her head resting on his chest, but even in the stillness, her thoughts swirled. This weekend had been a dream—a perfect, glittering facade—but what would come next?

Sunday Morning

The sunlight filtering through the curtains was soft and warm, the kind of light that made it easy to linger in bed. Sterling stirred beside her, his hand sliding over her hip as he pressed a kiss to her shoulder.

"Morning, beautiful," he murmured, his voice husky with sleep.

Zariyah stretched, her body pleasantly sore, the memory of the night before still lingering in her mind. "Morning," she replied softly, her gaze meeting his.

Sterling's eyes softened, and in that quiet moment, the world outside their suite seemed to vanish. He leaned in, brushing his lips against hers in a kiss that started tender but quickly deepened, reigniting the intimacy they'd shared the night before.   Their movements became instinctive, their connection magnetic, as if every unspoken word between them could be conveyed through touch.

After checking out of the hotel and enjoying a leisurely brunch, Sterling surprised her with a detour to Stone Mountain. They spent the afternoon walking barefoot along the lakeside, hand-in-hand, the quiet rhythm of the water easing some of the tension that lingered between them.

For a moment, things felt simple again. Peaceful.

But as they drove home that evening, the weight of reality began to creep back in. Despite the romantic moments, the fancy dinners, and the stolen glances, Zariyah's thoughts wandered back to what had been left unsaid.

Will the truth bring us closer together, or will it push us further apart?

Her usual Monday session with Dr. Monroe had been moved to Tuesday, giving her a full day to let the weekend's memories settle—and the questions to linger a bit longer.

Chapter
20

The familiar warmth of Dr. Monroe's office wrapped around Zariyah like a comforting embrace, but it did little to calm the whirlwind of emotions churning inside her. She sat with her legs crossed tightly, her fingers absently tracing the seam of the armchair. The soft ticking of the clock on the wall seemed louder than usual, its rhythm amplifying the silence between them.

Dr. Monroe tilted her head slightly, her expression gentle but curious. "How was the weekend?"

Zariyah hesitated, her mind darting back to the vivid moments of the past few days—the elegance of the rooftop dinner, the intimacy of the suite, the way Sterling's arms had felt so familiar yet foreign around her. "It was... nice," she said finally, her voice tinged with uncertainty. "Sterling went all out. A private jet, luxury suite, fancy dinners. It was everything you'd expect from him."

Dr. Monroe nodded, her pen poised over her notepad. "He wanted to make it special for you."

"Yes," Zariyah admitted, twisting the rings on her finger. "He did. He kept saying he wanted us to reconnect. And for a while, it worked. We laughed, we danced, we were intimate." Her cheeks flushed at the memory, and she glanced away, embarrassed by how raw the words felt leaving her mouth. "It felt... good to be wanted."

Dr. Monroe offered an encouraging smile. "And yet?"

Zariyah let out a shaky breath, her hands gripping the armrest as if bracing herself for what was coming next. "And yet, I couldn't fully let go. Even in the moments that felt perfect... I was holding back without even meaning to."

"Why do you think that is?" Dr. Monroe asked softly, her tone devoid of judgment.

"I don't know," Zariyah murmured, her voice barely audible. "Maybe because I know he doesn't see all of me. Or because I'm afraid of what'll happen if he does."

Zariyah hesitated, her gaze dropping to her lap as she twisted her rings again. The silence stretched, her words caught somewhere between her throat and her heart.
Finally, she spoke, her voice barely above a whisper. "I don't know. Maybe... fear. Fear of losing him. Fear of being seen for who I really am—damaged, messy." Her voice cracked, betraying the pain she had worked so hard to bury.

Dr. Monroe's brows furrowed slightly, her expression shifting to one of quiet concern. "Did you just say you were damaged?"

Zariyah shook her head quickly, then stilled. "Yes." The word lingered in the air, heavy with the weight of old wounds.

"Where did that come from?" Dr. Monroe's tone was soft but insistent, like a hand gently coaxing her out of hiding.

Zariyah took a deep breath, her chest tightening as the memories resurfaced. "It's one of the things Ben used to say... when he'd get angry. He'd tell me I was damaged. That I wasn't good enough. That nobody else would ever want me." Her voice wavered, and she clenched her hands to keep them steady.

Dr. Monroe exhaled, her pen resting on her notepad. "Zariyah," she said firmly, her eyes locking onto hers, "you are not damaged. What happened to you was damaging, but it does not define who you are. You survived. That's not damage—that's strength."

The words hit Zariyah like a wave, both soothing and jarring. She wanted to believe them, to let them sink in and wash away the years of self-doubt. But the echo of Ben's voice still lurked in the corners of her mind, a ghost she hadn't yet exorcized.

Dr. Monroe leaned forward slightly, her tone calm yet probing. "You've built walls to protect yourself, Zariyah. And that's understandable. Vulnerability is risky—it can feel like handing someone a weapon and trusting them not to use it. But vulnerability is also the foundation of intimacy. It's what allows us to truly connect."

Zariyah's throat tightened, her gaze fixed on her hands. The weight of Dr. Monroe's words settled over her like a heavy blanket, too familiar to shake off. She wanted to argue, to push back, to retreat into the safety of her walls. But deep down, she knew the truth: those same walls had kept Sterling—and everyone else—at arm's length.

"Do you think he'd use that weapon against you?" Dr. Monroe asked gently.

Zariyah looked up, her hazel eyes glistening with unshed tears. "I don't know," she admitted. "But I'm scared to find out."

Dr. Monroe nodded, her gaze steady and reassuring. "That fear is valid. But Zariyah, what if he doesn't? What if he surprises you? What if he's stronger than you think?"

The question hung in the air, its weight pressing on Zariyah's chest. For the first time, she allowed herself to consider the possibility—that maybe, just maybe, Sterling was strong enough to handle the truth. And maybe, just maybe, she was too.

Dr. Monroe's pen hovered over her notepad for a moment before she spoke again.

"Sometimes, the things we keep buried seem bigger and scarier than they are because they've been hidden for so long. Have you thought about what it would feel like to share even a small piece of that with Sterling?"

Zariyah bit her lip, her fingers knotting together in her lap as a storm of uncertainty churned in her chest. "I don't know. What if it changes how he sees me? What if... he looks at me differently? Her voice wavered, and she blinked rapidly, trying to keep the tears at bay.

Dr. Monroe's expression softened, her gaze steady but encouraging. "And what if he doesn't?" she countered gently. "What if sharing brings you closer instead of pulling you apart? Isn't it exhausting, Zariyah, carrying this weight on your own?"

The words hit like a quiet thunderclap, and Zariyah nodded slowly, the tears she'd been holding back spilling over. "It is," she admitted, her voice trembling. "But... at least I control it. If I keep it to myself, no one can use it to hurt me."

Dr. Monroe leaned back slightly, giving Zariyah the space to process the magnitude of her own admission. Her voice, when she spoke, was calm but firm, each word deliberate. "Do you really control it, or is it controlling you?"

The question hung in the air, and Zariyah froze, the weight of it pressing down on her. She wanted to argue, to defend her need for control, but she couldn't deny the truth in Dr. Monroe's words. The walls she'd built to keep her safe had become a prison, confining her and keeping the people she loved at a distance.

"What happened to you," Dr. Monroe continued, her voice unwavering, "doesn't define your worth, Zariyah. It doesn't make you broken, or unlovable, or weak. But hiding it? Pretending it doesn't exist? That's what's keeping you from fully stepping into the life you want—the relationship you deserve."

Zariyah's breath hitched as the words washed over her, peeling back layers of fear and shame she hadn't even realized she was still carrying. Her chest tightened, not with the suffocating grip of anxiety but with the overwhelming weight of possibility.

Zariyah pressed her fingers against her temples, her thoughts a swirl of doubt and yearning. "I just... don't even know where to start. What if I'm not strong enough to tell him? I haven't even told you the whole story yet."

Dr. Monroe leaned forward slightly, her gaze meeting Zariyah's with quiet intensity. "Then we work on that, together. One step at a time. Because you are strong, Zariyah. Even if you don't feel it yet, it's there. You've survived so much. Now, it's time to start healing."

The words hung in the air, heavy with truth and possibility. Zariyah exhaled shakily, the tears she'd been holding back spilling over.

Dr. Monroe offered her a tissue, her voice softening further. "I want you to think about this, Zariyah: What would it look like for you to prioritize your healing?"

Zariyah hesitated, the question catching her off guard. "I honestly don't know. I've spent so much time worrying about everyone else," she murmured, almost to herself. "Fixing their problems, protecting them."

Dr. Monroe nodded knowingly. "And neglecting you. Who was protecting you?"

The words hit Zariyah harder than she expected, and something deep stirred within her—a flicker of realization, painful yet undeniable.

Dr. Monroe set her notepad down and leaned forward, her tone resolute yet kind. "You are stronger than you think, Zariyah. And you deserve to live a life where you're not just surviving but thriving. Let's start small. What's one thing you can commit to doing this week for yourself? Something that moves you toward healing."

Zariyah wiped her cheeks, her thoughts racing. "I don't know. Maybe... writing. I used to journal a lot in college. It helped me sort through my feelings back then."

Dr. Monroe's smile softened. "That's a great start. How about this—write a letter to the little girl who was hurt. Speak to her like you would to a child you love. What would you want her to know?"

Zariyah's breath caught in her throat, the suggestion both daunting and comforting. She nodded slowly, her voice barely above a whisper. "Okay. I'll try."

"That's all I'm asking," Dr. Monroe said warmly. "One step at a time."

The idea of writing a letter to her nine-year-old self was terrifying, but it was a step.

Chapter
21

Zariyah stood in front of her closet, the doors wide open as she stared at the rows of dresses hanging in perfect order. The Jasper Ball was only days away, and until Dominic told her he was catering the event, she wasn't excited about attending.

The Jasper Ball was more than just another social event; it was the highlight of the season, the kind of affair where the weight of your presence was measured in your attire, your connections, and your ability to navigate the room with grace. Held annually in the grand ballroom of the historic Montgomery Estate, the event brought together business elites, philanthropists, and old Southern families whose names were woven into the fabric of local history.

Word had already spread about Dominic's signature pecan-crusted lamb chops, bourbon-glazed oysters, and the sweet potato tartlets topped with candied ginger that would be making their debut tonight. Dom's involvement alone was enough to make this year's event an experience. Everyone who mattered had secured their spot months ago.

The ballroom itself was always a spectacle. Towering arrangements of red and white roses usually adorned every table, and the crystal chandelier, the estate's crown jewel, as it cast a warm glow over the room, its countless facets scattering light like stars on the polished marble floors.

The night had a purpose beyond glamour and indulgence. Every year, the Jasper Ball raised funds for local charities, with a focus on education and community development. This year's cause—a mentorship program for underprivileged youth—had drawn an especially passionate crowd, eager to support and be seen supporting such a noble endeavor.

Zariyah smiled faintly, thinking of Dom's excitement. He had called her twice already to discuss his plans for the menu, his enthusiasm infectious. She was proud of him— not just for the culinary mastery that had earned him this opportunity, but for the way he had built a name for himself through sheer determination. Dom had always been the steady one, the sibling who could balance ambition with heart. Sometimes, Zariyah envied that about him—the way he seemed to know exactly where he belonged.

Zaryiah's fingers brushed lightly over the fabric of a few gowns, pausing briefly on a midnight blue dress she had worn years ago. She sighed, shaking her head. Too much history, she thought, sliding it back into place. None of these felt right—not for the way her emotions were unraveling or the questions swirling in her mind.

Then her gaze landed on the far corner of the closet, where a garment bag hung, slightly dusty at the top. Her heart skipped as she reached for it, her mind suddenly tugged back to the day she bought it.

It had been three years ago, at a boutique she loved but rarely indulged in. She had walked in with every intention of buying something practical, but the ruby-red gown had stopped her in her tracks. The color was so striking, so daring, that it felt almost like an act of rebellion to try it on. The moment she saw herself in the mirror, she knew she had to have it.

She had been planning to wear it to a gala, but the day before the event, an emergency with Aimee had derailed her plans. Zariyah had spent the evening consoling her best friend, the gown left unworn, still hanging in its bag. After that, life had simply gotten in the way. Every time she considered wearing it, something always seemed to come up—work, family, Sterling. It was almost as if the dress had been waiting for her to be ready.

Zariyah unzipped the bag slowly, revealing the gown in all its untouched beauty. The deep ruby fabric seemed to shimmer in the soft light, its layers of satin and chiffon flowing like liquid fire. The structured bodice was sleek and modern, with a sweetheart neckline that hinted at elegance without being overbearing. It was bold, commanding attention without asking for it.

She held it up to her body, catching her reflection in the mirror. The rich hue complemented her café au lait skin, the warm tones glowing against the vibrant red. Her molasses-colored hair, loose and cascading in natural waves over her shoulders, framed her face like a soft halo. For a moment, she could almost imagine herself at the ball, standing tall and confident, her presence undeniable.

But the doubts crept in just as quickly. Was it too much? Would she feel out of place, like a child playing dress-up? And Sterling—would he even notice? He always said the right things, but lately, it felt like his attention drifted elsewhere at the moments when she needed him most. She wasn't sure if it was intentional or just habit, but the sting was the same.

She took a deep breath, forcing herself to silence the

inner critic. This isn't about them, she told herself. *This is about you.*

Sliding the gown back into its bag, she resolved to make a decision tomorrow. For now, the thought of wearing it—the possibility of standing out, of standing tall—felt like a quiet rebellion against everything she had buried. Maybe, just maybe, it was time to stop hiding.

Chapter 22

The aroma of freshly brewed coffee laced with a hint of chicory and buttery sweet pastries wrapped around Zariyah the moment she stepped inside Charades. It was the kind of scent that hugged you, filled the gaps you didn't know were empty, and whispered that everything might just be okay for a little while. This smell had been a constant in her life—a grounding thread through the chaos. It reminded her of Sunday mornings spent with Dominic, their laughter mingling with the clatter of dishes, and how Charades had always been more than a restaurant. It felt more like home.

But today, even the warmth of the familiar wasn't enough to untangle the knot in her chest. While the weekend away had been good, she and Sterling had pretty much returned to the routine and then there was the upcoming ball—she was anxious about seeing Richard after all these years.

Dominic spotted her immediately, his smile as wide as the world. "Look who finally decided to stop by," he teased, drying his hands on a dish towel. "What's the occasion? You run out of coffee at home?"

Zariyah rolled her eyes, but her sigh gave her away. This wasn't a casual drop-in; it carried the weight of sleepless nights and thoughts too heavy to hold alone.

"Uh-oh," Dominic said, his playful tone softening as he studied her face. "You've got that brooding heroine look again. Spill it before it eats you alive."

Zariyah let out a heavy sigh, blowing the steam off her coffee. "That obvious?"

Dominic set a mug of coffee in front of her, leaning against the counter with an air of ease that only he could pull off.

"To me? Yeah. You forget, I've known you your whole life," Dominic said. He had in fact since he was four years older.

Zariyah smirked at him, but her expression quickly faded into something more serious. "It's been a week." She took a sip, her gaze distant. "Sterling and I went out of town last weekend, I told you."

Dominic nodded. "Didn't he whisk you off in a private jet and spoil you rotten?" He said sarcastically, even though he knew all about his brother-in-law's grand gestures.

He'd been on the receiving end a time or two.

"He did," she said looking over the rim of her cup with a whimsical grin to see her brother's reaction.

Dominic raised an eyebrow, waiting for her to finish. "Well, dang."

"It was really nice," Dom. "I needed it," she said, her voice quiet.

"But…"

"But now that we are home it all felt performative, like we were playing roles, trying to convince each other that things have been off for years."

Dominic's brow furrowed, and he pulled out a chair to sit across from her. "Sis, have you said anything to him? Does he know how you're feeling?"

Zariyah hesitated. "I don't even know how I'm feeling half the time. And even if I did, I'm not sure he'd want to hear it. I think he's just trying to distract me."

Just as she was about to tell Dom about her therapy sessions, a sous chef asked him to step in the kitchen for a minute.

Zariyah leaned back in her chair, and watching her brother move about the restaurant before he returned to her table. Dominic's path through the restaurant brought him to Felicity, Charades' hostess. She was talking to a customer, her soft laugh floating through the air as she handed them a to-go bag. Felicity was striking, with warm milk-chocolate skin, a halo of curls pulled into a loose bun, and curves that gave her an effortless elegance. Her easy demeanor seemed to put everyone at ease.

Zariyah couldn't help but notice the way Dominic lingered near her, the way his usual quick stride slowed just a bit as he exchanged a few words with her. Whatever he said made Felicity laugh again, her smile bright enough to rival the sunlight streaming through the windows.

Zariyah found herself smiling. Felicity was good fit for Charades, a steady presence in the whirlwind that was her brother's restaurant. Maybe she was even good for Dominic.

As Dominic returned to the table, Zariyah tilted her head, a knowing look in her eyes.   "Felicity is so sweet."

He shrugged, trying and failing to look nonchalant. "She's good people. Works hard, gets along with everyone."

"Hmm," Zariyah murmured, her tone teasing.

Dominic shook his head, his grin returning. "Don't start, Z." He said wiping his hands on a towel. "Where were we? Oh … Sis, relationships go through stuff. Especially when there's history—good or bad. But you two? You've always been solid. Don't overthink it."

Zariyah's lips twitched into a smile, but it didn't reach her eyes. "Yeah, but what if we are just pretending? What if he's only doing all these grand gestures because he feels guilty about something?"

Dominic raised an eyebrow. "What, you think Sterling's up to no good?"

"I don't know," Zariyah whispered, her voice barely audible. "I don't want to think that, but..."

Dominic folded his arms over his chest. "Sterling loves you, Z. Always has. You've just gotta figure out if these feelings are coming from him... or if they are something els."

Zariyah's gaze dropped to her hands, "You sound like Dr. Monroe."

"Who the heck is Dr. Monroe," he asked leaning forward looking worried.

"My therapist."

"Therapist?" He asked lowering his voice.

Zariyah nodded. She told him she'd been seeing Dr. Monroe for the past month or so. "It's been... eye-opening. Dr. Monroe's been helping me unpack a lot—stuff I didn't think was still affecting me, but it is."

Dominic leaned back, his gaze thoughtful. "Like what?"

Zariyah hesitated, her fingers tightening around her mug. "Aimee's back with Richard, and it's stirring up memories. Old wounds. Stuff I thought I'd buried."

Dominic nodded, listening intently. "Yeah, that's usually how it goes. Old wounds have a way of sticking around, even when we think we've buried them." She knew instinctively, he was thinking about his failed marriage.

She exhaled shakily. "It's just... I don't want her to get hurt like before."

Dominic groaned, rolling his eyes. "Honestly, I don't know what she's thinking."

"She's not," Zariyah said softly. "And that's what scares me. Richard apparently has already started his back and forth game. I can't watch her go through that again."

"Sis, she's a grown woman. All you can do is be there when she needs you."

Zariyah sighed. "I know. But every time I think about Aimee with Richard, I can't help but remember how it feels to be used, discarded, damaged."

Dominic's expression softened. "You're not damaged, Z. Annoying, but not damaged," he said, his playful demeanor back.

Zariyah blinked back the tears that threatened to spill.

Dominic leaned closer, his voice gentle. "Healing isn't a straight line, Z."

They sat in comfortable silence for a moment, sipping their coffee. Zariyah could feel the tension in her chest loosening, even if only slightly. Dominic had always been her anchor, the one person who could steady her when she felt like she was drifting too far. But could she let Sterling be that for her too?

Her brother's voice pulled her from her thoughts.

"So, Richard and Aimee are really back together, huh?" Dominic's tone was casual, but something about the way he asked made Zariyah pause.

She tilted her head, studying him for a moment. Dominic had never shown much interest in Aimee's love life before— or at least, not enough to ask this directly. Does Dom have a soft spot for Aimee? The thought was so out of left field, she nearly laughed, but she let it slide. For now.

Instead, she gave a small shrug. "They are, for now. But enough about them. Are you ready for the ball? What's on the menu?"

Dominic leaned back, his easy grin returning. "Wouldn't

you like to know."

"Yes, I do," Zariyah pressed, giving him a playful punch on the arm.

Dominic leaned in, lowering his voice as if sharing classified information. "Pecan-crusted lamb chops, bourbon-glazed oysters, and—wait for it—sweet potato tartlets with candied ginger."

Zariyah's eyes widened. "Sweet potato tartlets? Dom, you've officially outdone yourself."

"What can I say? I aim to impress," he replied, his pride evident. "Just make sure you're not too busy playing belle of the ball to grab a plate."

Zariyah rolled her eyes but couldn't help smiling. "Fine, but only if you save me one of those tartlets. You know I'll cut someone if they run out before I get one."

Dominic laughed, shaking his head. "Noted. One tartlet reserved for the queen herself."

As Zariyah left Charades, the scent of coffee and pastries still lingering in her mind, she felt a little steadier. But the ball was only a day away, and with it came the promise of old memories and fresh complications. She wasn't sure if she was ready—but there was no turning back now.

Chapter
23

Zariyah adjusted the fabric of the gown, the soft navy-blue material cascading over her hourglass figure like liquid midnight. She hadn't noticed Sterling enter the walk-in closet until his reflection appeared behind her in the mirror. His gaze was unmistakable—a blend of admiration and pride, as though she were a masterpiece he'd envisioned and brought to life.

"I had a feeling this would look perfect on you," Sterling said, his voice low and warm.

Zariyah's puzzled expression deepened as she turned slightly toward him. Sterling grinned, almost sheepishly, and rubbed the back of his neck. "I spotted it in that last boutique we visited—the one where you bought the cocktail dress. I had it shipped to my office."

Sterling stepped closer, his hands resting lightly on her shoulders. "I snuck it in yesterday and asked Ms. Emma to steam it and hang it up this morning."

Zariyah stared at him through the mirror, her fingers brushing over the smooth fabric as the realization sank in. "You... planned all this?" she murmured, her voice tinged with surprise.

He nodded, his grin softening into something more sincere. "Tonight, we dazzle them together," he said, his tone laced with quiet confidence.

Her eyes flickered to the note she'd found tucked neatly into the folds of the dress earlier. The handwritten words were a perfect match to the sentiment in his voice, and for a moment, the tension in her chest eased. Sterling's thoughtfulness had always been one of his strengths, even when it felt contrived.

Zariyah turned to face him fully, her lips curving into a soft smile. "Thank you, Sterling. It's... perfect."

He cupped her face gently, his thumb brushing over her cheek. "You're perfect," he whispered, his gaze steady and unyielding.

Sterling disappeared into the bathroom to shower and start getting dressed. Despite his tendency toward a touch of vanity, he never took long. Maybe it was because he didn't need to—God seemed to have made him that way, already so put together that even minimal effort yielded maximum effect.

Zariyah slipped out of the gown carefully and took a seat at her vanity to do her makeup. Her hair, which she usually wore in its natural voluminous state, had been pressed into silky, loose waves for the occasion. The delicate updo, artfully styled, accentuated the graceful curve of her neck. Soft tendrils cascaded down, catching the light with hints of auburn and honey, especially at the edges. She leaned forward, applying a touch of shimmer to her eyelids, then finishing her look with a nude lip that brought everything together effortlessly.

Once her makeup was complete, Zariyah stepped back into the gown, letting it flow around her, giving her a sense of confidence she hadn't felt in a long time. She was standing at her jewelry box, debating which piece would complement her look, when Sterling walked into the closet.

Sterling stepped back into the closet, and Zariyah's breath caught before she even realized it. He stood there, adjusting the cuffs of a crisp white dress shirt that hugged his athletic frame perfectly, its tailored lines emphasizing his broad shoulders and narrow waist. Over it, he wore a deep navy tuxedo with a subtle satin sheen, the midnight blue bow tie at his neck adding a touch of old-world elegance.

His cinnamon-toned skin seemed to glow against the richness of the fabric, and the low lighting in the room caught the fine texture of his neatly trimmed beard, making him look as if he'd just stepped out of a high-fashion campaign. He'd been to the barber so his curls had just enough tousle to soften the precision of his look.

As always it was his confidence—easy, unforced—that made the entire ensemble breathtaking. The faint smirk playing on his lips told her he knew he looked good, but it was the way his eyes lingered on her that made Zariyah's heart skip.

"You're not the only one dazzling tonight," he teased, reaching for the lapel of his tuxedo to smooth it.

She tilted her head, taking him in from head to toe, her lips curving into a smile. "You bought that when we were out of town, didn't you?"

Sterling chuckled, his deep voice sending a shiver through her. "Guilty. Figured if I wanted to stand next to the most stunning woman in the room, I'd better step up my game."

Sterling took a step closer, his cologne—clean, with hints of sandalwood and spice—filling the space between them. "We're a pretty good-looking team, don't you think?" he murmured, his voice low, as his hand found the small of her back.

Zariyah laughed softly, shaking her head. "You clean up well, Sterling Ellis. Almost too well."

"Almost?" he asked, raising a playful brow.

"Don't get used to me admitting it," she teased, feeling the warmth of his touch steadying her. For a moment, she allowed herself to enjoy the magnetic pull of the man standing before her.

With a chuckle, Sterling took a step back, letting his eyes linger on her as she turned back toward her jewelry box. Zariyah sifted through her options, lifting a delicate gold chain and then setting it down again, none of the pieces quite feeling right for the gown or the moment.

"Maybe you can wear these," Sterling half asked, the hope in his voice drawing her attention. She turned to see him pulling a blue velvet box from his pocket, opening it to reveal the blue sapphires he'd given her weeks ago.

Zariyah's breath caught in her throat. The pendant was exquisite, the deep sapphire surrounded by diamonds that sparkled like stars. Sterling stepped closer, his fingers brushing hers as he took the necklace from the box. "Turn around," he said softly.

Sterling's warm hands worked deftly to clasp the pendant around her neck. The cool weight of the jewelry settled against her skin, and as she turned back to the mirror, the effect was dazzling. The sapphire pendant rested perfectly above the sweetheart neckline of her gown, the color an exact match to Sterling's cufflinks, which caught her eye as he adjusted his sleeve.

Her gaze flicked to his wrist and back to the pendant, a small smile curving her lips. "Your cufflinks," she said softly. "They match."

Sterling grinned, his reflection in the mirror radiating pride. "I told you, Z. Tonight, we dazzle them together."

* * *

The Jasper Ball was a dazzling display of Birmingham's finest—a convergence of old money, new ambition, and timeless elegance, all housed in the historic Montgomery Estate. Towering marble columns framed the grand ballroom, where crystal chandeliers hung like celestial constellations, casting fractured rainbows over the polished floors. Zariyah paused at the entrance, the swell of a live orchestra reverberating in her chest.

For a moment, she couldn't help but drink in the scene: women gliding across the room in gowns of satin and sequins, men in impeccably tailored tuxedos offering laughter and charm. The air shimmered with the soft hum of conversation and the faint clinking of champagne flutes. This was where the city's power players gathered to see and be seen, but for Zariyah, it was more than that—it was a stage, and tonight, and now that she was here, she wasn't sure if she wanted to play her part.

Sterling's warm hand on her lower back anchored her. His navy tuxedo fit him so perfectly he might have stepped from the pages of a fashion editorial, the deep hue a striking contrast against his cinnamon-toned complexion. "Ready?" he asked, his voice low and intimate, yet tinged with a quiet confidence that hinted he already knew the answer.

Zariyah met his gaze, the sapphire pendant at her neck glinting as she nodded. "Let's dazzle them," she replied, a small, determined smile playing on her lips.

As they stepped into the ballroom, memories of their first Jasper ball flooded her. They were young and impossibly in love, dancing under these same chandeliers as if the rest of the world didn't exist. But tonight carried a different energy—a mixture of nostalgia, unspoken words, and the lingering shadows of their recent struggles.

Sterling leaned in, his voice a gentle murmur. "You're stunning, Zariyah. Everyone here will know it too."

Her heart gave a little tug, equal parts gratitude and hesitation. She offered him a soft smile, the kind that didn't quite reach her eyes, and let him guide her deeper into the thrumming heartbeat of the crowd.

A voice called out, cutting through the hum of the crowd. "Zariyah!"

She turned to see Aimee weaving through the sea of gowns and tuxedos, her amethyst-purple dress catching the light with every step. The gown hugged her figure elegantly, its shimmering fabric a striking match for her unique eyes—a shade of blue so deep they almost seemed violet, adding an air of mystery to her already captivating presence. The rich hue of the dress seemed to glow against her warm, sun-kissed complexion, creating a contrast that was both striking and ethereal. Her dirty blonde curls tumbled over one shoulder in soft waves, framing her radiant smile.

"Zariyah," Aimee said, her voice light with excitement as she pulled her into a hug. She stepped back, giving Zariyah a once-over with an approving smile. "Girl, you look like like a goddess. That dress is perfection."

Zariyah laughed softly, the warmth of Aimee's compliment easing some of the tension in her chest. "Look who's talking. You're stunning, Aimee. That color was made for you."

Aimee did a playful twirl, her smile widening. "You really think so? I wasn't sure at first, but Richard said it was perfect."

At the mention of his name, Zariyah's gaze shifted to Richard, who lingered just behind her. For his faults, had dressed impeccably in a sharp black tuxedo that highlighted his clean-cut, polished demeanor.

"Hello, Richard," Zariyah said coolly, her smile fading just slightly, barely masking the unease she felt at his presence.

"Zariyah," Richard greeted, his voice smooth yet guarded as he leaned in for a careful hug. The formal gesture felt more obligatory than warm, a stark contrast to the casual, half-embrace he and Sterling had exchanged earlier—the kind of brotherly greeting men default to without much thought.

Sterling stepped closer, a subtle yet protective gesture, his hand firm at the small of her back. The conversation moved forward—polite pleasantries and light laughter—but Zariyah's mind remained distant, her unease growing as she watched the familiar way Richard's eyes lingered on Aimee. It was the same look he'd given her years ago, just before everything fell apart.

The orchestra struck a softer note, and Sterling took her hand, leading her to the dance floor. "Let's dance," he said, his tone leaving no room for argument.

Zariyah let him guide her, the warmth of his hand and the rhythm of the music pulling her into the moment. The familiar intimacy of his touch—the way his fingers pressed lightly against the small of her back—felt like a balm, even if just for a little while.

"You're miles away," Sterling murmured, his breath warm against her ear.

She blinked, her focus snapping back to him. "Sorry," she said, offering a small smile. "Just… thinking."

"About?"

"Nothing important." Her response was automatic, but the heaviness in her voice betrayed her.

Sterling's eyes searched hers, his expression softening as if he wanted to press further. But instead, he pulled her closer, letting the music fill the space between them.

As they swayed beneath the glittering chandeliers, Zariyah tried to lose herself in the moment. But the questions lingered. Could Aimee trust Richard after everything? Could she trust Sterling with the truths she hadn't yet dared to speak?

* * *

In the dining hall, the table was a vision of opulence, draped in a deep crimson cloth that shimmered like silk under the golden glow of the grand chandelier overhead. Crystal stemware and gold-rimmed plates gleamed against the backdrop of delicate floral arrangements—roses, hydrangeas, and calla lilies in shades of ivory and deep burgundy. The flickering glow of tall taper candles in polished brass holders lent an air of timeless sophistication.

Zariyah's breath caught slightly when she saw Dominic and Felicity already seated at the table. While she had known her brother would be overseeing the catering, she hadn't expected him to join the ball as a guest. Dominic looked striking in a tailored black tuxedo with a subtle velvet trim, his sienna-toned skin glowing warmly against the classic white dress shirt and black bowtie. His goatee was neatly trimmed, completing the picture of suave confidence.

Felicity sat beside him, a vision in an off-shoulder champagne-colored gown that hugged her curves in all the right places. The satin fabric gleamed like liquid gold against her milk-chocolate complexion, and her natural curls were swept up into a sleek bun, with a few loose tendrils framing her glowing face. A simple diamond necklace and matching earrings added just enough sparkle to make her presence feel quietly commanding.

"You're here?" Zariyah said to Dominic as Sterling pulled out her chair.

Dominic smirked. "What, you thought I was just going to hang out in the kitchen all night?" Dominic smirked. "What, you thought I'd be stuck in the kitchen all night?" He exchanged a quick fist bump with Sterling before offering Richard a polite nod.

"We'll see how long that lasts," Zariyah teased as she settled into her seat. Sterling sat beside her, adjusting his cufflinks with a nonchalant elegance that drew approving glances from nearby tables.

Aimee and Richard completed the group on their side of the table. Across from them sat an older couple—a philanthropist and his wife, who greeted everyone with warm, practiced smiles.

As glasses of champagne were poured, the hum of the ballroom quieted, and the emcee for the evening took the stage. Dressed in a sleek black gown, she beamed at the crowd as she held the microphone.

"Ladies and gentlemen, welcome to the annual Jasper Ball! Tonight, we celebrate the beauty of coming together as a community, all while supporting a cause that touches lives and shapes futures. This year, the funds raised will support our mentorship program for underprivileged youth, ensuring they have the tools and guidance to create brighter tomorrows."

The crowd broke into polite applause, and Zariyah stole a glance at Dominic. Pride flickered in his expression. Charades had contributed not just its catering expertise but a portion of tonight's proceeds to the program as well.

The emcee continued. "Of course, this evening wouldn't be possible without the dedication of so many, including our culinary partners. Please join me in thanking Dominic Campbell and the team at Charades for tonight's extraordinary menu."

A spotlight swept across the room, landing briefly on Dominic, who gave a modest nod and raised his glass. The room erupted in applause, and Felicity leaned into him, whispering something that made him smile.

"You've done good, Dom," Zariyah said softly, her words carrying more weight than just the event.

Dominic shrugged, though his grin betrayed how much her words meant. "It's all in a day's work."

As the first course was served—an artfully plated appetizer of bourbon-glazed oysters atop a bed of seaweed—conversation around the table began to flow. The older couple regaled the group with stories of past balls, their anecdotes tinged with humor and a touch of nostalgia.

Richard leaned toward Sterling, discussing local real estate trends, while Aimee and Zariyah exchanged whispers about Felicity.

"She's gorgeous," Aimee said, her blue eyes alight with curiosity. "Dominic seems... different tonight."

Zariyah smiled knowingly. "Doesn't he? It's about time he let someone in."

Felicity dropped her gaze, blushing at what was being said about her.

The group laughed, and Dominic's mock exasperation made everyone relax further. As the program continued, the emcee introduced a few of the mentees who shared their stories of transformation. Their speeches brought a few tears to Zariyah's eyes, the depth of their gratitude resonating deeply.

When the final award was presented, Sterling leaned toward Zariyah, his hand resting lightly on hers. "You okay?" he asked softly.

Zariyah nodded, offering a small smile.

The dinner wound down with dessert—Dominic's famed

sweet potato tartlets topped with candied ginger. Zariyah savored every bite, silently daring anyone at the table to ask for a second. As the orchestra resumed, guests began migrating toward the dance floor, the night far from over but settling into its own rhythm.

"Shall we?" Sterling asked, extending his hand.

Zariyah hesitated, glancing at the people around the table, before slipping her hand into his. For tonight, she would let herself enjoy the magic of the moment.

* * *

The house was quiet when they arrived home, the soft glow of the foyer lamp casting long shadows over the walls. The warmth of their living room felt like an exhale after the glittering spectacle of the Jasper Ball. Zariyah slipped off her heels at the door, letting out a soft sigh as her feet met the cool hardwood. Sterling followed close behind, his jacket draped over one arm, his tie already loosened.

"Need some help?" he asked, his voice low, almost cautious.

She shook her head, her faint smile not quite reaching her eyes. Moments from the evening replayed in her mind— the way they'd danced all night, Sterling's touch grounding her, even as the weight of Richard's presence, Aimee's exuberance, and the unspoken truths she needed to share pressed heavily on her thoughts..

Sterling draped his jacket over the arm of the couch, the smooth fabric whispering against the leather. As he stepped toward her, his fingers moved deftly, unfastening his shirt with practiced ease. With each button undone, the strong, defined lines of his chest came into view, a sight that sent a ripple of warmth through her. He stopped just short of her, his movements slowing as his gaze locked on hers—soft, yet probing, as if searching for the unspoken words lingering in the space between them.

"Did you enjoy tonight?" he asked, the gentleness in his tone disarming her.

"I did," Zariyah replied quietly, as her fingers move to unclasp the sapphire pendant at her neck, Sterling reached for her hand.

"Leave it on," looking into her eyes, "for a little longer."

He stepped closer, his fingers brushing against the delicate chain, tracing the path of the pendant until they lingered at the edge of her heaving bosom.

Zariyah closed her eyes for a moment, willing herself to let go. She felt Sterling's hands settle lightly on her shoulders, warm and steady, his thumbs kneading gently at the knots of tension at the base of her neck.

A soft sigh escaped her lips as she leaned into his touch, but the weight in her chest refused to dissipate fully. Sterling slid his hands down to her waist, his fingers grazing her sides with a tenderness that sent a shiver through her. His forehead rested against hers, their breaths mingling as his hands stilled, anchoring her in the moment.

"Come on," he whispered, his lips brushing her temple. "Let's call it a night."

Taking her hand, he led her toward their master suite. Once inside, he turned her gently, his hands skimming down her arms as his eyes searched hers. "Where's the zipper?" he asked with a soft smile.

Zariyah giggled, her voice lightening the air. "It's on the side," she murmured, lifting her arms slightly.

He found the hidden zipper, his fingers brushing against her skin as he tugged it down. The gown slid effortlessly down her body, pooling at her feet in a cascade of navy satin. Zariyah stepped out of it gracefully, standing before him in a delicate strapless bra and matching panties, the same deep hue as her gown. Sterling's breath hitched, his gaze lingering, drinking her in as if seeing her for the first time.

For a moment, neither of them moved, the room crackling with unspoken words and electric tension. Then Sterling began to undress, his movements slow and deliberate, his eyes never leaving hers. When his pants finally dropped to the floor, revealing a pair of satin navy boxers that matched her lingerie perfectly, Zariyah couldn't help but laugh.

"You planned this," she teased, her voice warm with affection.

Sterling grinned, stepping closer until their laughter dissolved into something quieter, deeper. "Maybe," he admitted, his hands finding her waist again.

They laughed softly together, the sound intimate and grounding. The quiet filled the room as they stood there, their vulnerability as bare as their skin, the space between them shrinking with every breath.

* * *

Sterling took her into his arms, his hands warm against the small of her back. Zariyah's breath hitched as she anticipated the kiss, rising onto her toes to meet him halfway. His lips met hers softly at first, but the kiss deepened, carrying with it an unspoken promise. As their connection intensified, he began to guide her backward toward the bed, his movements unhurried, giving her every chance to stop if she needed to.

When the back of her legs brushed against the bed, Sterling broke the kiss, his gaze steady and full of care. He reached down, pulling the covers back, silently inviting her in. Zariyah scooted under the blankets, the cool sheets a comforting contrast to the warmth radiating from his touch.

Sterling joined her moments later, his body settling beside

hers. He draped the covers over both of them and drew her close, her back fitting perfectly against his chest. His arm slipped around her waist, holding her securely, as though his embrace alone could shield her from the heaviness of her thoughts.

He pressed a tender kiss to the nape of her neck, his voice a gentle murmur in the quiet room. "Get some rest. Whatever's weighing on you... whenever you're ready, I promise I'll listen."

Zariyah's throat tightened, his words stirring something deep within her. She closed her eyes, her body melting into his warmth. For the first time in what felt like forever, she exhaled fully, the tight coil of tension in her chest loosening.

Sterling's steady breathing against her back became a soothing rhythm, grounding her. The nightmares that so often haunted her seemed to hover at the edges of her consciousness but never broke through. Wrapped in his arms, she felt a fragile sense of safety—a tentative peace that she hadn't dared to hope for.

And as sleep finally claimed her, Zariyah allowed herself to believe that maybe, just maybe, they could find their way back to each other. One step at a time.

And the first step was to tell him the secrets she'd been carrying.

Chapter 24

The warmth of the weekend lingered in Zariyah's mind as she stirred awake, the soft hum of life pulling her from sleep. For two days, she and Sterling had slipped into an easy rhythm—dinners at home, lighthearted conversations, and stolen glances. It had felt like a reprieve, a pocket of peace they both desperately needed.

Monday morning, the shrill ring of the phone shattered the stillness—a sharp reminder that the world outside their cocoon hadn't paused. Of course, it was Noni. It was the end of the month, and that only meant one thing: more "bills" that needed paying, as if Zariyah didn't already know the drill.

Her mother's requests were as predictable as they were exhausting. Zariyah and Dominic took care of her utilities and basic expenses, even giving her a $2,000 monthly allowance. But by the middle of the month, it was usually gone, leaving Noni scrambling to fill the gap she had created. Most of the time, it wasn't even necessities—just indulgences she couldn't resist, leaving Zariyah to clean up the mess.

The familiar smell of bacon and coffee wafted in from

the kitchen, pulling Zariyah fully from bed. She exchanged a glance with Sterling, both of them grinning like children caught in a secret. In unison, they scrambled for their robes.

"Ms. Emma's here," Sterling said, cinching his robe as they padded toward the kitchen.

"Morning," they chimed together as they entered. Ms. Emma was already bustling around, placing plates of French toast, scrambled eggs, and bacon on the table. The sight was pure comfort, a slice of their routine that always felt like home.

"You eat up now," Ms. Emma said with a knowing smile, patting Zariyah's shoulder before bustling off. "I'll get to my housework."

Zariyah stared at her plate, the rich aroma of syrup and warm spices curling around her like a soft, beckoning hug. But even the comforting smell couldn't chase away the sharp sting of her mother's belittling words, still echoing in her mind. Her appetite, dulled by the weight of it all, left the beautiful spread before her untouched.

Sterling, more attuned to her mood these days, reached for a slice of honeydew from the fruit bowl, his fingers brushing hers lightly as he held it to her lips. His playful grin was disarming, a gentle attempt to pull her back into the moment.

"Come on," he teased, tilting his head and giving her that boyish smile that always melted her resolve. "No brooding over breakfast."

She smiled faintly, leaning forward as he fed her the fruit. When he swiped the last piece of bacon off her plate, her laugh bubbled up—light, fleeting, but real.

"You're impossible," she said, shaking her head, though her tone was tinged with affection.

"Impossible and charming," he shot back, his grin as

easy as ever.

"Arrogant and conceited," she countered, her brow lifting in mock challenge.

"Confident and irresistible," he corrected smoothly, leaning back with a smug expression, clearly enjoying himself.

For a moment, the levity was enough to pull her from her thoughts. But even as they joked, Zariyah couldn't escape what lingered between them. Secrets and thoughts yet to be shared.

After breakfast, Zariyah helped Ms. Emma tidy the kitchen. Sorting pantry shelves alongside the older woman, she felt the quiet comfort of routine work, the hum of domestic normalcy offering a brief reprieve.

"I'm heading out," Sterling called from the hallway. Moments later, he appeared in the kitchen, his keys in hand.

"I won't be long," he said, his voice calm and familiar. But there was something in his gaze that made Zariyah pause. Sterling stepped closer, his presence filling the room as he framed her face in his hands. He kissed her gently, his lips warm and steady against hers.

"I love you," he murmured, the words soft but deliberate.

Zariyah wanted to respond, to meet his sincerity with her own. But instead, she nodded, her smile faint. The door closed behind him, the sound reverberating in the quiet kitchen.

"That man just said he loved you, and you just nodded," Ms. Emma said, folding her arms over her chest, her sharp gaze cutting straight through Zariyah.

Zariyah looked down at the dish towel in her hands, twisting it nervously.

"Child, what's so hard about saying it back? Ain't like you don't feel the same."

"It's not that simple," Zariyah said, her chest tightening. "I do love him… but."

Ms. Emma tilted her head, her expression softening. "Honey, love ain't about having a closet where skeletons used to hang. It's about letting them see all of you—the cracks, the flaws, the parts you're still trying to figure out—and trusting they'll stay."

Zariyah swallowed hard, her eyes stinging. "But what if he does decided to run? What if knowing what the skeletons are change everything?" And the idea of him looking at me differently, even for a second would be unbearable, Zariyah thought.

Ms. Emma stepped closer, resting a warm hand on Zariyah's arm. "You ever think maybe it'll change things for the better? Keeping all that locked up inside ain't just hurting you, baby. It's keeping you from letting him in."

Zariyah blinked rapidly, trying to hold back the tears threatening to fall. "You sound like my therapist."

Ms. Emma smiled gently, her grip firm but reassuring. "If she we are saying the same thing, then she's a smart woman."

She lifted Zariyah's chin and looked her in the eye, "But don't let fear steal what you've got with that man. He's a good one, Zariyah. Don't push him away while you're waiting for the perfect moment."

Ms. Emma walked away letting her words settle over Zariyah. Fear was prolonging what needed to be said.

"Thanks, Ms. Emma," she whispered, her voice thick with emotion.

"You're welcome," Ms. Emma yelled from the other room.

"So you see everything and hear too," Zariyah laughed.

"Indeed I do," Ms. Emma called back, her voice steady.

Zariyah laughed softly, shaking her head. Of course, Ms. Emma had heard her—Ms. Emma always did.   Zariyah couldn't believe she'd heard her.

Chapter 25

Zariyah sat across from Dr. Monroe, her legs crossed, hands clutching a cup of tea that had gone cold. The soft ticking of the clock filled the room, a metronome for the thoughts racing through her mind.

Dr. Monroe tilted her head slightly, her expression patient and inviting. "How was the ball?"

"It was… nice," Zariyah said after a pause, her tone carefully neutral. "Sterling was attentive, charming, everything he's always been. But…"

"But?" Dr. Monroe's gentle prompt carried the weight of curiosity and care.

"But I still couldn't say it. Every time I tried, the words just… disappeared." Zariyah's grip on the mug tightened, her knuckles whitening. "I don't know what's wrong with me. "Why can't I just tell him?"

Dr. Monroe leaned back, her voice calm and steady. "You're still protecting yourself in ways you've learned over time. But you're here, and that's a start. Did you complete the assignment we talked about?"

Zariyah nodded, reaching into her bag for the leather journal Dr. Monroe had given her weeks ago. She opened it to a page where the ink looked slightly smudged, the edges crinkled from her nervous handling. She hesitated, fingers hovering over the paper.

"Take your time," Dr. Monroe said with an encouraging nod.

Zariyah swallowed hard and began to read aloud, her voice trembling at first but steadying as she went.

Dear Little Zariyah,

I see you. I see the fear in your eyes, the way you shrink into yourself, hoping that if you're quiet enough, still enough, the world won't hurt you anymore. I wish I could wrap you in my arms and tell you it's not your fault. None of it is.

You are just a child, too young to understand why the people who are supposed to protect you failed. Too young to know that what Ben did to you wasn't about you—it was about him and his brokenness. His cruelty doesn't define your worth, even if it feels like it does right now.

I know you blame yourself. I know you wonder if you did something wrong, if you weren't good enough or smart enough or strong enough to stop it. But you did nothing wrong. You are enough now, always.

You will carry the weight of Ben's actions for a long time, but you don't have to. You don't need to hide, to shrink, to disappear to survive. You're stronger than you know. You'll grow into a woman who is fierce, loving, and capable of building a life filled with beauty and meaning.

Know there will be nights when the nightmares creep in, when his words echo in your mind, making you doubt yourself. There will be times when you'll look in the mirror and struggle to see anything but the cracks he left behind. And there will be moments when you let someone else treat you like you don't matter because a part of you believes it.

But, Zariyah, those moments won't define you. They'll shape you, yes. They'll teach you what you deserve, and they'll remind you of your strength. But they won't break you.

You'll find real love one day. The kind that doesn't demand perfection. The kind that sees all of you—your scars, your fears, your strength—and embraces it.

Right now, you're surviving. And that's enough. But one day, you'll thrive. You'll learn to speak your truth, to let go of the shame that was never yours to carry, and to forgive yourself for the things you couldn't control.

I'm so proud of you. I'm proud of the little girl who endured and the woman she's becoming. You are worthy of love, of joy, of healing. Keep going, little one. You're going to be okay.

With love and strength,

Zariyah

Zariyah's voice broke on the last word, her hands trembling as she closed the journal. She couldn't bring herself to meet Dr. Monroe's gaze, afraid of what she might see.

Dr. Monroe's sniffle broke the silence. "That was incredibly brave, Zariyah. Thank you for sharing it with me."

A tear slid down Zariyah's cheek, and she quickly wiped it away. "I wrote it, but I don't know if I believe it yet."

"That's okay," Dr. Monroe said. "Belief takes time. But this letter? It's a step. A big one."

Zariyah exhaled, the tension in her chest loosening, only for a different kind of weight to settle. "It feels like there's so much I haven't said—to anyone."

Dr. Monroe leaned forward slightly. "Do you think you're ready to start? Even just a little?"

Zariyah hesitated, clutching the edges of her chair. Her

voice wavered as she spoke. "It started when I was nine…"

Her words tumbled out, jagged and raw, as she recounted the details of her abuse—Ben's manipulation, the constant fear, and the shame that had been her shadow for years. When she spoke of her teenage years, her voice faltered.

"I… slept around, a lot. I hated myself for it, but it felt like the only way I could feel… something. Anything."

Dr. Monroe nodded, her expression kind but firm. "Zariyah, what you're describing is something many survivors experience. Hating your body, seeking validation through physical intimacy—it's not a reflection of who you are. It's a response to what you endured."

Tears streamed down Zariyah's face, her hands twisting the tissue in her lap. "I feel so ashamed."

"There's nothing to be ashamed of," Dr. Monroe said gently. "You were a child navigating unimaginable pain. You did what you needed to do to survive, and that survival makes you strong—not weak."

For the first time, the shame didn't feel like it was solely hers to carry. Dr. Monroe's words wrapped around her like a balm, soothing wounds she had hidden for so long. She felt seen—not just for her pain, but for her resilience.

Chapter 26

Zariyah was in the middle of setting the table for dinner when her phone buzzed, jolting her out of her fragile calm. She sighed, glancing at the time. It was already 6:15. Who could be calling now? Her heart lightened when she saw Sterling's name flash across the screen, but the weight of the day still pressed heavily on her mind.

"Hey," she answered, balancing the phone between her ear and shoulder as she adjusted the silverware.

"Change of plans," Sterling said, his voice warm but matter-of-fact. "We're meeting Richard and Aimee for dinner at that new Italian place across town. Seven o'clock."

The words landed like a stone in her stomach. Her gaze drifted over the carefully set table, the quiet dinner she'd envisioned slipping further from her grasp. "Wait, what? Richard and Aimee?" Her voice wavered, though she tried to keep it steady.

"Yeah," Sterling said, as though it were nothing. "Ran into Richard earlier today. He said he'd love to catch up, and Aimee's free, so I figured why not?"

Zariyah gripped the edge of the table, her knuckles whitening. You figured why not? Without asking me? Her mind raced, the anxiety she'd been holding at bay surging forward. "It's already 6:15, Sterling. I don't even have time to change."

"You look good in anything," he said smoothly, his grin practically audible through the phone. "What you're wearing is fine, I'm sure. Don't make me wait too long, Mrs. Ellis."

The easy charm in his tone grated against her already raw nerves. "Fine," she said tightly, not trusting herself to say more. As the call ended, she stared at the table, a pang of disappointment settling deep in her chest. The quiet evening she'd planned—the chance to talk to Sterling and unpack her emotions—was gone, replaced with yet another encounter with Richard.

Her stomach churned as she pushed her chair back. It had been a week since the ball, and she still hadn't talked to Aimee. How was she supposed to face both of them tonight, with so much unresolved?

* * *

The Italian restaurant was sleek and modern, with dim lighting casting a warm glow over the tables. The smell of fresh bread and garlic filled the air, but Zariyah barely noticed. Her pulse quickened as she spotted Sterling, Richard, and Aimee seated at a corner booth, their laughter carrying over the low hum of conversation.

Aimee waved enthusiastically, her smile bright. "Zariyah! You made it!"

Zariyah forced a smile as she adjusted her coat and walked toward the booth. Aimee looked radiant—so carefree, so utterly unguarded—that it made Zariyah's stomach twist with unease.

"Hey," Zariyah said, sliding into the booth beside Sterling. His hand found hers under the table—a small gesture of reassurance—but it did little to settle the unease in her gut. She gently pulled her hand away, pretending to adjust her napkin.

"Zariyah, it's good to see you again," Richard said smoothly, his polished smile gleaming under the dim restaurant lights. The easy charm in his voice made her skin prickle.

Zariyah offered a polite, cool smile. "Richard," she said, her tone even. Her gaze flicked to Aimee, who was blissfully unaware of the tension brewing just below the surface. Zariyah's chest tightened at the sight of Aimee's hand resting lightly on Richard's arm, her eyes filled with unguarded adoration. The image sent a quiet alarm blaring in her mind. Breathe, she reminded herself, calling on the techniques Dr. Monroe had taught her. In through the nose, hold, out through the mouth.

The conversation flowed too easily over dinner. Richard was every bit the polished charmer, his laughter warm, his anecdotes perfectly timed. Everyone at the table seemed captivated by him—except Zariyah. To her, it all felt shallow, his charisma a carefully constructed facade. Every time his gaze lingered on her just a moment too long, her discomfort deepened.

She stole glances at Aimee, who laughed along with him, her posture relaxed, her guard completely down. The knot in her stomach grew tighter with every passing minute, every polished word, every practiced smile from Richard. By the time the waiter cleared their plates, Zariyah felt like she was hanging on by a thread.

Dinner dragged on, Zariyah's mind whirling with unspoken thoughts. She kept glancing at Aimee, searching for any sign of doubt, any hint that she might see Richard for who he truly was. But Aimee's laughter rang out freely, her guard entirely down.

As they stepped outside into the crisp night air, Zariyah stayed close to Sterling, her silence reflecting the storm inside her. Richard and Aimee walked ahead, their laughter ringing out like a cruel mockery of her unease. Aimee seemed so sure, so comfortable in Richard's presence, but Zariyah's instincts screamed that something wasn't right.

Sterling squeezed her hand, drawing her attention. "You okay?" he asked, his voice low and concerned.

Zariyah hesitated, her gaze fixed on Richard as he opened the car door for Aimee. "Yeah," she lied, her smile faint and unconvincing. "Just… a lot on my mind."

Sterling frowned, his grip tightening slightly. "I should've asked you first," he admitted, his voice tinged with regret. "I didn't think—"

"No, you didn't," Zariyah cut in softly, her tone neutral but firm. She let out a small sigh, trying to temper the tension rising in her chest. "It's fine. Let's just… talk later."

Sterling's hand lingered on her waist, his lips brushing her temple. "We will," he promised, his voice earnest. "I'm sorry, Z."

As she slipped into her car, the apology hung in the air, offering a fleeting moment of comfort that dissolved the moment she pulled away. Her thoughts churned relentlessly.   Richard's presence had stirred something dark and familiar, a whisper of the wounds she'd begun to unearth in therapy. The way he carried himself, the polished charm masking old cruelties—it gnawed at her. And Aimee, blissfully trusting, seemed oblivious.

But as she pulled into the driveway, the weight of everything settled over her like a storm cloud. Healing was supposed to bring clarity, to lighten the load. So why, she wondered, did it still feel so heavy?

Chapter
27

The hum of the small fan in Dr. Monroe's office filled the quiet space, a gentle backdrop to Zariyah's nervous tapping on the arm of her chair. She hadn't met Dr. Monroe's gaze since sitting down, her focus flitting to the notepad in the therapist's lap, then to the clock on the wall. Anything but herself.

"You're still avoiding the conversation," Dr. Monroe said gently, her voice calm but probing.

Zariyah sighed deeply, her hands gripping the armrests. "Everytime I'm ready to talk, something pops up—a last minute appointment, him coming home late, this, that and the other."

Dr. Monroe tilted her head, her pen still against the page. "We've already talked about this. Holding onto trauma is like clutching broken glass—it cuts deeper the longer you hold it."

Zariyah's throat tightened. "I don't even know if it matters any more."

Dr. Monroe leaned forward, her gaze steady. "Zariyah, it matters. You matter. But you have to love you enough to fully heal."

Zariyah swallowed hard, her fingers twitching in her lap. "How do I even start?"

Dr. Monroe paused, then offered a small, encouraging smile. "Healing isn't a solo act. I want you to think about something." She retrieved a brochure from her desk and handed it to Zariyah. "There's a faith-based conference coming up—Restored by Grace. It's about healing emotionally, mentally, and spiritually. No pressure, but it might be a good place to start."

Faith. Zariyah hadn't touched the concept in years. The thought of unpacking it now made her anxious. "I'll… think about it," she murmured, the words surprising her.

Dr. Monroe nodded approvingly. "That's all I ask."

* * *

Later that day, Zariyah stood in her kitchen, stirring a cup of tea. The house was quiet except for the soft hum of the refrigerator and Ms. Emma's gentle shuffling. The scent of lavender cleaning spray lingered in the air as Ms. Emma hummed a hymn.

"You've been quiet today," Ms. Emma said, pausing mid-wipe. "Something weighing on you?"

Zariyah hesitated, unsure how to voice what had been swirling in her mind since therapy. "Do you think… faith is enough to fix things?"

Ms. Emma set down the rag and turned to face her fully, her expression tender. "Faith isn't a fix, baby. It's a foundation. It doesn't erase the pain, but it gives you the strength to carry it."

Tears pricked Zariyah's eyes.

Ms. Emma stepped closer, resting a hand on Zariyah's arm. "You know, baby, I've been where you are. Not sure where I stood with God, not sure if I could face Him with all my pain. But when I finally sat still and let myself just…

be, that's when I started finding peace."

Zariyah smiled.

Come with me to church this Sunday. Just sit beside me. No pressure," Ms Emma invited.

The idea of returning to church after years away felt overwhelming. But Ms. Emma's invitation was gentle, not demanding. "Maybe," Zariyah whispered, her chest loosening slightly.

Ms. Emma smiled, her eyes warm. "God doesn't need you to be perfect, baby. He just needs you to show up."

* * *

The next morning, Zariyah sat in her home office, her planner open but untouched. The space was orderly but carried the energy of someone juggling a million thoughts. She glanced at the brochure Dr. Monroe had mentioned: Restored by Grace. The words felt heavier now, resonating in a way she wasn't ready to admit.

Before she could talk herself out of it, Zariyah clicked the registration link. The confirmation email arrived within moments. **Welcome to Restored by Grace.** The bold text stared back at herblike a challenge she wasn't sure she was ready to face. What if this conference didn't help? What if opening that door only made the wounds deeper? But deep down, she knew staying closed off wasn't working either.

Chapter 28

The day of the Restored by Grace conference arrived faster than Zariyah anticipated. The sleek, modern conference hall buzzed with quiet energy. She adjusted the strap of her bag as she picked up her registration packet, her name printed neatly on the badge. The soft strains of worship music played in the background, filling the space with a calm serenity that contrasted the nerves fluttering in her chest.

As she found her seat near the front, her gaze lingered on the illuminated cross on the stage. A symbol she'd once leaned on now felt distant, foreign. But today, something about it seemed to beckon her.

The keynote speaker took the stage, a poised woman with a story of overcoming trauma that struck a chord deep within Zariyah. Each session peeled back layers she hadn't realized she'd built, leaving her exposed yet strangely lighter. One workshop in particular brought her to tears. It focused on inner vows—the silent promises we make to protect ourselves from pain.

Vows like, I'll never let anyone hurt me again or I have to be perfect to be loved replayed in her mind. The speaker's words hit like a revelation: "Those vows might have protected you once, but now they're the walls keeping love out."

Zariyah's breath caught. She'd been doing exactly that—guarding herself, even from Sterling. Tears blurred her vision as the session closed with a quiet prayer: Healing begins when we release the control we thought we needed to survive.

The worship team began to sing, the soft harmonies growing stronger as the congregation joined in. Then the opening chords of Kirk Franklin's "Something About the Name Jesus" filled the room. The soulful, raw power of the song wrapped around Zariyah like a comforting embrace. She tried to hold back, but the dam broke. Tears streamed down her face as her hands lifted almost involuntarily.

Before she realized it, Zariyah found herself at the altar, surrounded by others seeking their own release, their own healing. Her sobs came in waves, her hands trembling as she surrendered everything she had been holding inside.

A warm touch brought her back to the moment. Someone was gently wiping her tears away. When her eyes could focus through the blur, she saw Ms. Emma standing in front of her, a soft, knowing smile on her face.

Ms. Emma pulled her into a hug, holding her close as if to shield her from every hurt she'd ever felt. "Let it out, baby," Ms. Emma whispered, her voice steady and full of love. "Let it all out."

Zariyah clung to her, the strength in Ms. Emma's arms grounding her as the music swelled around them. They stood there for what felt like forever, wrapped in a moment of shared faith and unwavering support. For the first time in years, Zariyah felt seen—not just for her pain, but for her strength. She wasn't alone.

* * *

The next day, Zariyah sat in Dr. Monroe's office, her emotions still swirling from the conference. The familiar warmth of the room felt more like a cocoon than usual, the ticking clock a steady reminder that this was her time—her space to unpack what she'd learned.

Dr. Monroe folded her hands in her lap, her expression calm yet expectant. "How was the conference?" she asked gently.

Zariyah let out a shaky breath. "Intense. It was like… they were speaking directly to me." She paused, choosing her words carefully. "There was this session on inner vows. It made me realize how much I've been holding onto—and how those things have shaped my life."

Dr. Monroe tilted her head slightly, her pen resting on her notepad. "What stood out to you the most?"

Zariyah's voice wavered. "The idea that these vows were meant to protect me, but they're keeping me from what I want most. Especially with Sterling. I've been pushing him away because I'm so scared of being hurt again."

Dr. Monroe nodded, her eyes filled with understanding. "That fear is valid, Zariyah. But the survival mechanisms that once served you as a child don't have to define your adult relationships. What vows do you think you've made?"

Zariyah's throat tightened. "I promised myself I'd never trust anyone—not fully. That I had to rely on myself because everyone else would let me down." Her voice cracked as she continued, "And I think… I promised myself I wasn't worthy of real love."

Dr. Monroe leaned forward slightly, her voice tender. "And do you believe those vows are still true?"

Tears slipped down Zariyah's cheeks as she shook her head. "No."

Dr. Monroe leaned forward slightly, her gaze never

wavering. "And how do you see these inner vows affecting your relationship with Sterling?"

Zariyah exhaled, her fingers tracing the outline of her coffee mug. "I've been pushing him away without even realizing it. It's like I'm always waiting for him to hurt me, or to leave me. I have to be on guard... always."

Dr. Monroe let the silence settle between them for a moment, allowing Zariyah to process. "Healing isn't linear," she said finally. "But every step you take—every truth you allow yourself to believe—is a step toward freedom."

The quiet encouragement of Dr. Monroe's words stayed with Zariyah as she sat back in her chair. Her thoughts swirled with the enormity of what she'd just begun to unpack.   She had spent years clutching the shards of her pain, too afraid to let go, yet now, for the first time, she could imagine what it might feel like to release them.

Dr. Monroe nodded, her voice gentle. "You've mentioned feeling emotionally neglected by your mother. Do you think that's where some of these vows originated?"

Zariyah's throat tightened. "I think it started there. After what happened with Ben, I promised myself I wouldn't trust anyone again. I wouldn't let anyone in, especially not a man. I was determined not to be vulnerable because I thought that's how I'd get hurt."

There was a pause as Zariyah stared at the ceiling, gathering her thoughts. "And then there's Sterling," she added, her voice quieter now. "He had to grow up fast when his dad died. He became the man of the house, but it's like... he never learned how to be vulnerable either. So we're both just... locked up."

Dr. Monroe's expression softened with understanding. "Sterling's experience with early responsibility, especially in the military, likely reinforced that emotional distance. He may think that providing is enough, but you're looking for more—a deeper connection."

Zariyah nodded, feeling the weight of it. "Exactly. I need more than just stability. I need him to let me in... and I need to figure out how to let him in, too."

Dr. Monroe's voice was tender but direct. "Those inner vows that once served to protect you—they aren't serving you anymore. They're keeping you from the connection and love you want with Sterling."

But how do I let them go?" Her voice cracked, the weight of the question pressing on her chest.

Dr. Monroe leaned forward slightly, her voice tender. "And do you believe those vows are still true?"

Tears slipped down Zariyah's cheeks as she shook her head. "No."

Dr. Monroe leaned forward, her gaze never wavering. "And how do you see these inner vows affecting your relationship with Sterling?"

Zariyah exhaled, her fingers tracing the outline of her coffee mug. "I've been pushing him away without even realizing it. It's like I'm always waiting for him to hurt me, or to leave me. I have to be on guard... always."

Dr. Monroe let the silence settle between them for a moment, allowing Zariyah to process. "Healing isn't linear," she said finally. "But every step you take—every truth you allow yourself to believe—is a step toward freedom."

The quiet encouragement of Dr. Monroe's words stayed with Zariyah as she sat back in her chair. Her thoughts swirled with the enormity of what she'd just begun to unpack.   She had spent years clutching the shards of her pain, too afraid to let go, yet now, for the first time, she could imagine what it might feel like to release them.

Dr. Monroe nodded, her voice gentle. "You've mentioned

feeling emotionally neglected by your mother. Do you think that's where some of these vows originated?"

Zariyah's throat tightened. "I think it started there. After what happened with Ben, I promised myself I wouldn't trust anyone again. I wouldn't let anyone in, especially not a man. I was determined not to be vulnerable because I thought that's how I'd get hurt."

There was a pause as Zariyah stared at the ceiling, gathering her thoughts. "And then there's Sterling," she added, her voice quieter now. "He had to grow up fast when his dad died. He became the man of the house, but it's like... he never learned how to be vulnerable either. So we're both just... locked up."

Dr. Monroe's expression softened with understanding. "Sterling's experience with early responsibility, especially in the military, likely reinforced that emotional distance. He may think that providing is enough, but you're looking for more—a deeper connection."

Zariyah nodded, feeling the weight of it. "Exactly. I need more than just stability. I need him to let me in... and I need to figure out how to let him in, too."

Dr. Monroe's voice was tender but direct. "Those inner vows that once served to protect you—they aren't serving you anymore. They're keeping you from the connection and love you want with Sterling."

Zariyah's voice cracked as she asked, "But how do I let them go?"

Dr. Monroe leaned forward, her voice firm yet compassionate. "You replace them with truths that reflect the life you want now, not the one you had to survive as a child. It's about transforming the pain into something that empowers you instead of controls you."

Zariyah nodded slowly, her trembling hands clutching

the tissue in her lap. "I've spent so long protecting myself that I don't even know who I am without the walls," she whispered. The admission felt like ripping open an old wound, raw and bleeding, but it also felt necessary.

Dr. Monroe offered a small, encouraging smile. "Healing isn't about demolishing yourself—it's about rebuilding. The walls you've built don't have to disappear. They can become boundaries, rooted in strength and love instead of fear."

She handed Zariyah a notepad. "Write down every inner vow you can think of. Then next to it, replace each one with a truth that aligns with the life you want now."

Her fingers hovered over the keyboard as doubt crept in. She typed: We need to talk. Then she deleted it, staring at the screen. A deep breath steadied her, and this time, her fingers didn't hesitate: *We need to talk.* No more avoiding it.

She hit send before she could second-guess herself. The walls she had built wouldn't crumble overnight, but this was a start.

Chapter
29

Zariyah left Dr. Monroe's office drained, her emotions swirling as she replayed the session in her mind. The weight of the inner vows she made lingered, each one a jagged brick in the walls she had built around herself. She couldn't keep living like this.

Sitting in her car, she hesitated before unlocking her phone. Her thumb hovered over Aimee's name. They hadn't spoken much since the dinner with Richard and Sterling. Taking a deep breath, she texted: Can we do lunch today? I feel like we haven't talked in forever.

The response came almost instantly: Yes, girl! Same spot as always?

Zariyah agreed, though unease settled, this was a conversation that needed to be had.

* * *

The sunlight streamed through the downtown bistro's large windows, casting a warm glow across the polished wood floors. Zariyah sat at their usual corner table, stirring her iced tea absently. Her journal and the new notebook tucked in her purse felt like lead weights—constant reminders of the truths she'd been wrestling with. She adjusted the silverware for the third time, her nerves manifesting in restless movements.

"Hey, girl!" Aimee's voice rang out, warm and familiar. Zariyah looked up to see her friend approaching, her polished exterior and confident stride an almost jarring contrast to the tension bubbling inside her. Aimee looked radiant, her hair perfectly styled, her smile bright—but Zariyah couldn't shake the feeling that it was all just a little too perfect.

"Hey," Zariyah greeted, forcing a smile as Aimee slid into the seat across from her.

They exchanged pleasantries at first—updates about work, a few light jokes about the weather—but the surface-level chatter only made the unspoken words between them more glaring. Zariyah took a sip of her tea, buying herself a few more seconds before she finally set the glass down and leaned forward.

"I've been meaning to check in with you," Zariyah began cautiously. "We haven't really talked about... Richard."

The shift in Aimee's demeanor was subtle, but Zariyah caught it—a flicker of unease in her eyes before her smile tightened. "What about him?" she asked, her tone carefully neutral.

"I just... I've been worried," Zariyah said, choosing her words carefully. "We haven't talked since the ball, and honestly, I couldn't shake the feeling that something was off. Especially after... well, you know, the way he showed up drunk that night."

Aimee's smile faltered, a crack appearing in her polished facade. "Richard's changed," she said quickly, her tone laced with defensiveness. "People can change, Zariyah."

"I'm not saying they can't," Zariyah replied gently, but her voice carried a firmness that cut through the air. "But after everything you went through—after the way he hurt you—I just don't want to see you get hurt again."

The words hung between them like a challenge. Aimee's expression darkened, and for a moment, Zariyah thought she might let the comment slide. But then Aimee's chair scraped loudly against the floor as she abruptly stood, her voice sharp and unsteady.

"You think your life is so perfect that you can sit here and judge mine?" Aimee's words lashed out like a whip, her eyes flashing with a mix of anger and pain. "Miss Perfect, always got it together, always knows best."

The accusation stung, catching Zariyah off guard. She opened her mouth to respond, but Aimee wasn't finished.

"You don't know what it's like," Aimee continued, her voice trembling. "To want something so badly—to believe in someone so much—only to have it all ripped away. You act like you've got it all figured out, but you don't. You're just as messed up as the rest of us."

The words struck like a punch to the gut. Zariyah blinked, stunned into silence. She hadn't expected this level of bitterness from Aimee, nor the intensity of the emotions pouring out of her friend.

Aimee's breathing was uneven as she sat back down, her hands gripping the edge of the table. "I'm sorry," she said, her voice softer now, though the anger still lingered in her eyes. "That was out of line. It's just... there's more to the story than you know."

"What do you mean?" Zariyah asked cautiously, her heart pounding.

Aimee hesitated, her gaze dropping to the table. "Back in college, when Richard disappeared, it wasn't just because he wanted out. His ex-girlfriend—who eventually became his wife—showed up. She was pregnant, Zariyah. And threatening to hurt herself and the baby if he didn't take her back."

Zariyah's breath caught in her throat. "Pregnant?" she echoed, barely able to form the word.

Aimee nodded, her voice cracking. "She was a mess. They'd broken up because she cheated on him, but then she showed up, claiming the baby was his—which it was. He didn't know what to do. So, he left."

The revelation hit Zariyah like a tidal wave. For years, she had believed one version of the story—a version where Richard was the villain and Aimee the heartbroken victim. Now, everything felt blurred, uncertain.

"Why didn't you tell me?" Zariyah asked, her voice trembling.

Aimee shrugged, tears brimming in her eyes. "I guess I was ashamed. Ashamed of still caring about him, even after everything. And part of me didn't want to admit how much it still affects me."

The silence between them was heavy, weighted with years of pain and unspoken truths. Finally, Zariyah reached across the table, placing a hand over Aimee's. "I'm not judging you," she said softly. "I just want you to be okay."

Aimee's lower lip quivered, but she managed a faint smile. "I will be," she whispered. "I'm not the girl I used to be, Z. I've learned how to protect myself."

Zariyah nodded, though a knot of unease still twisted in her chest. Something about Aimee's words felt more like a plea than a declaration of strength. As they parted ways, Zariyah couldn't shake the feeling that her friend was holding onto a pain she wasn't ready to share—not fully.

* * *

Back in her office, Zariyah closed the door behind her,

leaning against it as if the simple act might hold back the flood of emotions threatening to overwhelm her.

She reached into her bag and pulled out her notebook and journal, setting them on the desk with a weight that mirrored the heaviness in her chest.

For a long moment, she just stared at them. The notebook felt almost accusatory—a tangible reminder of Dr. Monroe's challenge to confront the inner vows that had shaped her life.

Finally, with a deep breath, she opened her journal, flipping to a blank page. She drew a line down the center, her pen poised over the left column. The words came slowly at first, then faster, as if the act of writing loosened something inside her.

Vows I Made to Protect Myself

I will never trust anyone.

I don't need anyone.

I will never let myself be vulnerable.

I will never ask for help.

I will always be alone.

No one will love me the way I need to be loved.

I don't deserve love.

I will never trust fully.

I am damaged.

I can't depend on a man.

I will never let anyone control me.

Zariyah stared at the list, her chest tightening as she took in the weight of each vow. They weren't just words on a page—they were the armor she had built over years of pain and survival. But now, looking at them, she saw them for what they truly were: walls. Walls that had kept her safe, yes, but also walls that had kept her isolated, unable to fully embrace the love she craved.

With trembling hands, she moved her pen to the right column. The truth. Dr. Monroe's words echoed in her mind: Replace them with truths that reflect the life you want now, not the one you had to survive as a child. The first line felt impossible to write, but she forced herself to start.

The Truth

Trusting others doesn't mean giving away all of my power.

I am not meant to walk this life alone.

Vulnerability is strength, not weakness.

Asking for help shows courage, not failure.

I am worthy of companionship and connection.

I am loved, even when I feel unworthy.

Love is not about perfection—it's about grace.

Trust takes time, but it's worth building.

I am not damaged; I am resilient.

I can depend on the right people.

I am in control of my choices and my life.

Tears blurred her vision as she finished the last line. The right column felt foreign, like trying on a new identity that didn't quite fit yet. But it also felt... possible. Like maybe, just maybe, she could step out of the shadows of her past and into a life where she didn't have to carry her pain alone.

Chapter

30

Zariyah sat at her desk, her cup of tea forgotten as her eyes lingered on her journal where she had poured out her most painful vows. The words stared back at her, heavy and unforgiving.

Her phone buzzed, the screen lighting up with Noni's name. Zariyah's heart sank. She knew this call wasn't about catching up or checking in—it was about control, guilt, and demands. Bracing herself, she answered.

"Hey, Ma."

"Finally!" Noni's voice was sharp, impatient. "I've been calling all morning. What are you so busy with? You don't even have kids to look after."

Zariyah closed her eyes, her grip tightening on the phone. "I've been working, Ma. I've got deadlines."

"Deadlines? When are you going to focus on what really matters? You're not getting any younger, Zariyah. You and Sterling should be thinking about starting a family."

The words opened familiar wound. "Sterling and I are doing fine, Ma. We're just taking things one step at a time."

"One step at a time? Baby, you're almost forty. What steps are left? It's already too late if you ask me."

The knot in Zariyah's chest tightened, her voice strained. "Ma, we've got it under control. Is there something you needed?"

Noni didn't miss a beat. "I'm short this month. Again. Your brother's not keeping up, and I can't keep living like this. You need to step up."

There it was. Zariyah's stomach churned as she gripped the edge of the table. "Ma, Dominic is doing what he can. And I'm—"

"Don't talk to me about your brother!" Noni snapped. "He's got enough excuses with his baby mama. I raised you better than this. I shouldn't have to beg my own daughter for help."

The words felt like a slap. They always did. "I'll send you something," Zariyah said tightly. "But you can't keep—"

"Ungrateful girl," Noni cut her off, her voice venomous. "I sacrificed everything for you, and this is how you repay me? If your father were alive, he'd be ashamed."

Zariyah flinched, her grip tightening on the phone. "Ma, I'm doing my best."

"Well, try harder," Noni snapped. "And while you're at it, think about what really matters. A career won't keep you warm at night, Zariyah."

The call ended, leaving Zariyah shaking, her breath coming in shallow gasps. She set the phone down and stared blankly at her journal. The words she had written echoed in her mind, louder now than ever: I will never be enough. I will never live up to my mother's expectations.

Her vision blurred with tears as she stood, her body trembling with the weight of it all. She needed to escape the suffocating energy left behind by the call.

"I can't keep doing this," she whispered, her voice breaking.

The sound of the front door opening startled her. Sterling's voice called out from the foyer. "Zariyah? You here?"

She wiped at her face quickly and walked out to meet him. Sterling stood in the kitchen sorting through the mail. The moment his eyes met hers, his brow furrowed with concern.

"Z, what's wrong?"

She shook her head, but the tears betrayed her. "It's nothing. I'm fine."

Sterling crossed the room in two strides, his hands gently cupping her face. "Don't do that," he said softly. "What's going on?"

The tenderness in his voice broke something inside her. She leaned into his chest, her tears soaking into his shirt. "It's my mother. She called again..."

Sterling's arms wrapped around her, strong and steady. "What did she say this time?"

Zariyah pulled back slightly, wiping her cheeks. "The usual. That I'm failing her and you. That I owe her more. And she brought up kids again."

Sterling's jaw tightened, his hands sliding down to hold her shoulders. "Z, you don't have to keep letting her do this to you."

"She's my mother," Zariyah said, her voice barely above a whisper.

"Start by setting some boundaries," Sterling said firmly. "You can't keep sacrificing your peace for her demands."

Zariyah searched his face, her own pain reflected in his eyes. Sterling's hands tightened on her shoulders. "You deserve to live your life without her voice in your head, making you feel like you're not enough. You're more than enough, Zariyah."

The sincerity in his voice brought fresh tears to her eyes. For the first time, she allowed herself to believe him, even just a little.

Sterling pulled her into another embrace, his voice a low murmur against her hair.

"Whatever you need, we'll figure it out. Together."

Zariyah clung to him, her mother's words slowly beginning to lift. For the first time in what felt like forever, she didn't feel alone. It was time.

Zariyah took a steadying breath, her hands trembling as she clasped them in her lap. "We need to talk. I need to tell you something."

Sterling's brow furrowed as he settled into the chair opposite her. "Okay. What's going on?"

She hesitated, the words sticking in her throat. "I've been going to therapy," she said finally, her voice soft but deliberate. "I've been working through some things from my past—things I've never shared with you."

His surprise was evident. "Therapy?" His tone carried a mix of curiosity and concern.

Zariyah nodded. "I needed to. I thought I had buried it all, but it's been affecting me... us. I've been scared, Sterling. Scared of being vulnerable. Scared you wouldn't understand."

Sterling leaned forward, his gaze searching hers. "Why wouldn't I understand? You didn't even give me a chance."

Her voice cracked as she pressed on. "Because there's more. I've been hiding something for years, and I didn't know how to tell you."

Sterling's expression shifted, concern deepening. "What haven't you told me?"

Zariyah's breath hitched, her chest tightening. "When I

was a child... I was abused. By Uncle Ben. I may have led you to believe it was beatings. It wasn't. He sexually abused me."

The words hung heavy in the air. Sterling's jaw dropped slightly, his eyes widening as if he hadn't fully processed what she'd said. "What?" he whispered, his voice barely audible.

Tears welled in her eyes. "I thought I could move on after he died. Pretend it didn't affect me. But it's always been there, in everything I do. I built walls to protect myself—even from you."

Sterling stood abruptly, pacing the room. "Why didn't you tell me this before?"

"I didn't know how," she said, her voice trembling. "I've spent my whole life trying to protect myself, to keep people out. It wasn't about you. It was about me not knowing how to trust."

Sterling stopped pacing, his face etched with frustration. "Trust. I've been here, every day, Zariyah. I'm working, I'm providing, I'm—"

"I don't need more things, Sterling!" she interrupted, her voice rising. "I need you. I need your heart, your attention. I need you to stop shutting me out."

His defenses rose like a shield. "Shutting you out! I'm making sure we have everything we need. What more do you want? Me to sit here and talk about my feelings? Is that it?"

Her heart broke at his sarcasm, but she didn't back down. "I want us to be partners, Sterling. Vulnerable. Honest. Because that's the only way this works."

He stopped in his tracks, his eyes blazing with a mix of anger and pain. "Maybe you're asking for too much."

Her breath caught, the words striking like a blow. But she didn't retreat. "I'm not asking for too much. I'm asking for what I deserve. For what we both deserve."

For a moment, something flickered in his eyes—understanding, maybe even regret—but it was quickly buried beneath his walls. "I've done everything I can. Maybe it's not enough for you."

Zariyah's voice softened, her anger giving way to heartbreak. "If we can't meet each other halfway... then maybe we shouldn't be together."

Zariyah gave him a brief look, her heart aching as she turned toward the bedroom. Each step felt heavier than the last, her mind swirling with the echoes of their argument. She had said the words she'd been too afraid to speak for years, and yet, instead of relief, all she felt was a hollow ache.

For a moment, Zariyah thought she heard Sterling shift behind her, as if he was about to call her back. But the silence stretched on, thick and suffocating. She didn't turn around.

The bedroom door clicked shut behind her, leaving Sterling alone in the quiet, staring at the space she had just occupied. Somewhere in the back of her mind, Zariyah wondered if they had just crossed a line they couldn't uncross.

Chapter
31

Sterling parked his car in front of the red-bricked building in Birmingham's Loft District, the city buzz faint in the background. The narrow streets were lined with converted warehouses and industrial-style apartments, the area reflecting a vibrancy that stood in stark contrast to the storm of emotions swirling inside him.

As he climbed the stairs to Dominic's loft, Sterling felt a knot tighten in his chest. The conversation with Zariyah had left him shaken, raw. Coming here wasn't planned, but he couldn't sit at home drowning in his thoughts. Dominic, with his straightforwardness and shared connection to Zariyah, might be the only person who could give him clarity—or at least some perspective.

Dominic opened the door, surprise flickering across his face. "Sterling? Didn't expect you."

Sterling shrugged, stepping inside. The open-plan loft, with its exposed brick walls and modern furniture, gave off a casual vibe. The scent of roasted coffee and the soft strains of jazz playing in the background made the space feel warm, even as Sterling's chest felt tight. "Sorry I didn't call. I need to talk to you."

"Come on in. You want a beer, wine, or something stronger?" Dominic asked, moving toward the kitchen.

"Just water," Sterling replied, his voice rough.

Dominic filled two glasses, handing one to Sterling before sitting down at the kitchen island. "What's up? You look... off."

Sterling stared into the glass, the words caught in his throat before they finally spilled out. "Zariyah told me last night she's been in therapy. For months."

Dominic's brow furrowed. "Yeah, she told me."

Sterling's head snapped up. "You knew?"

Dominic nodded slowly. "She mentioned it when we were talking about Mom. She didn't say much—just that she was working through some stuff. What happened?"

Sterling hesitated, running a hand through his hair. "She said... if I don't start meeting her halfway emotionally, it's over between us."

Dominic's jaw tightened, his gaze sharpening. "She said that?"

"Yeah." Sterling exhaled sharply. "I don't know what to do. I thought providing was enough."

Dominic set his glass down, crossing his arms. "Providing is part of it, but it's not everything. You can't just be there physically, man. She needs you to show up emotionally."

Sterling frowned, frustration bubbling. "What does that even mean? I've always thought being a good husband meant taking care of her, making sure she doesn't have to worry."

Dominic shook his head. "I used to think the same thing. But Camille—she needed more. And I couldn't give it to her. By the time I realized that, it was too late."

Sterling stared at him, his chest tightening. "It's different with Zariyah."

"Is it?" Dominic challenged. "She's asking for something you don't know how to give. You've got a chance to figure it out. Don't waste it."

Sterling rubbed his face, the weight of Dominic's words pressing down on him. "I don't know, man. I don't know how to fix this."

Dominic's tone softened. "Start by listening. Stop trying to fix everything and just listen."

Sterling nodded slowly, letting the words sink in. They lapsed into silence, the jazz music filling the air between them. After a moment, Sterling's voice broke through the quiet.

"So did you know about Ben?"

Dominic froze, his expression shifting instantly. "What about Ben?"

Sterling hesitated, his voice low. "That he sexually abused her."

Dominic's body stiffened, his fist tightening against the counter. "What?! She said that?"

Sterling nodded. "She told me last night."

Dominic's face darkened, and he stood abruptly, nearly knocking over the bar stool. His voice was heavy with disbelief and pain. "Are you serious? She never told me. Ben was... I looked up to him. He was there when Dad wasn't. How could I have missed this?"

Sterling leaned forward, his voice steady but pained. "She said she thought no one would believe her. And I... I didn't know what to say when she told me."

Dominic stared at the floor, his jaw tight as he tried to process the revelation. "She thought no one would believe her?" he echoed, his voice breaking. "She thought I wouldn't believe her? Damn it, Sterling. She's my sister."

Sterling placed a hand on his shoulder, his grip firm.

"She doesn't blame you, Dom. But this... it's broken her in ways I don't know how to fix."

Dominic's eyes filled with a mixture of anger and regret. "She shouldn't have had to carry that alone. None of this is her fault. None of it. But now? Now we step up. You hear me? You don't make her carry this by herself anymore."

Sterling nodded, his throat tight. "I hear you."

Dominic exhaled sharply, running a hand over his face. "That son of a..." His voice trailed off, the weight of the moment too much for words.

The two men sat in silence for a moment, the air heavy with unspoken pain. But as Sterling stood to leave, Dominic's voice broke through the stillness.

"Don't give up on her, Sterling. Don't let her down."

Sterling nodded, the weight in his chest lifting slightly as he left the loft. Dominic watched him go, his own thoughts spinning. Neither man knew exactly how to heal the wounds of the past, but one thing was clear—they couldn't let Zariyah face this alone.

* * *

Sterling wasn't entirely sure what drove him to Richard's place, but as he stood outside the brick apartment building, he realized he needed another perspective. Richard had been through his own emotional mess—maybe he'd have something to offer.

When the door opened, Richard's brows lifted in surprise. "Sterling? Didn't expect you."

Sterling nodded. "Got a minute?"

Inside, the apartment was cluttered but comfortable, with signs of a fresh start scattered across the room. Richard handed him a beer, gesturing to the couch.

"What's going on?" Richard asked, his tone cautious.

Sterling hesitated, the words thick in his throat. "Things

with Zariyah... they're bad. She's talking like it's over if I don't figure this out."

Richard leaned forward, resting his elbows on his knees. "And what are you doing about it?"

Sterling sighed, the weight of his uncertainty pressing down on him. "That's the thing—I don't know what to do. I thought I was doing enough, providing and handling everything. But it's not enough for her."

Richard's eyes softened, a flicker of understanding crossing his face. "Look, maybe I'm not the best person to talk to about your wife. You know she's not my biggest fan."

Sterling smirked despite himself. "Yeah, she's made that clear."

They both chuckled briefly before Richard got serious. "But here's the thing, man—Zariyah can handle herself. What she needs from you isn't the surface stuff. What's really going on?"

Sterling frowned, confusion flickering in his expression. "What do you mean?"

Richard exhaled deeply, leaning back against the couch. "When Aimee and I first started dating, I ghosted her. Just disappeared."

Sterling raised an eyebrow. "Why?"

"My ex came back," Richard said, his voice heavy. "She was pregnant and... manipulative. Remember, she cheated on me before we broke up?"

Sterling nodded, taking a sip of his beer. "Yeah, I remember."

"She threatened to hurt herself and the baby if I didn't take her back. I was falling for Aimee—hard—but instead of talking to her, I panicked and ran. Aimee didn't deserve that, but I was too scared to face the mess I was in."

Richard shook his head, his tone bitter. "For years, my

ex manipulated me, played on my guilt, and it almost broke me. It wasn't until I started therapy that I began to figure out how much I'd let fear control my life. Still go sometimes, especially when I feel myself slipping."

Sterling studied Richard, his chest tightening. "What about you and Aimee now?"

Richard shrugged, regret shadowing his face. "We're trying to rebuild, but it's not easy. I broke her trust, and that's not something you fix overnight. Hell, maybe you don't fix it at all."

The parallels to his own situation hit Sterling like a punch to the gut. Zariyah wasn't asking for more things; she wanted connection, something he'd been too afraid to give.

Richard's voice softened. "Don't make the same mistake I did. If she's asking for more, it's because she believes you can give it to her. Be real with her, Sterling. Whatever's holding you back, you've gotta face it."

Sterling nodded slowly, the weight of Dominic's and Richard's words settling heavily on him. Fear had been his armor, but now it felt more like a cage. If he wanted to save his marriage, he'd have to break free.

He set the beer down and stood. "Thanks, Richard."

Richard rose as well, clapping a hand on Sterling's shoulder. "Go fix it, man. Don't wait until it's too late."

As Sterling walked back to his car, the evening air felt thick with everything he had just heard. It wouldn't be easy, but he knew now that avoiding the hard truths was no longer an option.

Chapter 32

Returning to Dr. Monroe's office so soon wasn't part of her plan, but with everything spiraling, she knew she couldn't navigate it alone.

She let out a slow breath, her eyes drifting to the window where sunlight filtered through the blinds, casting fragmented patterns on the floor. The conversation with Sterling had opened wounds she wasn't sure she could heal. Now, sitting here, the weight of those wounds pressed down on her like an anchor.

Dr. Monroe's gentle voice broke through her thoughts. "You've been through quite a bit since our last session. How are you feeling today?"

Zariyah exhaled deeply, her shoulders slumping under the weight of her thoughts. "Like I'm standing at the edge of a cliff," she admitted, her voice tinged with weariness. "It's only been a couple of days, but it feels like everything is falling apart."

Dr. Monroe nodded thoughtfully. "It's a lot to process in a short amount of time. What's feeling most pressing to you right now?"

Zariyah considered the question, her fingers still tracing

the edge of her journal. "Honestly? I'm not sure. It's like I'm juggling too many things, and I can't afford to drop any of them. But I'm so tired."

Her throat tightened as the words began spilling out. "The conversation with Sterling... it was hard. He didn't know what to do with it, and I don't blame him—it's a lot. But his reaction..." She hesitated, her eyes shifting to the edge of the tissue box on the table. "It was like he didn't know what to do with me. It brought up everything else I've been trying to avoid."

Dr. Monroe leaned in slightly, her tone gentle but probing. "Like what?"

"My mother," Zariyah said, the words heavy on her tongue. She told Dr. Monroe about her mother berating her just before Sterling had arrived, replaying Noni's cutting words in her mind.

"Noni always makes me feel like I'm not enough," she continued, her voice cracking. "And I think... I know I've carried that into everything I do. Even with Sterling. I keep waiting for him to fail me so I can prove what I've always believed: that I can't depend on anyone."

Her voice cracked on the last word, and she quickly reached for a tissue, dabbing at her eyes. The weight of her admission pressed against her chest like a vise.

Dr. Monroe gave her a moment before speaking, her voice calm but firm. "And what would it mean for you to let go of that belief? To allow yourself to trust someone without the fear of being let down?"

Zariyah stared at her hands, her thumb tracing the soft leather cover of her journal. "I don't know. I don't know if I can. Every time I try, it feels like... like they prove me right. Sterling, my mom—they just expect me to hold it all together. To be strong. And I'm so tired, Dr. Monroe. I'm so tired of carrying it all."

Her voice broke, and tears slipped silently down her cheeks. She didn't fight them this time.

Dr. Monroe leaned forward slightly. "It's okay to be tired, Zariyah. You've been carrying far more than anyone should, and for far too long. But letting go doesn't mean you're weak. It means you're strong enough to stop fighting battles that were never yours to fight."

Zariyah's gaze met Dr. Monroe's, her eyes filled with a mixture of fear and hope. "But if I don't do it, who will?"

"That's the real question, isn't it?" Dr. Monroe said gently. "Who's responsible for carrying the weight of your happiness, your healing? And why can't it be you?"

The words landed like a thunderclap, reverberating in the quiet room. Zariyah had spent so much of her life trying to control the narrative, to manage everyone else's expectations so they couldn't hurt her. But now, faced with the truth of what that control had cost her, she wasn't so sure anymore.

"We're both stuck," Zariyah admitted, her voice soft but steady. "Sterling deflects everything, and I keep him at a distance. I thought being strong meant handling it all, but now... it just feels like too much."

Dr. Monroe nodded, her expression understanding. "Strength doesn't mean carrying it all alone. It means knowing when to ask for help, when to share the load. Have you talked to Sterling about what you need from him?"

Zariyah hesitated, her lips pressing into a thin line. "I've tried, but he just... he shuts down. And I don't know how to reach him."

"Zariyah," Dr. Monroe said softly, "he might not have the tools yet, but that doesn't mean he can't learn. Vulnerability is a practice, not a switch you flip. You've taken a huge step in sharing your story with him. That's not small—it's monumental. Now it's about figuring out what you need for yourself and giving him space to figure out his role in this."

Zariyah let the words settle over her, the truth of them cutting through her exhaustion. "I've spent so long protecting myself that I don't even know who I am without the walls," she whispered.

Dr. Monroe smiled gently. "That's what this journey is about—rediscovering yourself. You don't have to have all the answers today. Healing isn't about perfection; it's about permission. Permission to be messy, to stumble, to figure it out as you go."

For the first time in the session, Zariyah exhaled fully, the tension in her chest loosening ever so slightly.

* * *

Zariyah left Dr. Monroe's office, her mind swirling from their conversation. She barely registered the drive to Charades, her thoughts a tangle of past hurts, Sterling's reaction, and Noni's incessant demands. By the time she arrived, the familiar warmth of the bistro was almost jarring. Dominic had texted her earlier to meet him in his office, their usual spot when the weight of life pressed too hard.

The soft hum of activity in the dining area faded as she slipped into the private room. Dominic was already there, leaning back in his chair, his face etched with exhaustion.

"Hey, Z," he greeted, his voice low but warm. "Glad you made it."

She offered a faint smile, sinking into the chair across from him. The atmosphere between them felt heavier than usual, as though they both knew this conversation would touch on wounds neither of them had fully healed.

For over an hour, they talked, their words circling back to

the same subject—Noni.

"She asked for more money again," Zariyah said, her frustration barely concealed.

"We're already giving her $2,000 a month, Dom. It's like it's never enough."

Dominic let out a bitter laugh, rubbing a hand over his face. "What's she even doing with it? Her house is paid off, we cover her utilities, and she's not paying property taxes. But somehow, she's always short."

Zariyah sighed, the familiar knot in her stomach tightening. "And every time we try to help her budget, she acts like we're the problem. Like it's our job to fix everything."

"Because that's what we've always done," Dominic said sharply. "But it's draining us, Z. I've got my own bills, my own problems, and this place... it's barely staying afloat. She's bleeding us dry."

The weariness in his voice struck a chord deep in her chest. She had spent years trying to shoulder Noni's demands, sacrificing her own peace and financial stability to keep their mother happy—or at least placated. But it was never enough.

"I've been talking about this in therapy," Zariyah admitted quietly, her gaze dropping to the table. "Dr. Monroe's been helping me realize how much of this is tied to how we grew up. Mom's constant criticism, her making us feel like we were never enough... it's shaped everything. Even my marriage. I've been so busy trying to prove I'm not a failure that I've forgotten how to just... live."

Dominic's brow furrowed, his expression a mix of sympathy and frustration. "Therapy, huh? I don't know if I could do that. Too much crap to unpack. But you're right— Mom messed us up in ways we're still dealing with. And now... it's like we're trapped."

The silence between them grew heavy, filled with unspoken burdens neither of them could name.

"I've been thinking about making some big changes at Charades," Dominic said after a moment, his tone softer. "Maybe bringing in investors, renting it out more, or even switching up the business model completely. I love this place, but right now... it feels like I'm suffocating with Mom always leaning on me. I don't know how much longer I can keep it together."

Zariyah reached across the table, her hand covering his. "You're not alone in this," she said firmly. "We'll figure it out together."

Dominic gave her a small smile, but the strain in his eyes remained. "I guess we're all we've got, huh?"

"Yeah," she replied softly. "We are."

They sat in silence for a while, the weight of their shared history pressing down on them like an invisible force. For Zariyah, the conversation with Dr. Monroe echoed in her mind: letting go doesn't mean you're weak. It means you're strong enough to stop fighting battles that were never yours to fight.

Dominic broke the silence, his voice quiet but resolute. "We need to do something, Z. We can't keep living like this. I think... I think we need to cut her off. Completely."

Zariyah's head snapped up, her heart pounding. "What? You mean... stop giving her money?"

Dominic nodded, his expression firm. "Yeah. She's never going to stop unless we make her. We've tried everything else—helping her budget, covering her expenses—but it's never enough. Maybe it's time we let her figure it out on her own."

The idea hit her like a slap, her mind racing with the implications. Cutting Noni off felt impossible—unthinkable.

But as Dominic's words sank in, she realized he might be right. They couldn't keep living like this, trapped in a cycle of obligation and guilt.

"Do you really think we could do that?" she asked, her voice barely above a whisper.

Dominic's gaze met hers, steady and unyielding. "I think we have to. For us. For our sanity."

Zariyah felt her chest tighten, the enormity of the decision weighing on her like a stone. The thought of standing up to Noni, of setting boundaries that would likely be met with anger and manipulation, terrified her. But as she looked at her brother, at the strain etched into his features, she agreed—something had to change.

Chapter
33

Zariyah woke to the soft light filtering through the blinds, but the ache in her chest was anything but soft. The tightness had been there for days, an ever-present reminder of the distance between her and Sterling. She lay still for a moment, staring at the ceiling, her thoughts swirling in the silence of their fractured home.

He hadn't been sleeping in their bed. She wasn't sure if he was avoiding her, or if he simply didn't know how to face her after everything that had been said. Either way, the void between them felt insurmountable. She sighed, the weight of their unresolved conversation pressing down on her chest.

With a deep breath, she swung her legs over the side of the bed, the cold floor grounding her as she moved through her morning routine. By the time she made it to the kitchen, she had prepared herself for the possibility that Sterling would already be gone, retreating into his work as he so often did when things got hard.

But he wasn't gone.

There he was, sitting at the table, a cup of coffee in hand, staring out the window. His shoulders were hunched, his posture tense, and his expression unreadable. Zariyah froze in the doorway, uncertain of how to bridge the gap between them.

Sterling glanced over his shoulder, sensing her presence. His tired eyes met hers, and for a moment, something flickered there—regret, maybe. "Morning," he muttered, his voice rough.

"Morning," Zariyah replied softly, stepping into the room. The awkwardness between them was palpable, settling like a thick fog. She made her way to the counter and poured herself a cup of coffee, her hands trembling slightly. She wanted to say something, to break the silence, but the words wouldn't come.

Sterling spoke first. "I've been thinking about our conversation."

Zariyah's heart quickened, her pulse thudding in her ears. She turned toward him, watching as he turned his mug in his hands, his gaze fixed on the swirling liquid.

"For once in my life... I don't know if I can do this," he admitted, his voice low, almost hesitant.

The pressure in Zariyah's chest intensified, her throat tightening as his words sank in. "Sterling..." she began, her voice trembling. "I didn't mean to hurt you. I—"

"It's not about that," he interrupted, finally looking up at her. His jaw was tight, his expression conflicted. "I've never been the kind of person who... dwells on feelings. That's never made sense to me. But after what you said, after everything we've been through... I think I'm starting to get it."

Zariyah froze, her breath catching in her throat. She hadn't expected him to say that.

Sterling exhaled heavily, running a hand through his hair. "I don't know how to do this, Z. I've spent my whole life avoiding this kind of stuff. But... I'm willing to try. For us."

The vulnerability in his voice broke something open in her, and for the first time in days, she felt a flicker of hope. Sterling met her gaze, his eyes earnest. "Maybe... maybe I can come to therapy with you."

Zariyah blinked, caught off guard by his offer. "You'd do that?" she asked, her voice barely above a whisper.

Sterling shrugged, a hint of nervousness in the motion. "I don't know if it'll help. I just... I want to understand."

Her chest swelled with fragile hope, a spark of light breaking through the darkness. "That would mean so much to me," she said, her voice trembling with emotion.

Sterling nodded slowly, the corner of his mouth twitching in the smallest hint of a smile. "Okay," he said softly. "We'll start there."

As Sterling's hand lingered in hers, Zariyah felt a faint glimmer of hope. Their relationship wasn't fixed, but the willingness to try—to even consider therapy together—was more than she'd dared to expect. It wasn't a solution, but it was a start.

Later that morning, she found herself sitting at the kitchen table, her journal open before her. Dr. Monroe's words from her last session echoed in her mind: "Sometimes, moving forward means clearing the table. Confront the things weighing you down, one by one. Some you'll resolve, and others you'll need to let go of entirely."

And then the conference speaker's voice joined the chorus: "Forgiveness isn't about excusing someone's actions—it's about releasing their hold over your peace."

Zariyah had taken those words to heart. Forgiveness wasn't absolution; it was freedom. Though the prospect of confronting her mother felt like trying to move a mountain, it wasn't just for herself—it was for Dominic, too. He deserved better than to be trapped in the same exhausting cycle she'd been living in.

Her chest tightened as she picked up her phone and dialed Noni's number. When the call went unanswered, she clenched the phone tighter, resolving that she would face her mother today—phone call or not. There was no easy way to do this, no perfect words to soften the blow. But for once, Zariyah wasn't looking for perfection. She was looking for freedom.

Zariyah gripped the steering wheel tightly, her car idling in front of the small bungalow. The modest home stood quietly beneath the soft morning light, its exterior clean but weathered—much like her relationship with her mother.

She shoved the thought aside and focused on her mantra: This is for me. The words repeated in her mind, a drumbeat that kept her grounded.

Finally, she stepped out of the car, her heartbeat pounding in her ears. She approached the door slowly, every step feeling heavier than the last. When Noni opened it, her expression shifted from mild curiosity to irritation in an instant.

"What are you doing here? I thought you'd just send the money," Noni snapped, her tone sharp.

Zariyah swallowed the retort rising in her throat and forced herself to stay calm. "We need to talk, Momma."

Noni stepped aside, crossing her arms as Zariyah walked in. The living room was neat, the faint scent of lavender hanging in the air. It was always lavender with Noni— her signature, her constant. Zariyah froze mid-step as the realization hit her like a wave of nausea.

Lavender.

The candles on her desk, the sprays in her home—it wasn't just a scent she'd chosen because she liked it. She had chosen it because of Noni. Her stomach twisted, the air in the room suddenly feeling thick and suffocating. *How did I not see this?*

All these years, she had surrounded herself with lavender, thinking it brought peace. But now she knew: it was a subconscious tether to a mother who made her feel small, inadequate. The realization churned in her gut as Noni's sharp voice snapped her back to the moment.

"What are you doing here? If you didn't come to tell me you're pregnant, I don't see what we need to talk about."

Zariyah's chest tightened, the words hitting like a slap, but she forced herself to stay calm. "This isn't about that, Momma. This is about setting some boundaries."

"Boundaries?" Noni scoffed, her lips twisting into a smirk. "You're talking like one of those therapists you're probably wasting your husband's money on. Whining about all the things I did and didn't do for you."

Zariyah lowered herself into the armchair across from her, her hands clasped in her lap to keep them from trembling. "Yes, Momma, boundaries. I'm going to need you to keep your opinions to yourself. I no longer care what you think or say about me. Maybe you love me, maybe you don't. It doesn't matter anymore."

She took a slow breath, her voice steady despite the storm brewing inside her. "And it may be better if you don't call me unless it's a dire emergency. And you," she paused, locking eyes with her mother, "needing more money is NOT an emergency."

Noni's eyes narrowed dangerously. "Now you wait a minute," she said, standing abruptly, her hands on her hips. "Who do you think you're talking to? I sacrificed everything for you and your brother."

"I know, Momma." Zariyah stood, leveling her gaze.

"And I've sacrificed for you—since I was old enough to work. Dominic and I have covered your bills, paid off your house, given you an allowance, and extra every single month. But it's never enough."

Noni's lips curled in a sneer. "You think you're better than me now, huh? Just because you've got your rich husband and your little business? You're still that selfish, ungrateful—"

"Stop," Zariyah cut her off, her voice calm but firm. "I'm not doing this anymore. We'll keep covering the bills and giving you the allowance, but not one penny more. So don't ask me. I'm done being your safety net."

Noni's face twisted in anger, her voice rising. "You'll regret this. You think that man of yours is going to stick around when you can't even give him a child? Men like that stray, Zariyah. Yours is a fine, strapping man, and another woman—one who can give him a child—will find it easy to take him from you."

The words hit like a slap, slicing through the air and landing squarely on Zariyah's chest. Her hands trembled, the nausea from earlier threatening to resurface. For a moment, she simply stared at Noni, the sheer audacity of her mother's cruelty leaving her breathless.

But then, something shifted. The anger that surged through Zariyah wasn't the kind that weakened her—it was the kind that sharpened her resolve. She straightened her spine, her voice cold and unwavering.

"I pity you, Momma," Zariyah said, her tone cutting through the tension like a blade. "You think tearing me down will make you feel better about your own choices? It won't. But here's the thing—you don't have any power over me anymore. None. You can say whatever hateful thing you want, but it doesn't change who I am. It doesn't change what I'm worth."

Noni's mouth opened as if to retort, but Zariyah didn't give her the chance. "And I'll tell you this one last time: we're keeping the allowance and the bills we already cover, but that's it. Don't ask for anything more because you won't get it."

At the door, Zariyah paused, her hand on the doorknob. She didn't turn around, but her voice was steady. "I love you, Momma. I hope you find some peace. But I won't be the one to give it to you."

Chapter
34

Zariyah parked outside Aimee's building, her emotions still raw from her confrontation with Noni. She had taken a moment in the car to steady her breathing, convincing herself that coming here wasn't a mistake. She needed her friend.

When Aimee opened the door, she looked surprised but quickly offered a smile. "Hey, Z! What are you doing here?"

Zariyah hesitated in the doorway. "I needed to talk. Is this a bad time?"

Aimee stepped back to let her in. "Uh, no. Not really. Come on in. I was just cleaning up a little, but we can talk."

The living room was pristine, as always, but there was an underlying tension in Aimee's movements. She adjusted a vase on the coffee table, picked up a magazine that was already perfectly aligned, and tucked it neatly into a drawer. Her laptop sat open on the dining table, notifications pinging softly in the background.

"Sorry about the mess," Aimee said absently, rearranging pillows on the couch.

"It's fine," Zariyah replied, sitting down cautiously. The knot in her chest tightened when Aimee didn't sit beside her but instead stood near the table, checking her phone.

"So, what's going on?" Aimee asked lightly, her tone distracted.

Zariyah swallowed hard, trying to ignore the sinking feeling in her stomach. "I had a fight with Noni this morning. A bad one."

"Again?" Aimee said nonchalantly, still scrolling on her phone. "What now?"

Zariyah blinked, caught off guard by the dismissive tone.

"It's always the same thing with you and Noni—m-o-n-e-y," Aimee replied, finally setting her phone down. "I mean, Z, at some point you've got to let it go. Like with me and my dad—I stopped letting his crap get to me years ago."

Zariyah's jaw tightened. She knew all about Aimee's father, about the unresolved pain of his abandonment, but this was different. "This wasn't just a little argument," Zariyah said. Her voice wavered as she recounted the cruel things her mother had said to her that morning.

Aimee tilted her head, frowning slightly but not meeting Zariyah's eyes. "That sucks," she said finally. "Sounds like that one time my dad told me I wasn't his real kid. Remember?"

Zariyah stared at her, anger simmering beneath the surface. "Aimee—"

"And let me tell you about Richard," Aimee cut in, grabbing her wine glass and filling it. "He's been texting me nonstop since last night, and I don't even know what to say to him. Like, how do you even deal with someone who's all 'I've changed' when you know they haven't?"

Zariyah clenched her fists, her body rigid. "Seriously? You're not even going to ask how I feel about what I just told you?"

Aimee paused, finally looking at her. "Z, you've been dealing with this for so long—what's really different this time?"

Zariyah's breath hitched, her voice rising despite herself. "What's different is I needed you today, Aimee. I needed you to be a friend for once. And instead, it's the same thing. You, your dad, and now Richard."

Aimee bristled, her eyes narrowing. "That's not fair, Z. I didn't ask you to come over here and dump all this on me. I'm trying to deal with my own stuff."

The words hit harder than Zariyah expected, leaving her momentarily speechless. She stood abruptly, her chest heaving. "You're right. You didn't ask me to come here. That's on me."

"Z—" Aimee started, but Zariyah shook her head, her voice trembling.

"I'm tired, Aimee. I'm tired of being the friend who's always there for everyone else but can't count on anyone to be there for me."

Without waiting for a response, Zariyah grabbed her bag and walked out, her heart pounding. She didn't look back.

As she got into her car, the tears came in waves, hot and unrelenting. This wasn't how she had imagined things going, but maybe that was the point. Maybe this was another weight she needed to let go of.

Chapter
35

Zariyah gripped the steering wheel, her knuckles white against the leather as she sat in the parking lot outside Charades. Her breath came in shallow bursts, the weight in her chest pressing harder with each passing second. She felt like she was unraveling.

The confrontation with Noni still echoed in her mind—sharp, cutting words that had left invisible scars. Aimee's indifference, her inability to see Zariyah's pain, had only added salt to the wounds. Every moment replayed on a loop in her head, a suffocating reminder of how much she was carrying.

Zariyah glanced at her phone. Dominic was expecting her at Charades to go over plans for a party. A normal day, a familiar space. It should've been grounding. But even the thought of stepping inside felt like climbing a mountain.

I'll cancel, she thought, but her fingers didn't move to dial. Instead, she exhaled shakily and opened the car door, letting the brisk air sting her cheeks.

Zariyah stepped into Charades, her legs trembling under the weight of her emotions. The dim interior, usually a sanctuary, felt stifling today. Her breaths came shallow, the air thick and heavy. Felicity greeted her with a warm smile, but Zariyah barely registered it.

"Dominic's running late," Felicity said, her tone cheerful. "You can wait in his office, though."

Zariyah nodded absently, her vision narrowing as she made her way to the back. The hallway seemed longer than usual, the walls closing in around her. When she finally reached the office, her legs buckled slightly, and she gripped the doorframe for support.

Inside, she sank into the chair, her heart hammering in her chest. Her phone buzzed on the desk, but even reaching for it felt insurmountable. The edges of her vision blurred, black dots dancing before her eyes. She tried to steady her breathing, but her chest tightened further, each breath more shallow than the last. The room began to spin, the dizziness consuming her until the ground gave way beneath her.

Felicity heard the thud before she realized what had happened. Her eyes widened as she rushed into Dominic's office, her heart dropping at the sight of Zariyah crumpled on the floor.

"Zariyah!" she cried, kneeling beside her. Her hands trembled as she checked for a pulse, relief flooding her when she found it—weak but steady.

She grabbed her phone, her voice shaking as she spoke to the 911 operator. "Please hurry," she begged, glancing back at Zariyah's pale face. "She's not waking up."

The minutes stretched into an eternity, and Felicity fought the rising panic in her chest. "It's going to be okay," she whispered, as much to herself as to Zariyah. But the sight of her boss's sister lying there, so still and vulnerable, made her question if she believed it.

* * *

Sterling paced the waiting room, his mind racing with

a thousand thoughts. He replayed every argument, every moment he'd ignored the signs of her stress. He thought of the late nights when she'd stayed up working, her shoulders tense as she stared at her laptop. The mornings when her smile didn't reach her eyes. The countless times she'd said she was fine when he knew she wasn't—but he'd let it slide anyway. Because it was easier to believe her than to ask what was really wrong.

The weight of his guilt was crushing, his breath coming in shallow gasps.

When Dominic arrived, his face was set with a grim determination; he sat heavily beside Sterling. "Any updates?"

Sterling shook his head, his voice tight. "Not yet. They're running tests."

Dominic's expression darkened, and he stood abruptly, pacing the room with his phone in hand. He dialed Felicity again, muttering under his breath when it went to voicemail. "She's strong," he repeated, almost like a prayer, his voice faltering as he sank back into the chair beside Sterling. "I should've been there."

Before Sterling could respond, the door to the ICU swung open, and a doctor walked toward them.

"Mr. Ellis?" the doctor asked, his expression professional yet sympathetic.

Sterling's heart dropped. "Yes. How is she?"

"Zariyah is stable for now. We've diagnosed her with Takotsubo cardiomyopathy, often called 'stress-induced cardiomyopathy.' It's not a heart attack, but it mimics one. Her heart was weakened by extreme emotional stress."

Sterling's stomach churned. Stress… caused by me.

"Can I see her?" His voice cracked.

The doctor nodded. "She's still unconscious, but you can sit with her."

Dominic gave Sterling a reassuring nod. "Go, man. I'll be here."

Sterling walked through the ICU doors, every step feeling like a thousand. When he reached Zariyah's room, he froze in the doorway. She lay so still, pale against the white hospital sheets, surrounded by beeping machines. His heart clenched painfully as he took in the IV line that snaked around her wrist and all the other chords attached to her chest.

Sitting by her bedside, he took her hand in his, the warmth of her skin grounding him. He rested his head on their intertwined hands, a tear slipping down his cheek. "I'm sorry, Z," he whispered. "I should've been better. I should've seen what this was doing to you."

The door creaked open, but Sterling didn't move. A nurse stepped inside quietly, offering a soft smile. "Take your time," she said gently before leaving.

Sterling stayed by Zariyah's side for hours. Exhaustion tugged at him, and at some point, he drifted off to sleep, his head resting on the edge of the bed, his hand still wrapped around Zariyah's.

* * *

Sterling woke to the faintest squeeze of his hand.

His heart leaped into his throat as he jerked upright, blinking against the soft morning light filtering through the blinds. He looked at Zariyah, her eyelids fluttering open. Relief flooded him.

"Zariyah," Sterling breathed, his voice thick with emotion.

Her gaze found his, weak and unfocused. "Sterling…" Her voice was barely audible, but it was enough.

"I'm here," he said, his voice thick with emotion. "You're okay. You're going to be okay."

Zariyah blinked slowly, confusion knitting her brow. "What… happened?"

Sterling brushed a stray curl from her forehead, his movements slow and deliberate. "You collapsed at Charades."

Her lips parted as if she wanted to say more, but her strength faltered. Instead, she closed her eyes, her voice a faint whisper. "Don't… leave me."

Sterling's chest tightened. He leaned closer, his forehead resting lightly against their intertwined hands. "I won't," he promised, his voice raw. "I'm not going anywhere."

As she drifted back to sleep, Sterling sat back, his own exhaustion pulling at him. He stayed by her side as the hospital morning routine stirred around him—nurses coming and going, machines humming faintly. He wouldn't just be here for her now; he would be better for her.

No more silence. No more avoiding the hard conversations.

Chapter 36

After four long days in the ICU, Zariyah had finally been moved to a private room. The steady beeping of the heart monitor filled the silence, a constant reminder of how fragile she was. Every moment spent here wasn't just about recovery; it was a reckoning with the weight of silence— words and wounds carried over a lifetime.

The door creaked open softly, and she didn't need to open her eyes to know who it was. The heavy scent of Noni's perfume hit her first—a familiar assault that stirred both nausea and unwelcome memories.

When she opened her eyes, Noni stood at the foot of the bed, immaculately dressed, her sharp gaze sweeping the room before landing on Zariyah. "I didn't realize hospital rooms came with a view," she said, her tone clipped and cold.

Zariyah's chest tightened, the beeping of the monitor quickening slightly as her mother stepped closer.

"Look at you," Noni continued, her voice laced with mockery. "Laid up like some helpless child. I hope you're not expecting pity because you won't get it from me."

"Momma, please," Zariyah whispered, each word

strained. "Go. I need to rest."

"Rest?" Noni scoffed, crossing her arms. "You've been resting your whole life, Zariyah. Always running from reality. Do you think Sterling is going to keep putting up with this?" Her lips curled into a smirk. "A man like him doesn't stick around for long when his wife becomes dead weight."

The words hit hard, but Zariyah stayed silent, refusing to rise to the bait. Noni's eyes narrowed, clearly irritated by the lack of reaction.

"I raised you to be strong, but you've turned into a disappointment," Noni pressed, her voice rising. "And let me tell you something—men don't stay where there's weakness. Mark my words, the first woman who can give him a child will snatch him right out from under you."

The heart monitor's beeping spiked, a loud, erratic rhythm that filled the room. Zariyah's breaths grew shallow, her chest rising and falling rapidly as the pressure she'd worked so hard to manage threatened to overtake her.

The door swung open, and Sterling strode in, his face tight with concern. His eyes locked on Zariyah before darting to Noni. The tension in the room became palpable as he crossed to her side and gently took her hand.

"What are you doing here, Noni?" Sterling's voice was low, but it carried a sharp edge. "She doesn't need this."

Noni turned to face him, her chin lifting in defiance. "I'm her mother. What makes you think you know what she needs better than I do?"

Sterling's jaw tightened, and his voice dropped even lower. "A mother who cared would focus on helping her recover—not tearing her down."

Before Noni could respond, the door opened again, and Aimee stepped inside. She stopped in her tracks, her gaze flicking between Zariyah's pale face and the heart monitor's frantic beeping. Without hesitation, she strode forward, placing a firm hand on Noni's arm.

"Ms. Noni," Aimee said, her tone calm but steely. "It's time for you to leave."

Noni's eyes narrowed, her lips curling in disdain. "And who do you think you are?"

"Someone who actually cares about Zariyah," Aimee replied, her voice unwavering.

For a moment, Noni seemed poised to argue, but the monitor's erratic beeping finally caught her attention. Her gaze flicked back to Zariyah, her face unreadable. Without another word, she turned on her heel and stalked to the door.

Before leaving, she glanced over her shoulder. "You'll regret this, Zariyah. Mark my words."

The door clicked shut, leaving the room heavy with silence. Sterling turned back to Zariyah, his grip on her hand firm but gentle. "Breathe, baby," he murmured. "Just breathe."

Aimee moved closer, her touch light on Zariyah's shoulder. "It's okay, Z. She's gone. Just focus on us."

The heart monitor's beeping gradually slowed, the tension easing as Zariyah focused on their voices. Exhaustion dragged at her, but before sleep overtook her, she squeezed Sterling's hand weakly and whispered, "Thank you."

Sterling pressed a kiss to her forehead. "I'm here. I've got you."

Aimee wiped at a lone tear as she reached for Zariyah's other hand. "We've got you, Z. You're not doing this alone, not anymore."

Zariyah squeezed both their hands lightly before her eyes drifted shut, the steady rhythm of the heart monitor finally reflecting the peace she desperately needed.

Chapter
37

The room was filled with the soft fragrance of fresh flowers when Zariyah stirred. Her eyes fluttered open, drawn to the bouquet on the bedside table. Tulips, hydrangeas, and roses—her favorites. She smiled faintly, though her body still felt heavy, weighed down by both the physical toll of her collapse and the emotional wreckage of the past week.

The door creaked open, and a nurse entered with a clipboard, her steps efficient yet unhurried. "Good morning, Mrs. Ellis. How are you feeling today?"

"Better," Zariyah murmured, her voice hoarse. She glanced at the flowers.

The nurse reached for the small card tucked among the blooms and handed it to Zariyah before raising the bed into a sitting position. "They were delivered early this morning. Looks like you have some people who really care about you."

Zariyah opened the card, her heart warming as she read the neat handwriting: Love, Dominic and Amara.

The nurse smiled as she checked Zariyah's vitals. "Your husband said to tell you he'd be right back. Can I get you anything?"

Zariyah shook her head just as Sterling stepped into the

room, carrying a basket. His eyes softened as they met hers, and he leaned down, kissing her softly, cautiously.

"How are you?" he asked, setting the basket on the table and pulling a chair closer to her bed.

"Better," she said again, her voice steadier this time.

"Have you eaten? Ms. Emma sent these." He opened the basket, revealing two carefully labeled plates. One was filled with fresh fruit and a cranberry muffin, the other a mix of bacon, a biscuit, fruit, and a cinnamon roll.

"She's too much," Zariyah said, laughing lightly as Sterling handed her a fork.

"You gotta love her," Sterling said, his tone warm. "I ran into a Joshua downstairs. He said Ms. Emma made sure I didn't leave the house without these."

As they ate, Zariyah recounted the countless stories Ms. Emma had shared about her grandson—his love for football, academic achievements, and even his baking skills. Sterling listened, the quiet moment between them feeling normal.

They had just finished eating when the door opened, and Dr. Holden stepped in, his expression warm but professional.

"Good morning, Mrs. Ellis," he greeted, pulling her chart from the end of the bed. "How are we feeling today?"

"Stronger," Zariyah replied.

Dr. Holden nodded approvingly, checking her chart. "Your heart is recovering well, but it's going to take time. Stress-induced cardiomyopathy can mimic a heart attack, but it's brought on by emotional or physical strain. Rest and reduced stress are crucial."

Sterling leaned forward slightly, his brow furrowed. "So, this was all stress?"

"Primarily," Dr. Holden confirmed. "It's a reminder that the heart and mind are deeply connected. The good news is, we've seen significant improvement since you were admitted last week."

Zariyah nodded slowly, her hand brushing against her stomach—a subconscious movement. Dr. Holden's gaze flicked briefly to her movement before returning to her chart.

"There's one more thing," he added, his tone careful but steady. "We've gotten some of your test results back, and while everything with your heart is improving, there's something else we discovered."

Zariyah and Sterling exchanged a glance, worry flashing across their faces.

Dr. Holden's tone softened. "Looks like you're pregnant."

For a moment the room was utterly still.

Sterling's voice cracked. "What did you say?"

"Your wife is pregnant," Dr. Holden repeated. "It's early—about six weeks—but the tests confirm it. Given the recent cardiac event, you'll need close monitoring. But so far, there's no reason to believe the pregnancy is at risk."

He placed the chart back. "I'll get your discharge papers ready, and you should follow up with my office next week. Congratulations to you both." He shook Sterling's hand and left them alone.

Sterling turned to Zariyah, his expression a mix of wonder and apprehension. "We're going to be parents," he whispered, his voice thick with emotion.

Zariyah's hand trembled against her stomach. Tears welled up, a mix of fear and hope flooding her heart. "Sterling… there's something I need to tell you."

Still holding her hand, Sterling sat next to her on the bed. "I'm listening."

Zariyah's voice wavered. "Early in our marriage, I was pregnant. I didn't tell you because… I was scared. And then I lost it before I could figure out how."

Sterling's grip on her hand tightened, his expression softening with regret. "Z… you shouldn't have gone through that alone."

"I thought it was my fault," she whispered, tears slipping down her cheeks. "I thought I wasn't meant to be a mother."

Sterling leaned forward, pressing his forehead gently to hers. "It wasn't your fault, Z. You've been carrying this too long."

He wrapped his arms around her, holding her close. "I can't change the past, but I can promise you this—whatever happens, we're in this together. I'll be here. For you, for this baby, for us."

A soft knock interrupted the moment, and Dr. Monroe stepped inside. She smiled gently at the couple before pulling up a chair. "I hear you're going home?"

"Yes," Zariyah whispered, her voice fragile but genuine.

"Good," Dr. Monroe said. "That is good to hear."

Sterling rose from the bed and looked between the two women. Dr. Monroe extended her hand. "Nice to finally meet you, Sterling… is it alright if I call you Sterling?" she asked warmly. "I'm Dr. Monroe, Zariyah's therapist."

Sterling shook her hand firmly, then moved a chair to the other side of the bed for her. He returned to Zariyah's side, his hand resting protectively over hers.

Dr. Monroe glanced between them, a light smile playing on her lips. "So…your walls came tumbling down?" she teased, directing her question to Zariyah.

Zariyah let out a soft laugh, her smile tinged with irony. "Yep, and I was Humpty Dumpty."

They all chuckled at the lame joke, the moment easing some of the tension in the room.

But Dr. Monroe's tone turned serious as she leaned forward slightly. "Before we send you off, I think it's important to talk about where you go from here," she said, her gaze flicking between the two of them. "This hospitalization should be a wake-up call—for both of you."

Sterling shifted on the bed, his jaw tightening briefly before he exhaled a deep breath. "I know I haven't been... emotionally present for Zariyah," he admitted. "But I want to change that."

Dr. Monroe nodded thoughtfully. "Sterling, acknowledging that is an important first step. But it's going to take more than that. Zariyah has been carrying trauma that shaped her entire view of herself and her relationships. She's spent years building walls to protect herself, and those walls have impacted your marriage."

Zariyah glanced down at her hands, her fingers nervously brushing the edge of the hospital blanket. "It's hard to believe I can be vulnerable without getting hurt," she whispered.

Sterling leaned closer, his voice low but firm. "Z, I get it. And I've been hiding too. But I'm ready to put in the work. I don't want to lose you."

Dr. Monroe smiled softly, her warmth filling the room. "Healing doesn't happen overnight, Zariyah. And it's not a straight path. But the fact that you're both here, ready to confront these things together—that's what matters."

They sat in silence for a moment, letting her words settle between them. Sterling tightened his grip on Zariyah's hand, his resolve clear in his expression.

Dr. Monroe rose, preparing to leave. "I'll leave you with this one piece of advice: the key to moving forward is to stay connected. Don't retreat into your old habits. Keep talking, keep listening, and when things get hard, lean on each other."

Sterling nodded, his hand still firmly clasping Zariyah's.

"We will," he promised, his voice steady.

Chapter 38

The drive home was quiet. Sterling held Zariyah's hand much of the way, glancing at her occasionally. Each time their eyes met, he offered a soft, boyish grin that tugged at her heart. She couldn't help but smile back. Though her body was still weak, the sense of safety in his presence was something she hadn't felt in a long time.

When they arrived, Ms. Emma met them at the garage door, pulling them both into warm hugs. Sterling carried Zariyah's overnight bag to the bedroom, leaving the two women in the family room. Ms. Emma fussed over Zariyah, making her sit down and draping a lightweight blanket over her lap before heading to the kitchen. She returned moments later with a warm cup of tea, placing it gently in Zariyah's hands.

"I'll have your lunch ready shortly," she said as she bustled back to the kitchen, humming softly.

Zariyah sipped the tea, savoring the warmth, though her emotions churned beneath the surface. Ms. Emma's presence was steady, comforting—everything her own mother had failed to be. Her thoughts flickered back to Noni's cruel words at the hospital, and the weight of it pressed harder on her chest.

"Ms. Emma," Zariyah said softly, her voice barely carrying over the quiet.

The older woman paused, drying her hands on a dish towel before turning to face her. "Yes, baby?"

Zariyah hesitated, her throat tight as emotion swirled inside her. "I don't know how to thank you… for everything."

Ms. Emma's eyes softened as she crossed the room and sat beside her. "Sweetheart, you don't need to thank me. Family shows up, no matter what."

Zariyah's breath hitched. "You… you consider me family?"

Ms. Emma placed a warm hand on her knee. "Of course, I do. You've been family from the moment I laid eyes on you. Family isn't about blood, baby—it's about love and showing up for each other, especially when it's hard."

The words unraveled something inside her. Zariyah's tears spilled over, her voice breaking. "I don't feel like I deserve it. I've been so lost. So far from Him, from myself, from everyone."

Ms. Emma pulled her into a tight hug, rocking her gently. "None of us deserve the love we get, but that's the beauty of it, honey. God's love doesn't require you to earn it. And you're not alone, Zariyah. Storms don't last forever, and when they clear, you'll be stronger on the other side."

Zariyah sobbed into Ms. Emma's arms, the release long overdue.

After a while, Ms. Emma pulled back, wiping Zariyah's tears with a tissue. "You've been carrying too much on your own. It's time to let it go, baby. Give it to God and let Him carry the weight for you."

Zariyah sniffled, her voice fragile but sincere. "I know."

Ms. Emma cupped her face gently. "Start by reaching

out. He's never been distant from you. And when you're ready, come to church with me. You don't have to walk this journey alone. You've got people who love you."

A soft knock interrupted their conversation.

Dominic stepped into the room, his tall frame filling the doorway. A bouquet of hydrangeas—her favorite—was tucked under his arm.

"Hey, sis," he greeted, his voice warm but tinged with something heavier. "Sterling let me in. You up for some company?"

Zariyah smiled faintly, setting her cup aside. "Hey, Dom."

Ms. Emma took the flowers to the kitchen. Dominic sat next to his sister, his movements slower than usual, as though he carried something heavy on his mind. After a few moments of light conversation about her recovery, the topic shifted to Charades.

"I took your advice about promoting events," Dominic said, his eyes lighting up. "We're booked solid through the holidays—baby showers, anniversaries, the works. People are loving the space."

Zariyah beamed. "That's amazing! I told you it would work."

They laughed, the moment briefly lifting the weight of everything. But Dominic's expression grew serious, and he glanced toward the kitchen before leaning forward, his hands clasped tightly.

"There's something else I wanted to talk to you about," he said quietly. "About Uncle Ben."

Zariyah's smile faded, her stomach twisting. She hadn't expected this conversation so soon. She squeezed his hand.

"Ms. Emma, I think I'd like to eat out on the patio." Zariyah stood quietly, beckoning her brother to follow her.

"Alright, it'll be another twenty or thirty minutes. Take

that blanket with you," she said.

Once the door was closed and they were seated at the table, Dominic continued, his voice strained. "Sterling told me."

"I didn't know, Z. I should have known. I should've protected you."

"Dom, you couldn't have known. I didn't tell anyone because I was scared, and Ben told me repeatedly that no one would believe me."

Dominic's jaw clenched. "I would've believed you. I would've done something."

Zariyah squeezed his hand. "You were a kid too. It wasn't your job to protect me. Ben was the one who did wrong. Not you."

Dominic's eyes filled with guilt and anger. "It's been eating me up. All these years, and I didn't know you were carrying this on top of how momma was with you."

Zariyah let his hand go, her voice softened. "They both hurt us in different ways."

Dominic nodded, his shoulders sagging as he let out a deep breath. "I'm here for you, don't ever forget that. No matter how ugly it is."

"I know," Zariyah said, her voice steady. "And I'm here for you too."

Ms. Emma, who had been quietly observing from the kitchen, tapped on the door and announced that lunch was ready. Dominic opened the door and took the tray from Ms. Emma. The two plates had fried chicken, creamy mashed potatoes smothered in gravy, and green beans cooked with just a hint of smoky bacon. The comforting aroma filled the air, and Zariyah couldn't help but smile at the sight. She'd missed Ms. Emma's cooking.

Ms. Emma took the plates off the trays with a flourish,

then revealed a smaller dish covered with a linen napkin. "And for dessert, my peach cobbler bars," she announced, her tone proud.

Zariyah's eyes softened, her gratitude evident. "Ms. Emma!"

Ms. Emma waved a hand dismissively, her smile bright. "Good food heals the soul, baby. Now, y'all dig in while it's hot." She handed Dominic a fork, giving him a pointed look. "And don't let her try to skip those green beans, you hear?"

Dominic laughed, playfully nudging Zariyah. "You heard the boss."

She looked from one to the other. "Ain't nothing like a strong brother-sister bond." She placed a hand on each of their shoulders, offering a gentle squeeze before returning inside.

As they ate, Dominic caught Zariyah up on Amara, his daughter, and everything else that had happened since the Jasper Ball—including being asked to do a feature in an upcoming issue of Ebony magazine. The pride in his voice was unmistakable, and for a moment, it felt like they were just siblings again, sharing each other's victories without the shadow of their past lingering overhead.

As the sun began to dip lower in the sky, Zariyah's eyes grew heavy. Dominic noticed and stood, helping her to her feet. He gently escorted her to her bedroom, making sure she was settled comfortably before pulling the lightweight blanket over her legs. He leaned down and kissed her forehead.

"You get some rest, Sis," he said softly. "And don't hesitate to call me if you need anything, okay?"

Zariyah nodded, her smile faint but genuine. "Thanks, Dom. I mean it."

Dominic lingered for a moment, his gaze soft, then

glanced back at her one last time before heading out. His voice carried down the hall as he called out to Ms. Emma, thanking her for lunch.

Later that evening, Ms. Emma gently woke Zariyah from her nap. Ms. Emma helped her sit up and fluffed the pillows behind her before returning a moment later with a hearty bowl of homemade chicken noodle soup.

"Now, you eat every bit of this," Ms. Emma said, setting the tray across Zariyah's lap. "You've got to keep your strength up."

Zariyah glanced down at the steaming bowl, the aroma warming her senses, but she couldn't help the smile tugging at her lips. Her voice was soft as she spoke. "Ms. Emma, this baby is going to be so blessed to have you as its god-grandmother."

Ms. Emma froze mid-step, her back to Zariyah. She turned slowly, her face lighting up with pure joy. "Wait—what did you say?"

Zariyah's eyes glistened with unshed tears, but her smile didn't waver. "I said this baby's going to be blessed to have you as its god-grandmother."

Ms. Emma's mouth dropped open, and for a split second, she just stood there, stunned. Then, with a burst of energy, she let out a joyous laugh, clapping her hands together. "Well, look at God!"

Her joy overflowed, and she did a little two-step praise dance right there in the bedroom, her laughter bubbling over as she danced her way back to Zariyah. She wrapped her arms around her in a tight hug, rocking her gently as she let out a joyful shout. "Oh, baby, this is a blessing! You hear me? A blessing!"

Zariyah laughed through her tears, her heart swelling at

the sight of Ms. Emma's joy.

Ms. Emma stepped back, wiping her own eyes now. "God is good, baby. God is good. You just wait and see— all of this, everything you've been through, it's leading you right where you need to be."

As the evening settled into quiet stillness, Zariyah lay back in bed, the soft hum of the house around her. Sterling had returned and was working quietly in the adjacent room, giving her the space she needed while remaining close.

She placed her hand on her stomach, a small, tentative smile playing at her lips. For the first time in weeks, she allowed herself to hope—for her marriage, for her family, for the new life growing within her.

Chapter
39

The ride home from Dr. Monroe's office was quiet, but it wasn't the uncomfortable silence they'd grown used to. It was a new kind of stillness—one that felt like progress, like space for thought.

Zariyah leaned her head against the window, watching the passing trees blur into a watercolor of greens and browns. Her mind lingered on the session, Dr. Monroe's steady voice still ringing in her ears: ""Healing isn't about finding the perfect solution overnight. It's about showing up for the hard conversations, the uncomfortable moments, and letting your partner know you're there—even when you don't have all the answers."

She had been skeptical at first. Letting Sterling see her fears, her wounds, and her vulnerabilities felt like handing him a fragile glass vase with no guarantee he wouldn't drop it. But today, for the first time, it felt possible. The way Sterling had listened—truly listened—made her feel like she would be okay.

Sterling's hand brushed hers as he shifted gears, and she smiled softly. His actions—small and big—had been different since the hospital. He wasn't just there; he was present.

"I was thinking about what Dr. Monroe said," Zariyah said quietly, her voice cutting through the hum of the car.

Sterling smiled faintly, the tension easing from his shoulders. "Me too," his voice loud, but clear. His hands gripped the steering wheel, his knuckles relaxing as he glanced at her. "About showing up. About really seeing you."

Zariyah turned her head to look at him, her heart catching at the sincerity in his eyes.   Her voice soft, "I want to let you in… not just tonight, but always."

His words settled over her and she reached for his hand, "One step at a time."

Sterling's lips curved into a faint smile, the kind that made her heart ache in the best way. "One step at a time," he echoed.

As they pulled into the driveway, the calm between them felt like a fragile thread, but it was there. And for the first time in a long time, Zariyah felt like they were walking the same path—together.

Chapter
40

When they pulled into the driveway, Ms. Emma was already at the door, her warm smile and outstretched arms a welcome sight. She wrapped them both in a big hug.

"Now, you get yourself settled," she said to Zariyah, guiding her gently toward the bedroom. Sterling excused himself, muttering something about "handling a quick errand," leaving Zariyah in Ms. Emma's capable hands.

Earlier that morning, Sterling had enlisted Ms. Emma and Dominic to help with a surprise for Zariyah. He wanted to show her how much he was committed to their healing and to making things right. Ms. Emma, ever the nurturer, had eagerly agreed, and Dominic had jumped in with just as much enthusiasm.

By late afternoon, Ms. Emma arrived with a basket of freshly baked bread, herbs, and colorful wildflowers from her garden. Humming softly, she arranged the blooms in vases and scattered them around the veranda. Shortly after, Dominic showed up, stringing twinkling lights along the canopy and helping Sterling rearrange furniture to create a cozy, intimate setting. Together, they transformed the outdoor space into something magical.

The table was set with elegant simplicity: flickering candles, soft linens, and the warm glow of the nearby fire adding to the ambiance. The air carried the rich aroma of grilled herb-crusted salmon, roasted vegetables, and creamy risotto—all of which Dominic had prepared with care. A fresh salad with mixed greens, candied pecans, and goat cheese, drizzled with balsamic glaze, completed the meal.

As Dominic placed the final dish on the table, he gave Sterling a nod of approval. "It's all set," he said, his voice low but filled with quiet pride. "She's going to love this."

Sterling stepped back, taking it all in. "I hope so," he murmured. "It's been a rough few weeks. She's healing, but I know it's not just her body. There's still a lot weighing on her."

Dominic nodded, his expression softening. "Yeah, but you're showing up now. That counts for a lot. Zariyah's tough, but she's got a heart that needs care. You're giving her that."

Sterling rubbed the back of his neck, glancing toward the house where Zariyah rested. "I didn't realize how much I was failing her until everything came crashing down. I just want to be better. For her."

"You're doing the right thing," Dominic said firmly. "She's starting to heal, but don't rush it. Just keep showing up."

Sterling gave a slight nod, gratitude flickering in his eyes. "Thanks, Dom. I needed to hear that."

Dominic clapped a reassuring hand on Sterling's shoulder before stepping back. "Alright, I'm out. You've got this."

Sterling watched him leave, the soft click of the door behind him leaving him alone with the warm glow of the veranda.

Inside, Zariyah stirred. The warmth of the bed lulled

her in and out of light sleep, but something—the faint hum of activity outside or perhaps the enticing smell of food—pulled her fully awake. She blinked, glancing toward the window, where the fading light of day had given way to the soft glow of evening. Curiosity stirred within her.

She slipped on a sweater and padded toward the veranda, her bare feet brushing the cool hardwood floor. When she stepped outside, the sight stopped her in her tracks. Twinkling lights cast a golden glow over the space, while the soft crackle of the fire added warmth to the crisp evening air.

Sterling stood by the fire, tending to the flames. For a moment, Zariyah simply watched him, her heart swelling at the scene before her. This wasn't like the dinner party she'd planned that spring, the one he missed, leaving her with cold food and colder disappointment. This was different. There was intention in every detail—a tenderness she hadn't felt in a long time.

Sterling turned, as if sensing her presence. When his eyes met hers, his face lit up. "I was just about to call you," he said with a warm smile. He crossed the veranda, pulling out a chair for her. His hand brushed her back gently as she sat. "I thought we could use a night like this."

Zariyah smiled, her eyes flickering over the table, the fire, the lights. "It's beautiful," she said softly, her voice thick with emotion. "Thank you."

They ate in comfortable silence at first, the fire crackling beside them, the warmth wrapping around them. The meal was perfect, but it was the thought behind it that touched Zariyah the most. Conversation flowed easily as they ate, punctuated by soft laughter and stolen glances. For the first time in months, everything felt lighter.

Zariyah's presence grounded Sterling in a way he hadn't

felt in years, but his thoughts wandered to the conversation he'd had with Richard just a few days ago.

Richard's words still echoed in his mind—*Focus on understanding, not fixing*. For the first time, Sterling felt he truly grasped what that meant."

As the evening wound down, Zariyah spoke, her voice soft but firm. "You've changed."

Sterling's eyes met hers. "I had to," he admitted. "I almost lost you. And now... I want to be here. Really be here. Not just as your husband, but as your partner."

Zariyah reached across the table, taking his hand. "I see that," she said quietly, her heart swelling with a mix of hope and warmth.

Later, as they lingered by the fire, Sterling's voice broke the comfortable silence. "Aimee called earlier. She wanted to know if you're up for a visit."

Zariyah hesitated, her chest tightening slightly. The thought of facing Aimee stirred unresolved emotions, but tonight—here, in this moment—she felt ready to take the first step. "I think I am," she said, her voice steady. "I think I'm ready."

Sterling nodded, his hand tightening gently around hers. "One step at a time," he said softly.

Zariyah smiled, the crackle of the fire and the warmth of Sterling's presence anchoring her. One step at a time. For the first time in a long time, that felt like enough.

Zariyah hesitated, the thought of seeing Aimee stirring up a mix of guilt and apprehension. But sitting there, feeling Sterling's presence—it felt possible. "I think I'm ready," she said softly.

Chapter
41

The morning light filtered gently through the curtains as Zariyah stirred in bed. The coolness of the early fall air seeped into the room, mingling with the quiet hum of hope she'd felt since last night's dinner with Sterling. It hadn't fixed everything, but it had reminded her that healing—for both of them—was possible.

Today, however, held its own challenge. Aimee was coming over, and the thought settled heavily on her chest.

A soft knock at the door pulled her from her thoughts. Ms. Emma peeked in, her smile warm and understanding. "Good morning, baby. Breakfast is ready, and your friend will be here soon."

Zariyah offered a faint smile. "Thanks, Ms. Emma."

As she dressed, her nerves hummed beneath the surface. The confrontation with Aimee had left raw edges. Could they truly mend their friendship? By the time Zariyah entered the kitchen, the smell of coffee and the gentle clatter of dishes greeted her. Ms. Emma had set a cozy breakfast spread, and just as Zariyah reached for her coffee, the doorbell rang.

Aimee stood on the porch, pausing before she rang the bell. The weight of their last conversation hung between them like a fog. When Zariyah opened the door, neither woman spoke at first. Finally, Aimee broke the silence. "Hey," she said softly. "I wasn't sure if you'd want to see me."

Zariyah stepped aside, her voice calm. "Come in."

They moved into the kitchen, where Ms. Emma welcomed Aimee with a warm smile and a cup of coffee before retreating to the garden. The silence lingered until Zariyah finally spoke. "I wasn't sure I was ready for this, either," she admitted. "But I think we need to talk."

Aimee nodded, her eyes heavy with emotion. "I know I hurt you, Z. I leaned on you so much without realizing how much you were carrying. When you confronted me, I didn't want to face it. And when you ended up in the hospital…" Her voice broke. "I hated myself for not being there for you."

Zariyah took a deep breath. "I've been working through a lot in therapy—boundaries, my fears, my walls. I realize now that I didn't just let you lean on me. I encouraged it, because it made me feel needed. But I was drowning, and I didn't know how to tell you."

The honesty in her voice seemed to unravel something in Aimee. "I don't know how we move forward," Aimee said, tears brimming. "But I want to try. I miss my friend."

"I miss you, too," Zariyah whispered, her voice tinged with vulnerability. "But I think we need to rebuild this friendship differently—healthier. For both of us."

Aimee nodded, and for the first time, the tension between them began to ease. Ms. Emma returned then, her timing impeccable, carrying plates of warm food. "No more heavy hearts, now," she said with a gentle smile. "Eat your breakfast before it gets cold."

Zariyah and Aimee exchanged a soft laugh, the moment

lightening further.

* * *

Later that afternoon, Zariyah and Sterling sat side by side in Dr. Monroe's office. The soft hum of a white noise machine filled the air as they recounted their recent progress.

"We're talking more," Zariyah said, her voice steady. "Really talking, not just skimming the surface. It's been... hard, but good."

Sterling nodded. "I'm not to fix, but to listen to understand. That's been a challenge for me, but I'm trying."

Dr. Monroe smiled. "That's wonderful progress. Again, healing is a process, and the two of you are taking important steps together."

As the session wound down, Sterling took a deep breath. "Dr. Monroe, I've been thinking about starting individual therapy. There's a lot from my past I've ignored, and I think it's time I deal with it."

Dr. Monroe's expression softened. "That's a courageous step, Sterling. Therapy is about growth, and I'm here for you if you're ready to take that journey."

Zariyah squeezed his hand, pride swelling in her chest.

"Before you go," Dr. Monroe said, her eyes flicking to Zariyah's small but unmistakable bump, "is there something you'd like to share?"

Zariyah exchanged a glance with Sterling, both of them smiling. "We're expecting," she said softly. "We only told Ms. Emma, our housekeeper, but we wanted you to know."

Dr. Monroe's face lit up. "That's wonderful news. Congratulations to both of you."

* * *

The final piece of the day brought them to a doctor's office. Zariyah lay on the examination table, Sterling's hand tightly clasping hers as the Doppler whirred to life.

240

"There it is," the doctor said, smiling as the sound of their baby's heartbeat filled the room.

Sterling's eyes widened, his voice thick with emotion. "That's our baby," he whispered.

Zariyah felt her heart swell as she looked at him. The baby's heartbeat, the progress they'd made in therapy, and the tentative rebuilding of her friendship with Aimee—it all felt like pieces of a puzzle falling into place.

As they left the doctor's office, Sterling turned to her, his grin wide and unguarded. "I don't think I've ever been this happy."

Zariyah smiled, her hand resting protectively over her bump. "Me either."

This was the start of something new—something whole.

Chapter 42

The early light streamed through the windows of the nursery, highlighting the soft pastel walls and the tiny crib Sterling had assembled the night before. Zariyah stood in the middle of the room, her hand resting gently on her bump. The space was peaceful, yet her heart felt heavier than she'd expected.

Sterling entered with a small stack of baby clothes, his smile warm and unguarded.

"What do you think?" he asked, holding up a onesie covered in tiny stars.

Zariyah smiled faintly. "It's perfect," she said softly, but her thoughts were elsewhere. As Sterling busied himself arranging the clothes, she slipped away, needing a moment to process the swirl of emotions building inside her.

She found her favorite chair by the living room window, the one where she often journaled or prayed. The quiet of the morning wrapped around her as she picked up her journal, her pen moving instinctively.

Journal Entry: *Lord, I've spent so much time being afraid—of failing, of not being enough. But you've shown me, again and again, that I'm more than my mistakes. I'm scared, but I'm also ready. Thank you for bringing me to this moment. Help me to be the mother you've called me to be.*

The words flowed easily, carrying away some of the heaviness she'd been holding. Closing her journal, Zariyah leaned back, her hand resting on her belly, a quiet peace settling over her.

In the weeks since coming home, life had felt like a slow but steady rhythm of healing. She and Sterling had started going to church with Ms. Emma and her family—a decision that had felt daunting at first but quickly became a source of strength. Sitting in the pews, surrounded by Ms. Emma's warmth and the gentle encouragement of her community, Zariyah found herself reconnecting to her faith in ways she hadn't expected.

Sterling, too, seemed to find solace in the sermons and the quiet moments of prayer. She often caught him closing his eyes during service, his head bowed slightly as if laying his burdens down at last. It was a new kind of intimacy for them, one that stretched beyond words and into the quiet, sacred spaces they were learning to share.

Later that afternoon, Ms. Emma joined her for tea, their conversation easy and familiar. "I've been thinking a lot," Zariyah admitted, her voice reflective. "About what kind of mother I want to be."

Ms. Emma smiled knowingly. "You've come a long way, baby. You're going to be just fine."

Zariyah nodded, her hand instinctively brushing her belly. "I believe that now. But there's still so much to face."

Ms. Emma's expression grew thoughtful. "Have you talked to your mama yet?" she asked gently.

Zariyah hesitated, her gaze dropping to the table. "No," she said quietly. "I haven't   told her about the baby...

or anything else."

Ms. Emma reached across the table, her hand covering Zariyah's. "Don't let fear keep you from sharing your joy. You've done the work, Zariyah. You're stronger than you think."

Zariyah thought back to the recent Sunday service, the way Ms. Emma had squeezed her hand during the closing prayer, the way Sterling had rested his arm protectively around her shoulders. It had been the first time in a long time she'd felt truly supported, not just by those around her but by something greater.

The words lingered in the air long after Ms. Emma had left. Zariyah knew she couldn't avoid her mother forever.

Chapter
43

The hum of the car engine filled the air as Zariyah rested her hand over her growing bump. Sterling's hand occasionally drifted to her leg, giving a reassuring squeeze.

"Five months," he said, breaking the peaceful silence. "We're getting closer."

Zariyah smiled, her excitement mixed with a hint of nervousness. "It's surreal sometimes."

Their OBGYN visit had gone well, and the reassurance of a healthy baby made the world feel lighter. As they turned onto their street, Zariyah spoke up. "I've been thinking... what if we host a Friendsgiving dinner? It'd be the perfect time to tell everyone about the baby."

Sterling's face lit up. "You mean we finally stop hiding under hoodies and blankets?" he teased, gesturing to her oversized sweatshirt.

She laughed, nodding. "Yes, it's time."

"Let's do it," he agreed. "My brother's coming into town—he's going to flip when he finds out he's going to be an uncle."

Later that evening, after dinner, they settled on the couch, the flickering fireplace casting a warm glow. Zariyah curled up under a blanket, her thoughts lingering on an unresolved matter.

"Sterling," she said softly, drawing his attention away from his book. "I've been thinking about my mom."

Sterling set his book aside, his face softening. "What about her?"

Zariyah sighed. "I haven't spoken to her since the hospital, and it hurts. She hasn't called or checked in... and I'm still sending money through Dominic so she doesn't know it's from me."

Sterling raised a brow but kept silent, giving her space to continue.

"I know I've forgiven her in my heart," Zariyah said, her voice cracking slightly. "But I'm not ready to face her yet. I talked to Dr. Monroe about it, and she reminded me that forgiveness doesn't mean reconciliation."

Sterling reached for her hand, his thumb brushing gently over her knuckles. "You'll know when the time is right. And whenever that is, I'll be right there with you."

Relief washed over her. "Thank you."

The next morning, Zariyah and Sterling gathered in the kitchen, a notepad between them as they planned the dinner. Ms. Emma, ever the gracious helper, had already offered to take the lead in the kitchen.

"Turkey, ham, mac and cheese, and Ms. Emma's cornbread dressing are non-negotiable," Sterling said, jotting down the staples.

"Sweet potato casserole, collard greens, fried okra, and pecan pie for dessert," Zariyah added, grinning.

"We'll need a separate table just for the food," Sterling joked, his excitement clear.

Later that evening, they sent out electronic invitations

to their closest friends and family. The RSVPs rolled in quickly: Aimee, Dominic, Felicity, Richard, and Sterling's brother and his wife all confirmed.

"It's official now," Sterling said, wrapping an arm around Zariyah.

She rested her head on his shoulder, her heart full. "This is going to be unforgettable."

Chapter
44

The house was alive with warmth and laughter, the aroma of Ms. Emma's cooking filling every corner. Zariyah sat comfortably on the sofa, her growing bump concealed under a soft blanket. She radiated joy in her fitted dress, the deep autumnal hue complementing her glowing complexion. Sterling moved around the house, ensuring every detail was perfect. His gaze frequently drifted toward Zariyah, admiration in his smile.

"You look beautiful," he said, pausing briefly beside her.

"Thank you," she replied softly, her hand resting on her belly. "I'm glad we're doing this."

The doorbell rang, and the evening officially began.

One by one, friends and family arrived, filling the house with energy. Aimee, Richard, Dominic, Felicity, and Sterling's brother and his wife greeted Zariyah warmly.

None seemed to notice the secret beneath the blanket, their focus on the warm atmosphere Sterling had created. The tables, dressed with autumn-colored linens and flickering candles, were set for a feast: turkey, honey-glazed ham, cornbread dressing, mac and cheese, collard greens, and sweet potato casserole. Ms. Emma even added some extras to the menu—green beans with new potatoes, candied yams, a corn casserole, and mashed potatoes.

As the final dishes were placed, Ms. Emma smiled, wiping her hands. "Y'all enjoy this feast. Don't forget to save me some pie," she teased, earning a round of gratitude before heading out.

"Which kind?" Dominic asked bending to get a whiff of the maple and cream apple pie she'd just taken out of the oven and placed next the the bourbon pecan pie and sweet potato pie.

Sterling stepped forward, his grin widening. "Alright, everyone, dinner's ready. But before we dig in, Zariyah and I have something to share."

All eyes turned to the couple as Sterling gently folded the blanket from Zariyah's lap. She stood, revealing her baby bump. Gasps echoed around the room, quickly replaced by cheers and laughter.

Sterling's voice brimmed with pride. "We told y'all in the invitation we had a lot to celebrate."

Hugs and congratulations followed, with each guest offering words of love and encouragement.

Later, as dessert was served, Zariyah slipped out to the veranda for a moment of quiet. The cool night air brushed against her skin, offering a reprieve from the warmth inside.

Richard soon appeared, his expression soft. "Mind if I join you?"

Zariyah nodded, gesturing to the chair beside her. They sat in companionable silence for a moment before Richard spoke.

"You look happy," he said sincerely. "I'm glad."

Zariyah smiled faintly. "I am. It's been a long road, but we're in a good place now."

Richard nodded. "Sterling seems different, too. More

grounded. You've brought out the best in each other."

Zariyah glanced at him, her thoughts drifting to what Sterling had shared about Richard and Aimee's past. Though the revelations had been painful, they brought understanding, allowing her to see Richard in a new light.

"We've all changed," she said softly. "And I think that's what matters most."

Richard smiled, gratitude in his eyes. "Thank you, Zariyah."

Sterling appeared in the doorway, his protective presence grounding the moment.

"Everything alright out here?"

Zariyah smiled up at him, her heart full. "Yeah, everything's good."

Sterling extended his hand, helping her up. "Come on, sweetheart. Everyone's waiting on you."

* * *

As the evening began to wind down, Zariyah sat comfortably on the sofa, her legs tucked beneath a soft blanket that she draped casually over her growing belly. Her radiant glow was enhanced by the soft autumnal hues of her dress and her signature curls, pinned up elegantly.

Sterling, ever the attentive host, moved through the family room, catching last-minute details while sneaking glances at Zariyah. He paused beside her, leaning down with a warm smile. "You look beautiful," he said softly.

Zariyah returned his smile, her heart full. "Thank you."

As they shared a quiet moment, Felicity and Aimee exchanged knowing glances before Aimee leaned forward, unable to contain her excitement. "We've got to see the nursery before we leave!"

Chloe, Sterling's sister-in-law, smiled warmly. "Count me in. I'd love to see it too."

Zariyah laughed, nodding. "Alright, let's go."

Sterling gave her a playful wink as the women stood to head toward the hallway. "Show off that masterpiece," he teased.

The three women made their way upstairs, their footsteps soft on the carpeted stairs. Zariyah opened the door to the nursery, stepping inside and flipping on the light. The soft glow of the nursery light illuminated the pastel walls as Zariyah stepped aside to let the group enter. The room was a serene blend of comfort and whimsy: a delicate mobile of stars and clouds hung over a small crib, and the shelves were lined with books, stuffed animals, and keepsakes lovingly selected by Zariyah.

Aimee gasped, taking in the space. "Z, this is stunning. It's perfect."

Felicity ran her fingers along the edge of the crib. "This room feels like a hug," she said softly. "Your baby is going to be so loved."

Chloe stepped closer, her eyes misting. "It's beautiful, Zariyah. You can feel the care and love in every detail."

Zariyah's voice was quiet but filled with emotion. "I wanted it to be a place where our baby feels safe and cherished from the very beginning."

Aimee wrapped an arm around her shoulders. "You've done just that."

They lingered, admiring the tiny clothes hanging in the closet and sharing light-hearted jokes. Aimee, feigning seriousness, placed her hands on her hips. "Alright, Z. Did you leave anything for the rest of us aunties to buy?"

The women burst into laughter, their joy spilling into the cozy nursery.

Back in the family room, the men had gathered near the

dining table, chatting over the remains of dessert. Sterling's brother, Malcolm, leaned back, his grin teasing. "So, how's married life treating you, big brother?"

Sterling chuckled, shaking his head. "It's good. Really good. But it's been a journey, you know?"

Malcolm's expression shifted, sensing the weight behind Sterling's words. "What do you mean?"

Sterling exhaled, his gaze distant for a moment, remembering that only Richard and Dom knew what had been going on. "Zariyah's had some serious health issues a few months ago. We thought I might lose her."

The room grew quiet as the gravity of his words settled over them.

Dominic, standing nearby, broke the silence, his voice heavy with emotion. "She scared all of us. But Zariyah— she's tough. Too tough."

Sterling nodded, gratitude in his eyes. "Yeah. But she's also been carrying so much on her own for years. I didn't see it until it was almost too late."

Malcolm placed a hand on Sterling's shoulder as he listened to him and Sterling recount the past few month. His voice filled with pride when he said, "You kept it together when it mattered most. I don't think I've ever been prouder of you, Sterling."

Richard, standing quietly nearby, spoke up. "You've got a strong woman, Sterling. And she's got a good man. You're both lucky."

Sterling gave a small, appreciative nod. "Yeah. We are."

The women returned to the family room, their laughter filling the space. Aimee, still glowing from the nursery visit, turned to Sterling with a grin.

"Alright, Dad. You've got some serious competition in

that nursery. It's absolutely perfect."

Sterling chuckled. "Well, it's all her. I just followed orders."

The group gathered once more, the camaraderie of the evening wrapping around them like the warm glow of the fireplace.

Malcolm raised his glass, his tone light but meaningful. "Alright, a toast. To Zariyah and Sterling—and the little one on the way. And to family, because that's what nights like this are all about."

Everyone lifted their glasses, the room alive with cheers and laughter.

"To family," Zariyah said softly, her voice filled with gratitude as she met Sterling's gaze.

Everyone pitched in to clear the table and tidy the kitchen. The aroma of leftovers lingered in the air as laughter and soft conversation filled the space.

Dominic, drying a dish, looked over at Sterling. "Hey, Sterling—" He paused, a grin tugging at his lips.

Sterling glanced up from the sink, amused. "What is it?"

"Never mind," Dominic said with a laugh. "I was going to ask for a to-go plate, but I think I'll just come back tomorrow to help you guys finish off this food."

Zariyah laughed softly from the sofa, her eyes flicking between Dominic and Felicity, who was wiping the counter a little too intently. "What time's the game tomorrow?" she asked, her voice teasing.

Dominic exchanged a quick look with Felicity, trying to act casual. "Around one," he said, while Felicity avoided Zariyah's knowing smile.

One by one, the guests said their goodnights, leaving behind hugs and well-wishes for the parents-to-be.

"Tonight was perfect," Aimee said, pulling Zariyah into a tight hug.

"It really was," Zariyah replied, her heart full.

Once the house was quiet, Sterling and Zariyah found themselves curled up on the sofa, the fire casting a warm, intimate glow over the room. The sounds of the evening had faded into the stillness, leaving just the crackle of the flames and the steady rhythm of their breathing.

"You think Dominic and Felicity think they're being slick?" Sterling asked, his voice laced with amusement as he gently rubbed Zariyah's back.

Zariyah smirked, her head resting on his shoulder. "Oh, absolutely. But they'll figure it out soon enough."

Sterling chuckled, his chest rumbling softly against her. He shifted slightly, brushing a kiss to her temple. "You okay, Z?" His voice was quieter now, laced with concern.

Zariyah nodded, her voice low and content. "Yeah. Tonight was everything I needed."

Sterling pulled her closer, his arms tightening protectively around her. "It was good seeing everyone together like that."

She tilted her head up to meet his gaze, her eyes soft and full of love. "I love you," she whispered, her voice carrying all the emotion she felt.

Sterling smiled, his fingers brushing along her cheek with a tenderness that made her heart swell. "I love you too."

For a moment, they stayed like that, their eyes locked as if the world had faded away, leaving only them in the warmth of the firelight. Sterling leaned down, capturing her lips in a kiss that started soft but quickly deepened, carrying with it all the gratitude, love, and passion he felt for her. Zariyah melted into him, her hands sliding up to rest on his chest as he cradled her face.

"Come here," he murmured, his voice low and gravelly as he stood, effortlessly scooping her into his arms. Zariyah let out a soft laugh, her arms looping around his neck as he carried her toward the bedroom.

Once inside, the firelight followed them, flickering in the background as Sterling set her gently on the bed. He knelt before her, his hands sliding up her thighs as he pressed a kiss to her belly, then her hips, his lips trailing a path that sent shivers down her spine.

"You're so beautiful," he whispered, his hands caressing her with reverence. "I don't know if I'll ever be able to say it enough."

"You keep telling me that," Zariyah said, reaching for him, pulling him up to her, their lips meeting again in a kiss that was both tender and searing. Sterling moved slowly, his hands cradling her as though she were the most delicate treasure, his touch careful but filled with passion.

He laid her back against the pillows, his lips never leaving hers as he took his time exploring every inch of her. Each kiss, each caress, was a silent promise—a vow that he was hers, fully and completely, that he would always cherish her.

Zariyah's breath hitched as his lips trailed down her neck, his hands finding hers and intertwining their fingers. "Sterling," she whispered, her voice trembling with emotion and desire.

"I've got you, Z," he murmured against her skin, his words a soothing balm and a spark all at once. "Always."

Their love that night was slow and unhurried, a dance of devotion and intimacy. Sterling treated her as both a delicate flower and a goddess, his every move a declaration of how much he cherished her.

And as they held each other afterward, wrapped in the quiet of their love, Zariyah felt at peace in Sterling's arms;

she felt safe, adored, and deeply, irrevocably loved.

Chapter
45

Thanksgiving Morning

The rich aroma of leftover roasted turkey and freshly brewed coffee filled the kitchen, mingling with the sizzle of butter in the pan as Dominic diced peppers and onions with precise, practiced movements. Zariyah leaned against the counter, a glass of water in her hands, watching her brother work.

"It's weird having you here this early," she teased, a playful smile tugging at her lips. "You're usually the king of fashionably late."

Dominic glanced up, a chuckle escaping him. "Turning over a new leaf. Thought I'd actually earn my plate for once."

Zariyah grinned, glancing toward the living room where the low murmur of Malcolm and Chloe's voices drifted in. Hosting her in-laws for the weekend had been a balancing act—equal parts joy and extra work. Having Dominic there, pitching in for breakfast, eased the load in ways she wasn't about to take for granted.

"It's nice, though," she admitted, her voice softening. "Having you here to help."

Dominic raised an eyebrow, still focused on the vegetables. "Don't get used to it. You know I have an ulterior motive," he added, his eyes twinkling. "To help finish off the food from last night and watch the game on that giant-ass TV your husband has in his office."

Zariyah burst out laughing. "There it is! The real reason you showed up early!"

"Hey," Dominic said with a laugh, tossing some diced peppers into the pan. "I never said I wasn't predictable."

She laughed, giving him a light swat on the arm, but her expression shifted a moment later. A flicker of hesitation passed through her eyes as she swirled the water in her glass. "Dom… can I ask you something?"

Dominic didn't answer immediately, instead wiping his hands on a towel and sliding an omelet onto a fresh plate. With a quick flourish, he added a sprig of parsley for flair and replaced the half-eaten slice of sweet potato pie and mug of coffee on the counter with the new dish and a tall glass of orange juice.

Zariyah raised an eyebrow at him, her lips twisting into a reluctant smile. "You trying to tell me something about my breakfast choices?"

"You're welcome," Dominic said, ignoring her mock glare as he returned to the stove.

She made an exaggerated face, crossing her eyes and sticking out her tongue before digging into the omelet. "Fine," she mumbled around a mouthful. "This is better."

Dominic smirked, glancing over his shoulder. "Now, what's your question?"

Zariyah exhaled slowly, setting her fork down. "Don't tell Momma about the baby. I'm not ready to deal with her. Okay?"

Dominic turned to her fully, his expression softening as he placed a hand on her shoulder. "Z, you know I wouldn't. It's your news, not mine. Whenever you're ready, I'll back you up. Always."

Her eyes flickered with gratitude, and for a moment, the usual banter between them fell away, replaced by the kind of unspoken understanding only siblings could share. She gave his hand a quick squeeze, a silent thank-you, before picking up her fork again.

The moment shifted as Zariyah changed the subject, her voice lightening. "Speaking of news, what's going on with you and Felicity? Don't think I didn't see those looks last night."

Dominic laughed, rubbing the back of his neck. "We're taking it slow. She's different, Z. I don't want to mess it up."

"You won't," she said firmly. "Just trust yourself, Dom. She's worth it, and so are you."

Before either of them could say more, Malcolm strolled into the kitchen, rubbing his belly dramatically. "I finally get to have some of Chef Dom's cooking," he said with a wide grin, his voice loud enough to announce his presence.

Chloe followed behind him, rolling her eyes as she smirked. "Don't let him fool you, Dom. He's been talking about this since we got here."

Dominic chuckled, turning back to the stove as Malcolm leaned against the counter. "Well, it's about time someone appreciates my genius in the kitchen."

Malcolm's grin widened. "Oh, I plan to appreciate every bite. Just make sure you don't let Z burn the toast."

"Excuse me?" Zariyah said, arching an eyebrow at him. "I made the pie you couldn't stop eating last night, thank you very much."

Chloe laughed as she grabbed a seat at the table. "And here we go again."

Just then, Sterling walked into the kitchen tying the sash

of his robe. "What did I miss?"

He crossed the room to Zariyah, wrapping an arm around her waist as he leaned down to kiss her softly on the temple. "Good morning," he murmured, his voice low enough that it felt meant just for her.

"Morning," she replied, nudging him gently with her elbow.

Dominic smirked, tossing another handful of diced vegetables into the pan. "Alright, alright. Get a room—or at least let me finish breakfast first."

Sterling chuckled, releasing Zariyah and heading to the counter to pour himself a cup of coffee. "You're just jealous, Dom."

"Maybe," Dominic admitted with a grin, stirring the eggs. "But I'd never admit it."

* * *

The house settled into a comforting quiet in the days after Friendsgiving and Thanksgiving, as though even the walls had absorbed the warmth and laughter shared that evening. Malcolm and Chloe's visit had transformed the house into a hub of easy camaraderie. The boys—Sterling, Dom, Malcolm, and even Richard—claimed the den for their makeshift sleepover, binging on NFL games and yelling through the infamous Iron Bowl showdown between Alabama and Auburn. The low hum of their banter and cheers filled the air, paired with the clink of beer bottles and munching on snacks.

Zariyah and Chloe, grateful for a reprieve from the "boy noise," carved out their own time. They ventured to the movies, sharing buttery popcorn and laughter, and capped the evening with a relaxed dinner at a quiet restaurant. For Zariyah, it was a chance to connect with Chloe on a deeper level, their easy conversation weaving the kind of bond that felt like it had been there all along, waiting to be uncovered.

Zariyah found herself replaying moments from that night—a room filled with laughter, Sterling's easy charm, the comfort of family and friends—holding onto them like a cherished melody.

Late November brought shorter days and cooler nights, and the couple fell into a peaceful rhythm. Their moments together felt both ordinary and extraordinary: Sterling playfully swiping flour on Zariyah's nose as they tested cookie recipes, Zariyah tucking away baby name lists scribbled on scraps of paper, and the two of them sitting hand in hand, savoring the quiet before life changed forever.

By the time December arrived on a brisk wind, carrying the scent of pine and cinnamon, it felt as if the world itself had shifted. Sterling strung lights around the porch with meticulous care, insisting every bulb be perfect. Zariyah laughed from her perch on the front steps, sipping cocoa as she watched him fuss over the symmetry of the display.

On Christmas morning, Zariyah curled on the couch, her hands resting on her belly. Sterling handed her a small gold box, his smile warm and excited.

Inside, a delicate silver locket glimmered, engraved with Our Family, Our Future.

Zariyah opened it, her breath catching as she imagined the tiny pictures it would one day hold.

"Sterling," she whispered, her voice thick with emotion. "It's perfect."

He wrapped an arm around her. "You're perfect. And this is just the start."

The days between Christmas and New Year's passed in a peaceful blur. The tree stood proudly in the corner, its lights casting a gentle glow in the evenings. Zariyah and Sterling spent their time savoring the calm, sharing whispered dreams about the year ahead.

Zariyah and Sterling opted for a quiet evening at home in front of a flickering fire while the world around them celebrated. Sterling reached for her hand, his thumb brushing gently over her knuckles.

"Next year," he said softly, "we'll have a little one here with us. Our first New Year's as parents."

Zariyah smiled, leaning her head against his shoulder. "It's hard to believe."

As the clock struck midnight, Sterling kissed her gently, his voice low and full of promise. "Happy New Year, sweetheart."

Zariyah's heart swelled as she whispered back, "Happy New Year. To everything that's coming."

Sterling held her hand, guiding her toward their bedroom. The moonlight spilled through the windows, casting silver streaks across the walls.

"You've made this the happiest start to a new year I've ever had," he whispered, his voice rich with sincerity.

Zariyah smiled, wrapping her arms around his neck. "You've made me believe in new beginnings," she murmured, her voice barely above a whisper.

Sterling cupped her face, his thumb brushing along her cheek as he leaned in, his lips capturing hers in a kiss that was slow, deliberate, and full of love. His lovemaking that night—like the many of late—wasn't rushed or frantic—it was a reaffirmation of everything they had been building together.

His hands slid to her waist, pulling her closer as the kiss deepened. Zariyah's fingers tangled in the short curls at the nape of his neck, a soft sigh escaping her as they melted into each other.

Zariyah reached up, her fingers grazing his jawline. "So are you," she whispered, her smile tender. "And you're mine."

Her words ignited something in Sterling. His kisses traveled from her lips to her neck, to the delicate curve of her collarbone. Zariyah's breaths grew shallower, her hands roaming across his back as their touches became more intimate, more intentional.

Sterling's hand came to rest protectively over her belly, his thumb tracing small circles. Zariyah nestled closer, resting her head on his chest. As sleep claimed her, lulled by the steady rhythm of his heartbeat, one thought lingered: the new year was already off to the perfect start.

Chapter 46

The early February morning was crisp, a slight chill lingering in the air despite the promise of spring on the horizon. Zariyah hadn't been expecting it—not yet. Her due date was still two weeks away, and everything about her pregnancy had been smooth and steady. But the familiar, insistent tightness in her belly told her their little one had plans of her own.

She turned to Sterling, her voice steady but tinged with excitement. "Sterling... I think it's time."

Sterling shot up from bed, his eyes wide, a mix of sleepiness and exhilaration in his expression. "What? Now?"

Zariyah nodded, a smile tugging at her lips. "Yeah, now."

Within minutes, they were dressed and ready, grabbing the hospital bag they had packed weeks ago. The drive to the hospital felt surreal—like stepping into a dream they'd been imagining for months. Sterling kept one hand on the wheel and the other on Zariyah's, squeezing gently each time she breathed through another contraction.

Hours later, after a whirlwind of effort, encouragement, and an overwhelming rush of emotions, Zariyah held their tiny baby in her arms for the first time. The room had quieted, filled now only with the soft, soothing sound of the baby's breathing and the occasional hum of hospital monitors.

Sterling sat beside her, his hand resting gently on the baby's head. His eyes brimmed with awe. "I can't believe it," he whispered, his voice thick with emotion. "You did it."

Zariyah gazed down at their daughter, her heart full in a way she'd never imagined possible. "She's perfect."

Born two weeks early, their baby girl had arrived on her own terms—healthy, strong, and already leaving an indelible mark on their hearts. They had chosen not to learn the baby's gender ahead of time, and now, holding her in their arms, they couldn't imagine it any other way.

"What should we name her?" Zariyah asked softly, looking up at Sterling, her eyes sparkling with emotion.

Sterling grinned, his gaze shifting to the tiny face cradled between them. "I've got a name in mind. How about Zoey Grace?"

Zariyah tilted her head, her lips curving into a soft smile. "Zoey Grace?"

Sterling nodded. "Zoey means 'life.' And Grace... well, that's exactly what she is. A gift of life and grace. It feels right—like she was always meant to be our Zoey Grace."

Tears shimmered in Zariyah's eyes as she leaned into Sterling. "It's perfect."

Two weeks after baby Zoey's arrival, Aimee hosted a small sip-and-see for close family and friends. The living room was transformed into a cozy, welcoming space, with soft pastel decorations and a table laden with light refreshments. Zoey, wrapped snugly in a pink blanket, slept peacefully in Zariyah's arms as guests arrived to meet her.

Dominic and Felicity were among the first through the

door. Dominic's usually sharp eyes softened as he leaned in to look at his niece. "She's beautiful, Z," he whispered, pressing a gentle kiss to Zariyah's cheek.

Felicity rested her hand on Dominic's arm, her smile warm and radiant. "You're glowing, mama. She's absolutely precious."

Aimee and Richard arrived next, their excitement bubbling over as they took turns holding Zoey. Aimee's eyes glistened with unshed tears as she squeezed Zariyah's hand. "I'm so happy for you both."

Not long after, Malcolm and Chloe joined the gathering. Chloe greeted Zariyah and Sterling with an embrace, her smile carrying an extra spark of excitement. "We've got news of our own," she said softly, placing a hand on her belly.

Zariyah's eyes widened. "No way! You're pregnant?"

Chloe nodded, beaming as she exchanged a loving glance with Malcolm. "We are. Looks like Zoey's going to have a cousin soon."

Laughter and cheers filled the room, mingling with heartfelt congratulations as the family celebrated not only Zoey's arrival but the promise of another little one to love.

Chapter
47

Spring had fully bloomed, and Zariyah and Sterling had settled into a new rhythm with Zoey Grace. Zoey's laughter filled the house, her tiny presence bringing a joy and peace that neither Zariyah nor Sterling could have imagined.

Ms. Emma had become Zariyah's surrogate mother and Zoey's doting grandmother, a constant source of love and wisdom for both of them.

As the days grew longer and warmer, Zariyah often found herself reflecting on how much had changed—not just for her, but for everyone around her.

As if on cue, the doorbell rang, and moments later, Aimee and Richard walked in, their faces glowing with excitement. Richard's arm was wrapped protectively around Aimee's shoulders, and Aimee held up her hand, flashing the sparkling engagement ring as soon as she entered the room.

"We have news!" Aimee announced, her smile wide and filled with joy.

Zariyah's eyes widened, a genuine smile spreading across her face. "Oh my goodness, Aimee, are you serious?" she exclaimed, her voice warm with excitement.

Richard chuckled, pulling Aimee a little closer as they

came to stand in front of Zariyah and Sterling. "Yep, it's official. We're getting married," Richard said, his voice carrying that deep sincerity Zariyah had come to appreciate in him.

Zariyah set Zoey gently in her bassinet and stood, wrapping Aimee in a tight hug. "I'm so happy for you both!" she whispered, her heart swelling with happiness for her friend.

Aimee pulled back, her eyes glistening with unshed tears. "I honestly didn't think I'd get to this place, Z. Not after everything... but Richard's been amazing. We've both grown so much."

Zariyah's gaze shifted to Richard, offering him a warm smile. "I've seen the change in both of you. You've worked hard for this—more than most couples would."

Richard met her eyes, his own filled with gratitude. "Thanks, Zariyah. We wouldn't have made it here without you and Sterling. You two have been an inspiration."

Sterling, who had been quietly watching from the side, stood and clapped Richard on the back. "You're both fighters. Marriage is tough, but you've already proven you've got what it takes."

The four of them stood there for a moment, letting the love and joy of the moment wash over them. Zariyah felt the warmth of the moment settle deep in her chest—this was more than just a celebration of an engagement; it was a testament to how far they had all come.

The wedding was set for June of the next year.

Chapter 48

In early April, Dominic and Felicity arrived at the house together, their laughter filling the entryway as they stepped inside. Zariyah noticed how naturally Dominic reached for Felicity's hand as they entered the room, the comfortable ease between them unmistakable.

"Hey, sis!" Dominic called out, giving Zariyah a warm smile as he leaned in to kiss her cheek. "And look at Zoey! I think she's gotten cuter since the last time I saw her."

Zariyah laughed, shaking her head. "She's definitely growing fast," she said, her eyes flicking between Dominic and Felicity. "And I see you two are still taking things... slow?"

Felicity blushed, but the smile on her face was soft and genuine. "We're getting there," she admitted, glancing at Dominic, who grinned down at her.

"We've had some long talks," Dominic added, his tone more serious now. "I've been working through a lot of stuff, with Dr. Monroe, but... Felicity's been patient with me."

Zariyah reached out to squeeze her brother's arm. "You're doing the right thing, Dom. And Felicity, thank you for being there for him."

Felicity met Zariyah's eyes, her voice soft but filled with certainty. "Dominic's worth it. I've always known that."

Dominic's grin widened, and he wrapped his arm around Felicity's shoulders, pulling her close. "We're taking our time, but this... this feels right."

Zariyah smiled knowingly. "That sounds like exactly what you need."

Chapter
49

Chloe and Malcolm's visit around Mother's Day brought not only familiar laughter, but also unexpected news. As they settled into the living room, Chloe placed a hand over her belly, her smile glowing with anticipation.

"We've got an update," she began, glancing at Malcolm. "We're not just getting ready for the baby—we're moving to Birmingham."

Zariyah's jaw dropped, her eyes wide with delight. "What? No way! You're moving closer? That's amazing!" She shifted Zoey in her arms and grinned. "I can't believe it—you're going to have us all spoiled, being so close."

Chloe laughed, her hand protectively resting over her bump. "We're excited. Nervous, but excited. Malcolm got an offer he couldn't refuse, and it just felt like the right time to make the move."

Malcolm chuckled, his deep voice warm as he added, "Definitely nervous. I thought I'd have a little more time before juggling work and chasing after a mini version of myself. But life, as usual, has other plans."

Sterling clapped a hand on his brother's shoulder, shaking his head with a grin. "Man, you're going to love it.

Birmingham's got everything you need, and being close to us? You'll have a built-in support system."

Chloe's expression softened as she looked at Zariyah, her eyes brimming with emotion. "I'm really looking forward to it, Z. You've been so inspiring, watching you and Sterling handle everything with such love and grace. I know there will be challenges, but I feel better knowing we'll have family nearby."

Zariyah felt a lump rise in her throat. "You're going to be amazing parents, Chloe. And you've got us, no matter what. If you need advice, help, or even just a nap break—we're here."

Chloe laughed, her hand brushing over her bump. "I'll hold you to that."

Malcolm leaned back, his smile reflecting his pride and excitement. "The move feels like the next step for us—starting our own little family. But I'll admit, the idea of moving with a baby on the way is... well, a little intimidating."

Sterling gave Malcolm a reassuring nod. "You'll figure it out. And the fact that you're even thinking about all this means you're already ahead of the game. Trust me— parenting isn't about being perfect; it's about showing up every day."

Chloe glanced at Malcolm, her smile widening. "We've got this," she said softly, her voice filled with quiet determination.

Zariyah felt her heart swell as she watched them. The way Chloe and Malcolm supported each other, balanced each other—it reminded her so much of the early days of her own journey with Sterling. The promise of a new beginning, of building something together, was written all over their faces.

"So when's the big move?" Zariyah asked, leaning

forward. "We should call Aimee. I'm sure she has some listings."

"End of August," Malcolm replied. "Plenty of time to settle in before the baby arrives in December."

Chloe added, "We're already looking at neighborhoods. It feels like a fresh start, like everything is falling into place."

Sterling grinned, raising an imaginary toast. "To fresh starts and growing families."

The room filled with laughter and warmth, and as Zariyah glanced between Malcolm and Chloe, she felt a deep sense of peace. Their journey, though different from her own, carried the same undercurrent of love, hope, and determination. Watching her family grow—both in numbers and in connection—filled her with gratitude and pride.

Chapter 50

Despite the joyful changes in her life, Zariyah knew there was one relationship she couldn't ignore: her mother, Noni. It wasn't easy to face, but the thought of keeping Zoey from her grandmother pushed her to take the first step. She invited Noni over to meet Zoey, bracing herself for her mother's attitude and silently grateful that Sterling would be there.

When Noni arrived that June afternoon, the tension was undeniable. Sterling stood beside Zariyah as they welcomed her into the family room. In his usual straightforward manner, Sterling made it clear how the visit would go. There was no room for debate—he'd drawn clear boundaries to ensure his wife's peace and well-being. Since Zariyah's incident, Sterling had quietly stepped into the role of her unwavering protector.

He'd taken to handling late-night feedings and soothing Zoey back to sleep, letting Zariyah rest without hesitation. His work schedule had shifted too—splitting his days between his downtown office and the home office above the garage. It was a sacrifice, but one he'd made without a second thought, because nothing mattered more than being there for his family.

Sterling had also remained committed to his own growth, continuing therapy sessions even when it felt uncomfortable. It was a quiet reminder that strength didn't mean going it alone—it meant showing up, even when it was hard.

He glanced at Zariyah now, her soft smile aimed at him as she leaned into the arm of the couch, her eyes tired but content. For Sterling, this was all that mattered—his family, his wife, his home.

To their surprise, Noni didn't respond sharply. She remained quiet, her eyes scanning the room with a reserved expression, but the usual edge in her gaze wasn't there.

Then Ms. Emma entered, carrying a cooing Zoey, who was dressed in a soft pink romper adorned with tiny bows and lace trim. A matching headband with a delicate satin bow crowned her dark curls, making her look every bit like a little princess.

Zoey nearly jumped out of Ms. Emma's arms when she saw her father, her tiny hands reaching eagerly toward him. Sterling chuckled, stepping forward to take her into his arms. He kissed her cheek with a grin before turning to introduce her to her grandmother.

"Noni, meet Zoey Grace," Sterling said gently, his tone softening as he cradled his daughter. He held her out toward Noni.

For a moment, Noni hesitated. Her stern expression faltered as she looked down at Zoey. Slowly, her hands lifted, trembling slightly as she took the baby into her arms. Her movements were cautious, unsure, as though she were afraid to disturb something fragile.

Zoey wriggled slightly, her tiny fingers brushing against Noni's chin before settling. A soft babble escaped her lips, and then she reached up, her hand grazing Noni's cheek with an innocent determination that froze the older woman in place.

Noni blinked, her lips parting slightly, and for a moment, she seemed almost breathless. Her hand came up instinctively to cradle Zoey's small fingers against her face, as if grounding herself in the moment.

"She's beautiful," Noni whispered, her voice almost reverent. The usual sharpness in her tone was gone, replaced by something soft, almost tender. Her eyes lifted to meet Zariyah's, and for the first time in years, there was no trace of judgment or criticism—only quiet vulnerability.

Noni stayed for nearly an hour, holding Zoey as though the weight of the baby anchored her to the moment. She asked questions with genuine curiosity, her gaze softening as Sterling or Zariyah answered. Each response seemed to draw her further in, her walls lowering with every tiny detail. When Zoey babbled again, Noni chuckled softly—a sound so rare it caught even Zariyah off guard. The sharpness that had once defined her presence seemed to fade as she stayed, letting herself be captivated by the little girl in her arms.

When Sterling finally took Zoey to change her, Noni turned to Zariyah, her expression still uncharacteristically soft.

"Thank you both for letting me meet her."

Zariyah swallowed the lump in her throat, her emotions swirling too fast to name. "I thought it was time," she said softly.

They sat together, the awkwardness lingering like a shadow but slowly fading as Zoey wrapped her tiny fingers around her grandmother's. There were no grand declarations, no sudden mending of old wounds. But as Zariyah watched her mother holding Zoey, the tension between them softened, layer by layer.

Later that evening, Zariyah found herself sitting in the nursery, the soft glow of the lamp casting warm light across the room. Zoey slept peacefully in her crib, her tiny chest rising and falling with each breath.

Zariyah's thoughts drifted to the sermon she had heard recently at church, where she and Sterling had started attending with Ms. Emma. The pastor's words played in her mind: "There is grace in letting go of the past and allowing space for new beginnings."

At the time, the words had felt impossible, almost hollow. But now, sitting here in the quiet, with the image of her mother holding Zoey still fresh in her mind, they made sense in a way they hadn't before. Forgiveness wasn't always loud, and healing didn't always come with words. Sometimes, it was simply allowing the weight of the past to loosen its hold.

Zariyah realized the silence between her and Noni had never just been about words left unsaid. It was about everything she had carried in that silence—the secrets, the fear, the shame she hadn't dared to voice. For years, that silence had been a crushing weight, something she bore alone. But now, as she thought of Noni cradling Zoey, something shifted.

The silence was still there—because some things didn't need to be spoken—but it no longer felt as heavy. It wasn't a burden to bear anymore. It was simply… the past.

Maybe that was the key. She didn't need to say everything out loud. She didn't need to confront every ounce of pain. Sometimes, the weight of silence could be lifted not by words, but by grace—by choosing to let go, even when the words remained unsaid.

For the first time, Zariyah felt the weight lift. She smiled softly, her gaze falling on Zoey's tiny fingers curled against her blanket. The silence between her and her mother wasn't gone, but its weight had lightened. And for the first time in her life, Zariyah knew she didn't have to carry it alone.

The weight of silence no longer bound her.

279

The End

BONUS CHAPTER

Every family has its secrets.
Peek into Dominic's story as he takes the spotlight in the
next installment of the Breaking the Silence series.

Dominic's Story

Dominic Campbell stood at the head of the sleek conference table, his deep voice steady and deliberate. Behind him, the screen glowed with the final slide of his presentation—a bold, vibrant campaign pitch he'd spent months crafting. Every word had been chosen with precision, every detail fine-tuned.

"This isn't just a campaign," he said, his gaze locking with the senior VP's. "It's a story—a narrative that connects people to the brand on an emotional level. And that's what drives loyalty."

A few murmurs of approval rippled through the room, breaking the charged silence. Dominic allowed himself a small, controlled smile. These moments were what he thrived on—the hum of anticipation, the quiet power of having every pair of eyes on him.

The senior VP leaned back, crossing his arms as he studied Dominic. "You're saying we could see a twenty percent increase in engagement within the first quarter?"

Dominic nodded, his confidence unwavering. "That's exactly what I'm saying. And if the numbers don't reflect that, I'll personally rework the strategy at no additional cost. That's how confident I am in this campaign."

The VP glanced at the CFO, who gave a slight nod. Then he turned back to Dominic, his expression firm. "Let's make it happen. You've got the green light."

The buzz of approval was immediate. As Dominic powered down his presentation, his colleagues offered murmurs of congratulations. "Killer pitch, Campbell," one said, clapping him on the shoulder.

He offered a polite smile but said little, already mentally moving on to the next task. The applause of a successful pitch never stayed with him long. It was fleeting. And Dominic had never been one for temporary things.

* * *

Back in his office, the rhythmic click of his shoes against the polished floor echoed in his ears. He shut the door behind him, loosening his tie as he moved to his desk. The satisfaction of the pitch faded into the quiet. He was used to this: the lull after the win, the creeping feeling that no amount of success could fill the void.

His phone buzzed on the desk. Before he could grab it, there was a knock at the door.

"Come in," he called, distracted.

The door creaked open to reveal a courier in a rumpled uniform, holding a slim envelope. "Dominic Campbell?"

Dominic frowned. "Yeah?"

The man crossed the room and placed the envelope on his desk. "You've been served," he said flatly before leaving without another word.

For a moment, Dominic didn't move. The envelope sat on his desk like an unwelcome guest, the words heavier than he'd anticipated. He tore it open, his fingers steady despite the tightening in his chest.

Petition for Divorce.

The words stared back at him in stark, unfeeling print. He sank into his chair, the weight of it pressing against his shoulders. His jaw clenched as he ran a hand over his face. He'd known this was coming, but knowing didn't make it sting any less.

* * *

The phone buzzed again, snapping him out of his thoughts. Zariyah's name flashed on the screen. He answered on the second ring.

"Yeah?"

"Dom, where are you? I just heard from your assistant about the campaign update. You killed it!" Her voice was warm, full of pride, but he couldn't match her energy.

He exhaled, leaning back in his chair. "My assistant told you?"

"Relax, Mr. Paranoid," she teased. "I called your office, and when I asked how the presentation was going, she couldn't stop gushing about how the room ate it up. "

"Own the win, Dom. You are brilliant, and you know it."Her voice was warm, full of pride, but he couldn't match her energy.

"Thanks," he said, the word flat.

"What's wrong?" she asked immediately, the shift in her tone as sharp as a blade.

"I got served," he replied, the words bitter on his tongue.

A pause. Her silence felt heavy with understanding. "Are you serious?"

"Dead serious."

A low, frustrated sound escaped her. "That woman… I'm coming over tonight. I'll cook. You'll vent. That's non-negotiable."

He chuckled despite himself, though the sound was hollow. "I'll think about it."

When the call ended, Dominic leaned back in his chair, his eyes drifting to the divorce papers still sitting on the desk. He considered calling her back, but stopped himself. Zariyah already had enough to deal with—her own marriage, their mother constantly pulling at her for support. She didn't need to carry his weight too.

Later that night, the loft was quiet, the city lights spilling through the massive windows in fractured patterns. Dominic sat on the leather sectional, a glass of whiskey in one hand and the divorce papers in the other.

A sharp knock at the door made him glance up.

"It's open," he called.

Zariyah stepped inside, the faint aroma of garlic and tomato sauce wafting from the bag in her hand. She set it on the counter and surveyed the room—the papers scattered across the coffee table, the loosened tie around his neck, the half-empty whiskey bottle.

"Wow," she said, arching a brow. "You really let yourself spiral, huh?"

He snorted. "What are you doing here?"

"I told you I was coming. You don't listen, remember?" She grabbed two plates and began dishing out food. "Are you going to talk about it, or should I start guessing?"

ABOUT THE AUTHOR

Zelda Oliver-Miles is a Southern author and former journalist based in Birmingham, Alabama. Her debut novel, The Weight of Silence, masterfully weaves themes of resilience, love, and family with heartfelt authenticity. When not crafting stories, she enjoys mentoring aspiring authors, immersing herself in books, and cherishing time with her family and friends. She is a wife and proud mother to two extraordinary adult children.

To connect with Zelda:
 Email:byzeldao@gmail.com
Instagram: @zeldaomiles
Facebook: @Zelda Oliver-Miles